On the Edge

Also by Margaret Visciglio and published by Ginninderra Press
The Blue Roses of Orroroo
Terra Nullius

Margaret Visciglio

On the Edge

To Liam Visciglio

a scholar and a gentleman

'Endless forms most beautiful and most wonderful
have been and are being evolved.'

Charles Darwin, *Origin of the Species*

1

Ahead, the dry grass shone white in the headlights. Then, as Bill hit a tree stump and the utility truck bounced, I saw the tops of the trees on the edge of Magnetic Hill. I hoped that the pillow that I had wedged behind Bill's back wouldn't slip loose. If it fell, his feet wouldn't reach the pedals and something very nasty might happen. A few more dents on the truck wouldn't matter, but if he rolled the vehicle, all of us kids could get hurt. I had taught Bill to drive six months ago, but his steering was still not good.

I held tight to the roll bar on the back of the cabin and gripped the rifle with the other hand. Bill whooped when the ute hit a large rock. I nearly flew off the tray. I wished I had another hand so that I could grab Emma, who was crouched on the floor beside me, sobbing and clinging to my legs. I should have been driving, because at fifteen I'm taller than Bill is, but Bill can't shoot for nuts, so he had to drive.

Of course, by rights, Dad would have been at the wheel, but Dad was sprawled on our couch back home with at least six empty beer bottles strewn around him and a half-empty bottle of Mr Flanagan's home-brewed hooch in his hand. Sergeant Wylie ought to arrest Mr Flanagan for selling that stuff, especially to my dad.

'The square of the hypotenuse is the sum of the two squares on both its sides,' I yelled. Was that correct? If I ever get to Greece, I'll spit on Pythagoras's grave. I was trying to remember stuff for my maths test tomorrow. I knew I'd get another D.

Until I got home from school, I had intended to swot tonight. Then, while I was serving up the mutton chops and mashed potato and tinned peas, Dad came in and announced that another sheep had been killed.

This was all Dad's fault. If he hadn't gone out to see why the crows had congregated by the fence in the top paddock, he wouldn't have found that dismembered sheep and he wouldn't have said that someone had to go out and shoot the wild dogs that had killed it. Dad was full of good intentions this afternoon but, like all of Dad's good intentions, they had evaporated by the time he opened the second bottle of beer.

'Please stop talking about hippopotamuses, Lizzie,' begged Emma from the floor, digging her nails into my flesh. I'd have to wear long pants to school tomorrow or everyone would ask why my legs were scratched. 'I'm scared enough already. I don't like guns and I don't like the dark and I'm frightened of the wild dogs.'

Her hot tears ran down my leg. Although Emma can be a pain in the butt at times, right now I felt sorry for her. Poor little kid, she should have been tucked up in bed by now. It must be at least ten o'clock. Way past her bedtime. Actually, I wished we were all safe in our beds. I was scared too. But at least if Emma was frightened, she'd stay awake and hold on tight and might not fall off the ute. It'd be hard to explain broken bones to the doctor and the school authorities. I'd brought her along to work the light and I needed her to be awake enough to shine the spotlight on the pack of dogs when we found it.

I knew that Emma would probably fall asleep at her desk tomorrow. Bill, too. Would one of the schoolteachers decide that the kids had been neglected, perhaps subjected to child abuse because they were so tired? Would some do-gooder decide to notify the child welfare people? I lived in fear of a social worker turning up on our doorstep, finding out that Dad was a drunk and that I was struggling to hold the family together.

I had already had a quiet word from Emma's teacher.

'It's up to you, Lizzie, to turn the television off and to make sure that your sister's in bed at a reasonable hour.'

It's not easy being fifteen, and the eldest kid in the family. Television! Those stupid teachers actually thought that we Epsoms watched television at night. When did they think we fed the chooks, did the cooking and the washing and the housework and everything else that kids have to do when their mum's dead and their dad's got problems?

The school had long ago decided that sending notes home to Dad was a waste of time and paper. My brother and sister must have made the same decision, because they chucked into the nearest bin anything handed to them. I kept telling Bill and Emma that I really needed to know what was going on in their classrooms, but either they didn't want to worry me or else they were as apathetic about authority as Dad was.

The truck hit another rock and flew up into the air. Bill whooped again. He was actually enjoying himself, the little sod. Emma wasn't, and neither was I. Bill seemed to be driving around in circles.

The circle, I reminded myself, has only one centre and a constant radius, which is why all circles are the same shape. Some ancient mathematician, who was called the Great Geometer, discovered that fact. Apollonius of Perga, that's him. I'm not sure if he was Italian or Greek. Whoever he was, it was a pretty simple discovery, really. It's the sort of thing that anyone with half a brain would have noticed, isn't it? He's remembered for noticing that all circles are the same shape. I ask you! He probably got the Nobel Prize, or whatever they had back then, for that discovery.

I bet the Great Geometer never had to go out in the dark with his younger siblings hunting wild animals. They didn't have cars in those days. Or rifles, come to think of it. Just bows and arrows. Old Apollonius just sat around in his cave, mulling over the obvious, making a simple statement of fact and people thought he was great. They probably put a laurel wreath on his head. A circular one.

But lots of people don't see the simple way out. What Dad should have done when he discovered the dead ewe was get the neighbours together, form a vigilante group, drive around the paddocks until they found the pack of dogs and shoot them. While I sat at home and did my homework. It's what adults usually do. That's what everyone else would have done. But Dad doesn't do what people usually do. I must admit he's not exactly popular in the district anyway, so maybe he thought no one would join his shooting party.

Bill steered the four-wheel drive car towards a clump of trees on the hilly side of the paddock, where I knew the land fell away steeply. From here, in the daylight, you can see the road where the cars roll up Magnetic Hill. It was dark now, of course, so you couldn't see the road.

The headlights distorted the trees and cast shadows that might have hidden ghosties and goblins or spaceships – or any of the things that the kids at school whispered lurked on Magnetic Hill. In the darkness, I almost believed the stories myself. I wished that I was back at home, preferably in my bed with the covers pulled over my head.

The wheels spun on the grass and went into a patch of dirt, and the dust rose up and made me cough. I hoped Emma wouldn't have an asthma attack from it. Did she have her Ventolin with her? Probably not, if I knew my sister. All she ever wanted to cart about was her teddy bear, but that didn't seem to be here either.

The car shot off at a tangent. I was supposed to learn something about tangents, but I couldn't remember what it was.

Emma lost her grip on my leg and was flung about on the floor of the utility. She screamed, squirmed on her tummy back towards me, grabbed my leg even harder and dug her fingernails deep into my flesh. I would probably be limping tomorrow and the other kids would ask why. I hate it when people think I'm different. You want to fit into the crowd when you're a teenager.

Lots of people think we're a bit odd anyway, because of where we live. There have been whispers about Epsom Downs ever since the Epsoms first settled on Magnetic Hill, about a hundred years ago. Magnetic Hill is near Bullyacre in the mid-north of South Australia, in case you've never heard of it. Our nearest big town is Orroroo. There are a lot of myths about Magnetic Hill. It's almost as bad the myths the ancient Greeks told.

Just after cars were invented, someone discovered that a stationary car would roll up Magnetic Hill if you took the brake off, and because of that everyone around here decided that the place is haunted or has some weird magnetic attraction about it. Ley lines or leprechauns, ghosts, or something else supernatural, depending on your point of view and which films you've watched. There are a couple of other places in the world where this happens. I think one is in Portugal, of all places. Look up 'magnetic hills' on Google if you don't believe me.

These days, the explanation is all UFOs and pseudo-scientific stuff. There's probably a perfectly good scientific explanation for the fact that cars roll up hill and also that mobile phones don't work well out here either. In the phone company's words, 'It's a black spot due to topography and coverage is difficult.' I have to use the Internet at school when I need to research anything. The other kids tease me about having no mobile phone or Internet access. They say I live in a pre-industrial revolution time zone and that one day I'll be attacked by vampires and zombies.

Lots of people don't believe the car thing happens, but it does. We get tourists coming here all the time. The town council tries to encourage tourists and they've put a big red artificial magnet at the top of the hill and a sign at the bottom telling them what to do and what to expect. The mayor will do anything to get tourists to come to Bullyacre, because he says the town needs the money and there's not much else here apart from the statue of Hugh Foulkes in the main street. Well, not until recently, anyway.

I taught Bill to drive on Magnetic Hill. You stop your car at the bottom of the slope, turn off the engine, then release the handbrake, and the vehicle rolls up the hill. Come out and try it if you don't believe me. My science teacher, Mr Williams, says that it's actually an optical illusion, and that you're rolling downhill when you think you're going uphill but it doesn't feel that way when you do it. But the scientific point of view doesn't always agree with what I've seen from our top paddock, where there's a good view of the road.

I don't know if it was science or the lack of it that drove Dad to drink. I think it was mostly the fact that Mum got cancer and died and left him with three young children to bring up alone. I've heard people say he's got a chip on his shoulder, whatever that means. He hasn't got many friends.

Still, I reckon if he'd asked around he could have found someone to help him hunt down those wild dogs. Farmers, even the ones who think you're crazy, don't say you're imagining stuff when you announce that your animals are being torn to pieces by wild dogs. They don't turn their backs when you need a hand. And they know that when those dogs have killed all your sheep, the next flock on the next property will be targeted.

But as I said earlier, Dad was snoring on the couch back in the house, and we kids were driving around the paddocks in the dark trying to save the farm. Bill laughed loudly as he jerked the steering wheel to miss some object, real or imaginary. I decided I would never let him watch grand prix racing on the television again.

Emma tugged my arm. 'It isn't a sheep,' she whispered.

'You'll have to speak up. I can hardly hear you over the engine,' I said.

'I said there are animals over near the trees, and they're not sheep,' she said, a little louder. 'They're really big. The eyes are shining at me and they're high off the ground so they must be big. I don't want them to hear me so I'm not going to speak loudly. Is it your hippopotamuses? Have they escaped from the zoo?'

'Shine the spotlight on them. It's a pack of wild dogs, you silly twit.'

'I can see something, Lizzie!' yelled Bill, sticking his head out of the car window and waving his arm to get my attention.

The Toyota veered off to the right as he took his eyes away from the windscreen. Then he over-corrected the steering wheel and we skidded on the dry grass. He slammed his foot on the brake and the car spun. Suddenly we were headed to the left at very high speed. Emma and I were jerked about and Emma lost her grip on my leg again, flew into the air, squealed and nearly fell overboard. I dropped the rifle and grabbed her. It was a good thing I had the safety on that rifle.

Bill stuck his head out of the window and yelled at me. 'Look over there, under those trees by the fence. It's got another sheep down. I'll head over there. That's a bloody big dog. The biggest I've ever seen. I reckon it's a bloody dingo.'

'I've told you not to swear, Bill. If you say stuff like that at school, I'm the one who's going to get told off by the headmaster. We don't get dingos around here. And keep your voice down, or the dogs'll take fright and run off and I won't be able to get a shot at them.'

The headlights illuminated something by the tree. Something big and dark that was crouched over a heap of white stuff on the ground. There was more white stuff spread around the area. Wool, that's wool from another one of our flock, I thought. That's another sheep gone, a sheep that we won't be getting fleece or meat from. Another step towards going broke and having to leave the farm. Maybe we'd be better off in the city. But then I thought about the suburban house my cousins live in, in a street that faces other houses, in a town full of people they don't even know. No trees, no hills, no birds, just television antennas and fumes from cars.

I bent over the side so I could speak into the car window without raising my voice too loudly. 'I can see the dogs now. There must be a whole pack of them. I can see three sets of eyes.' I leaned down to my sister, dragged her to her feet and whispered urgently. 'Pick up that spotlight, Emma. Shine it over there. Stop crying.'

Then I twisted towards the window again. 'Try to keep the car steady, Bill. I won't be able to get my sight on any of those dogs if you're changing direction and whizzing all over the place.'

I shook Emma and then I nearly fell over as the ute jerked forward.

'I've never seen dogs as big as them!' Bill shouted, driving at breakneck speed towards the trees. The headlights were going up and down so fast that I felt seasick. It was useless telling Bill to keep his voice down. When he's excited the decibels rise. I tried to concentrate on the spotlight that Emma was shining at the shadows under the trees, but the light was wavering because Emma's hands were shaking with fear.

'Those aren't dogs, they're cats,' whispered Emma, wiping her nose on my shirt.

I could feel her shivering as though she was cold, even though it was a hot night. I was trembling too. I hoped I'd be able to shoot straight, but I doubted it. 'Concentrate,' I ordered myself.

Emma pulled at my arm and whispered something. I bent to hear what she was saying and swore worse than Bill had done earlier. I'd had one of the animals in my sights but now I'd lost it again. I sighed and took another bead on the nearest dog. Even if I killed one of them, the rest of the pack would flee and we'd have to come out again tomorrow night. Bill was right: these animals were huge. But then everything looks bigger and scarier at night. The shadows distort and magnify stuff. They must just be ordinary dogs but the headlights and the spotlight made them appear bigger. And they looked monstrous. Could they be wolves? But I knew that was impossible.

I didn't want to do this again tomorrow night, or ever. Dad was going to have to pull himself together and take charge. I was angry with Dad, angry with the world. This was just not good enough. Kids should not be in this situation. Perhaps I could ask the neighbours to help. Would the police or the town council help if I contacted them? But then I'd have to admit that Dad was drunk and incapable, and that would be embarrassing. And it might even be dangerous. Some person in authority, Ms Wylie for example, might decide we kids needed to be taken into care. No, I'd have to take charge and sort things out. Just as I always did. And come back tomorrow night for another try if I had to.

'I'm glad it's not hippos,' Emma whispered. 'Hippos are the most dangerous animals in Africa. Maybe in the entire world. More dangerous than lions or crocodiles are. Miss Lennard said that in geography the other day. It's definitely cats, Lizzie.'

'Cats don't get that big,' I said. 'Even feral cats. They must be German shepherds. They're notorious for killing sheep. I would have said dingos, only we're below the dog fence. I don't like shooting someone's dogs, but it has to be done. People should control their animals.'

'The shape's wrong,' insisted Emma. 'I like drawing cats. I know what shape cats are, even in the dark. Those are really big cats, though. Perhaps they're panthers or leopards. But at least they're not big enough to be lions or tigers.'

'There aren't any panthers or leopards in Australia, Emma,' I said. 'They have to be dogs. Shine that spotlight on them and you'll see that they're dogs. And don't hold onto me, hold on to the roll bar. You'll spoil my shot if you knock me. Hold tight in case Bill jerks the car around again.'

'Now, Lizzie. Shoot now!' Bill shouted. 'You can't miss. They're dead ahead.'

'Lizzy,' shrieked Emma. 'It is a cat! There's just one cat, but it's really big.'

'Rubbish,' I yelled. 'I can see three sets of eyes. Let go of me.'

She tugged my arm. I pushed her away. She fell over and kicked me in the shin. She kicked again, even harder. She moaned and drummed her hands on the metal floor of the ute. If that didn't scare the dogs off, nothing would. But the shadow looming over the white shape on the ground didn't move and all those eyes kept glaring at me.

'Stop that, Emma,' I yelled. 'You'll ruin my shot.'

My sister had gone off her head, babbling nonsense the way she used to do when she was really little, just after Mum died. 'It's a monster cat with three heads, Lizzie. It's going to tear us to pieces! I want to go home,' Emma whispered frantically. She raised her head just enough to look over the edge of the ute. Her body shook violently.

I decided that my sister had gone crazy. Was she hallucinating because it was past her bedtime? I decided I would never let her watch David Attenborough shows on the TV again. Or horror films either.

'Lizzie…' Emma wept. 'Look at it! It's looking straight at me with all its eyes. And I don't like those long necks that look like snakes. The heads are twisting about and getting in each other's way and trying to decide what to tell the animal to do and when it works out what to do it's going to come over here and it's going to eat me the way it's been eating that sheep.'

I shook my head and kicked my sister just hard enough to shut her up. I had decided not to listen to her nonsense. I fired the gun. A .22 doesn't make all that much noise, but it sounded loud to me. Before I fired another shot, I glanced over at Emma, who, despite her sobs, had stood up and was valiantly shining the spotlight at my target. Poor kid. I reckon she was more scared of me than of whatever she thought she'd seen under the trees.

I peered back at the circle of light under the trees. I was hoping to see the body of a dog on the ground. I had never shot at anything bigger than a rabbit before, though, and I wasn't sure whether a .22 would bring a dog down at that range. Or whether I'd even hit an animal.

I hardly ever miss rabbits. A .22 works fine for rabbits. We eat a lot of rabbit. The only cost is the bullet, and there are lots of ways to cook them. You know when you've hit a bunny because the impact usually sends them flying up in the air. But this animal was a lot bigger than a rabbit and it didn't move at all. It was quite still. And it wasn't a dog, and it wasn't dead. The creature stood on four legs in the full glare of the wavering spotlight. The light was wavering because Emma's hands were shaking with terror, but it still showed the thing well enough. And this animal wasn't scared of us or the gun.

'Bloody hell!' Bill was yelling. He stuck his head out of the window, pointed at the beast standing rigid beside the pathetic pile of wool and flesh on the grass under the tree. 'That can't be real. Tell me it isn't there, Lizzie. Say I'm seeing things.'

That was when I decided we must all be hallucinating. I felt nauseous. Maybe that frozen pie we had eaten before we came out here had been past its use-by date. Perhaps we were affected by the fumes from Dad's beer. They say too much alcohol can give you the DTs and make you see things. Could breathing the gases from empty bottles harm our brains? But didn't you have to swallow the booze to be poisoned? And I usually pick up the empties and dump them in the recycling bin as fast as Dad drains them. Or maybe it was the influence of living near Magnetic Hill. Maybe it had finally affected us.

I pinched my arm to see if I was awake and not just dreaming. I was awake. Emma was right. The animal under the tree was a cat. Only it was the biggest cat I had ever seen in my life. And this cat was not only big. It was bizarre. I had to agree with Emma: the long necks did make it look like a snake. Or rather, like a nest of snakes.

When we did art history last year, I remember seeing a picture of Cerberus. Cerberus was a dog with three heads and I think it guarded the gates of hell or whatever. A mythical, mystical beast. Another Greek story. I asked the teacher why we have to learn all this stuff about Greece when we live in Australia, and I got told off for being disruptive. I reckon whoever sets the curriculum for secondary school is Greek.

But I have never seen anything, real or mythical, that prepared me for this. The animal stood there in the circle of light as if it was performing on a stage. All three heads, set on the end of impossibly long necks (I thought of swans because they were too flexible to compare with giraffes) twisted and swivelled to give the animal's six yellow eyes the best possible view of us. Three sets of implacable eyes glared straight at the truck. Three mouths full of bloodstained fangs gleamed in the headlights. One mouth had an untidy lump of sheep dangling from its incisors. There was nothing in Darwin's *Origin of the Species* about this thing. Well, not on the pages I'd seen.

Bill was safe. He had the windscreen between him and the monster, though he said later that his hands were frozen to the steering wheel and he wondered if he was going to need a clean pair of undies if he lived that long. On the back of the car, Emma and I were sitting ducks. Well, standing ducks, actually.

This was a big, powerful, angry animal, with big, powerful jaws. Three sets of jaws with lots of very large, very sharp fangs shining in them. One head with the usual number of jaws would have been bad enough. I suddenly realised why the sheep had been shredded. Three sets of jaws are better than one when it comes to tearing a corpse apart.

I hoped I had hit the thing, incapacitated it at least a little. Because there was no way a human, even an adult human, would be any match for this thing unless it was very disabled. Three kids were a dead loss. I wasn't sure that a .22 rifle was the right weapon to use against it. I wished I had something bigger. An elephant gun perhaps. But had I hit it?

As if to answer my question, one of the heads bent towards the monster's front left leg and began licking. I grabbed the spotlight from Emma's hands and directed the light down at the creature's leg. There was a thin stream of blood oozing from a wound just above the knee joint. Not enough to really stop a beast that size. Or that shape. I shone the light up and around the animal, still disbelieving what I was seeing.

It was definitely a feline of some sort, but just what sort, I had no idea. I had a feeling that even if I Googled this thing, I wouldn't get a result. Once again, I hoped that I was dreaming, that this was a nightmare brought on by too much stress. If so, maybe I'd wake up soon.

'What the hell is that, Lizzie?' yelled Bill. 'Shoot it again!'

So I wasn't dreaming. Bill couldn't sound as terrified as that if this was a dream.

'When my hands stop shaking, I will,' I promised. 'Emma, take that light and shine it on the cat.'

But now Emma was lying on the floor of the ute, her hands over her face, mewling like a kitten in pain. I gave up expecting her to help. I grabbed the spotlight and shone the beam on the monster myself. The two heads that were not engaged in licking the bullet hole glared back at me and I heard two low, menacing growls, just out of sync with each other. Then the third head stopped licking its wound, stretched its neck and looked straight at me. Its lips drew back in a snarl, exposing bloodstained teeth. It growled too. Under the cat noise and the engine noise, I could hear Bill sobbing in the cabin of the ute.

I realised how terrified the dying sheep must have felt. Sheep are the bottom of the food chain, unless you count grass. I had a feeling the kids and I weren't much further along the chain in this creature's view.

Now the head that had been inspecting the wounded leg rose and extended its neck, and three sets of golden eyes glared at me. Then all the eyes sank lower towards the dry earth. For a quarter of a moment I hoped, I wished, I prayed, that the cat was slipping to the ground as it slid towards death. Perhaps I had hit an artery in its leg and the thing was bleeding badly. But then I saw that the eyes, now barely above the grass, had begun to move slowly towards us. I knew the thing had decided we were its next meal. It was slinking towards us on its belly, calculating when to spring.

I've watched cats stalking birds or mice like that. They creep along almost imperceptibly, and when they're certain that they can launch themselves on their prey easily, they spring. Cats rarely miss.

I dragged Emma to her feet and thrust the light into her shaking hands. 'Pull yourself together and act like a big girl for a change,' I ordered. 'Shine that light on the cat and think about your teddy bear or something.'

'Shoot it again, Lizzie!' yelled Bill. 'Try for its head. You've wounded it. You can't leave it in misery. Dad says that's the first rule of hunting.'

Just like Bill, I thought. And I was feeling sorry for him a minute ago. Now he's worried about the monster being in misery. What about my misery? I was responsible for him, for Emma and for me. And for the bloody farm animals too. At this rate, soon there wouldn't be a sheep left in our flock.

'Which head?' I screamed. 'What's the point of shooting one head when it's got three of them?'

I raised the rifle. I aimed low and I pulled the trigger. I aimed the rifle at the middle of the animal. I don't like gut shots, but that was the biggest part of the creature, so it was the easiest target. I might get lucky and hit the heart. Even a monster this size must die if you put a bullet into its heart. I fired the rifle. I prayed harder than I had since the time I'd stood by my mother's death bed. To be perfectly honest, I don't actually think I've prayed much since then. And it didn't work then. Would it work this time?

The cat stopped crawling towards us. It pulled itself up. Two sets of eyes examined me malevolently. I watched as one head bent towards its belly and a tongue licked at a new trickle of dark blood that shone in the spotlight.

Then Emma dropped the lamp over the side of the truck. She moaned and threw herself down on the floor. She crawled into a corner, folded herself as small as she could, and wept. 'Dad's going to be so cross with me if the spotlight's broken,' she sobbed.

Now the only light we had was coming from the headlights, which were dimming. I realised that the battery was probably going flat again. I'd told Dad we needed a new battery for the ute, but he just kept putting the charger on the old one and saying he'd buy a new battery when he could afford it. Maybe next week, or next month. Next year, more likely. Let's be honest, probably never. All our family's money went on booze.

The ute slowed down but I could hear the motor still running weakly. Not all the cylinders were firing. Those spark plugs needed replacing, too. I knew that if Bill stalled the engine he wouldn't be able to start it again.

The panther began to pace slowly towards us, one head still inspecting its belly, another licking the wounded leg and the other one apparently calculating how far it had to go before it reached us. It was limping, so the leg must be troubling it. I didn't know whether it was worried about the belly wound or not. I wasn't going to stick around long enough to find out how badly it was hurt or how fast it could move. My stomach cramped as I thought of something else, something that really terrified me.

The engine spluttered and coughed and the headlights dimmed. I held my breath and listened to Emma's sobbing and Bill's curses. The car stalled. I could smell petrol.

'Don't flood the engine or you'll never get the ute going!' I yelled. I wondered whether to risk jumping off the tray of the vehicle and making a dash for the cabin, pushing Bill aside, and taking over the controls. I didn't think I would make it before the cat reached us. And dare I leave Emma in the tray on her own? I didn't think so.

The cat was closer now. I could smell the blood on its breath. Suddenly the truck shuddered and the engine roared as Bill flattened the accelerator.

'Turn round and get out of here!' I shouted. 'What if there are more of them out here? The countryside might be swarming with these things!'

I fired the gun once more at the cat just for luck. I shouldn't have missed at that range, but Bill was driving more erratically than ever and I couldn't see properly because of the dimness of the headlights. Even so, the bullet must have gone fairly close to the cat, because it faltered in its stride, three heads snarled at me, then it turned and headed off down the track towards the big gully on our property where the creek runs if and when we get a bit of rain. Bill revved the engine and we headed for home.

2

This time Dad was with us. It had taken me half the morning to get him and the ute going. I'd charged the vehicle's battery up overnight, cleaned the spark plugs with emery paper, checked the oil and filled the tank with petrol from a jerrycan.

I wished there was a way to charge Dad's battery up, but the only remedy I could think of was coffee. I'd made him drink three cups of coffee so thick you could just about stand a spoon up in it, but Dad was still pretty sluggish. He complained that he had a headache. I thought 'Serve you right' but I didn't say it out loud. Sore head or not, he was at the steering wheel now and I had my rifle and his between us on the seat. And a loaded shotgun, too, just in case.

Dad had driven the Toyota out to the place where we'd seen the cat dismembering the sheep the night before. Now he and I sat in the cabin of the ute and looked at the crime scene. The two kids were in the tray with the dogs. I figured they were safe enough sitting there because the last time I saw it, the cat had been limping down towards the creek. And I kept praying that there was only the one cat on Epsom Downs. God probably had a headache worse than the one Dad had, just from listening to me.

There wasn't a whole lot to see apart from a few strands of wool blowing about the paddock. The crows must have arrived and cleaned up most of the mess while I was persuading Dad to phone Mr Gonski, the headmaster at our school, and say that all of us kids had come down with diarrhoea overnight. It was a good excuse. No headmaster wants gastro spread through his school.

We got the dogs out of the vehicle and let them inspect the place. Toby, who's pretty old now and who never was much of a hunter anyway, inspected the few scraps of mutton still clinging to the bones that the crows had missed. I had to drag him away from the carcass. He might be old but he's always hungry. He probably has worms. Come to think of it, Bill probably has worms the way he eats. People can catch worms from dogs. I remember we were told about that in health and hygiene back in junior school, and urged to wash our hands after we touched dogs. The sheep have the worm eggs in their livers, and they crap on the grass and the dogs roll in the shit. I think that's the life cycle of the worms. Washing your hands all the time might be all right for city kids, but country kids are around dogs all their lives.

Banjo is younger than Toby and he sniffed the air with interest. Dogs have a better sense of smell than humans do, but even I could tell that there had been cats here. There's nothing like the smell of cat's urine on hot earth. Or was this cats' urine? Is a cat with three heads singular or plural? I should ask my English teacher about that one, if I lived long enough to go back to school.

Banjo put his nose to the ground and inhaled the other odours that had been left there. He found a patch of dark blood on the grass. I knew it wasn't sheep's blood because the hackles on his back stood up and his lips drew away from his teeth as he snarled and looked about him. Banjo's used to sheep blood. There's plenty of it around when Dad butchers one of the older ewes for our dinner table. This was a different smell. The dog knew something strange had happened here, something out of the ordinary.

Then Banjo raised his head and made a noise I'd never heard from him before. It wasn't a bark. That must be what baying sounds like, I thought. I'd read about baying in *The Hound of the Baskervilles* and in *Uncle Tom's Cabin*. It must have been terrifying for the escaped slaves in the deep south of America when they heard that sound behind them as they ran through the swamps trying to get away. Dad always said there's a bit of the bloodhound in Banjo. To be honest, there's a bit of most breeds in Banjo. Dad always says purebreds are useless, that mongrels are the best sheepdogs.

Then Banjo began to whine and tug at the leash that Bill held. I could see that Bill was having trouble holding onto the leash. The dog put his nose on the ground and pulled hard. He'd found a trail of scent leading from the killing ground.

'Banjo hates cats,' said Bill. 'I reckon he knows that there was a panther here. He probably even knows that it's got three heads. Dogs can work that sort of thing out better than people can.'

Dad shook his head. 'He'd probably act like that if there'd been a pack of strange dogs around. Or even a fox.'

I knew Dad still didn't believe the story we kids had yelled, screamed or sobbed (depending on who was doing the recounting) at him when we had burst into the house and shaken him awake last night. I knew the tale was a bit weird, but he hadn't lived through it. He wanted to know if we'd been watching horror movies on the TV. Come to think about it, Dad was complaining he had a headache this morning. What about me?

'Come off it, Dad,' I snapped. 'This place reeks of cat pee. It smells as if a mob of tomcats have been rampaging about in the bushes. This stink is worse than a tray of used kitty litter that's been left standing out in the sun on a hot day.'

I was hurt that Dad had said Bill and I were imagining things, embroidering the truth, when we told him about the cat. It wasn't until Emma drew a picture of the monster and had sworn, with tears in her eyes, that it was all true, that he began to think perhaps there was something nasty out in the fields. And even then I knew he had reservations.

Parents shouldn't have a favourite child. I know Emma is the youngest and the prettiest and she looks a lot like Mum did and she does have a talent for drawing that Dad tries to encourage, but Dad spoils her far too much, and he just ignores Bill most of the time. Bill's got a lot of good qualities too. I can't always recall what they are, but he's not a bad kid.

Of course, Dad gave in to Emma's whining even though I'd suggested that Emma stay at home while the rest of us went out to track the monster down, just because the rotten little brat became hysterical and threw one of the tantrums she's famous for.

'You might all get eaten and never come back and I'll be alone for the rest of my life,' she yelled, stamping her feet and banging her fists on the kitchen table. 'Or at least I'll be alone until the cat comes and jumps through the window and breaks the glass and eats me. If you're all going hunting, I'm coming too.'

So Dad said we had to bring the kid along. Now she clung to his arm and whispered that she was really, really scared but she knew her daddy would save her from being devoured.

'Devoured?' I thought. 'Where did she get that word from?'

'Do you think there really is a big pussy cat out in the paddock?' Dad asked Emma, stroking her hair.

I was pretty sure he thought we were having him on. He knew I had that maths test this morning, and from the way he looked at me when I handed him the phone with the school's number dialled in, I could tell he'd decided I just wanted to get out of school and have a day strolling around the paddocks picking off rabbits with the rifle.

I still wondered if he thought we'd invented the cat story to get him off the booze and onto the wagon. Bill and I had been trying to stop Dad's drinking for a long time. For his own good. And, I had to admit, for our good too. I hadn't thought of persuading Emma to ask him to curb his intake. Maybe that would work. It was disgusting how one golden tear running down her silky cheek often persuaded him to comply with whatever my sister wanted.

'Yes, Daddy,' said Emma, simpering and nodding vigorously. 'It's the biggest pussy cat I've ever seen. I was so scared, but Lizzie didn't care when I cried.'

She glared at me and I glared back. That's another ploy she uses. She says no one cares about her in order to get her way. It works every time with Dad. It doesn't work with me, though. I used to try that trick unsuccessfully on Mum, back when Mum was alive, so I know how little kids' minds work.

Emma had Dad's full attention, so she pouted at him and continued whining. 'It's either a panther or a leopard. It's got spots, so I think it's more likely to be a leopard, although the shape is right to be a panther, too. I looked at their pictures in the encyclopaedia. Look, Daddy, I brought the camera. If we find it, can we take a photo of it so I can show Miss Lennard at school? It would be great for show and tell.'

'You're an absolute drama queen, Emma,' I said. 'Anything to get attention, isn't it? Miss Lennard's got better things to do than look at your stupid pictures. She won't believe in a three-headed cat, anyway. She'll say we rigged the photo somehow. Like when you took photos of your dolls with paper wings on them and said we had fairies at the bottom of the garden. The whole class will laugh at you again. And then the whole school will be talking about our family and saying stuff about Magnetic Hill.'

Just like Emma to bring a camera. She'll be asking me to carry it for her next, because it'll be too heavy for her. At least she hasn't brought her teddy bear. Unless it's in her backpack. I'd told her to put the sandwiches I'd prepared into her rucksack, but I hadn't checked that she actually had done that. The bag was bulging with a teddy-bear-like fullness.

Banjo growled. He began to tug harder at the leash. Bill had to use both hands to restrain the dog, and gasped as he was dragged a couple of steps down the track.

'It must have gone that way,' said Bill. 'Banjo's's picked up the trail. Hey, Dad, there's footprints in the dust over there. And they look like cat prints. Bloody big cat prints. With drops of blood on them. You did hit it, Lizzie! Come on, Dad! I reckon we can corner it up there near those rocks.'

Bill stopped in his tracks and looked at me, wondering why I was hesitating. I shook my head. And grimaced. He gasped and swallowed, and I could see that my brother had realised that this move could be dangerous.

'Bill, slow down,' said Dad. 'Let's check this out before we go any further.'

'You stay well back out of the way, Emma,' I warned. 'That big pussy cat you were talking about has very big teeth and very big claws and it would enjoy devouring a little girl like you.'

'Don't frighten your little sister, Lizzie,' said Dad, grabbing the leash out of Bill's hands and tugging the dog back to his side. 'Sit, Banjo,' he ordered.

'Wait! I reckon the trail goes off into the gully,' said Bill, his voice suddenly a bit shaky. 'This could be tricky, Dad. There's a lot of really big gum trees down there by the creek. The cat could be sitting up there on a big branch, waiting to spring down on us. And there's a lot of big boulders along that creek bed, too. The cat could be hiding behind them, lying in wait for us.'

Dad bent over the prints to get a better look at them. He even picked up a bit of the dirt and sniffed it. 'I'm no expert tracker, Lizzie, but I've got to admit these prints don't look like anything I've ever seen. Still, I can't believe in big cats running around in the bush out here. This is near the home paddock, after all. Not that far from the house when you think about it.'

'We saw it, Dad, we all saw it last night. We watched it crunching up the sheep's bones like they were potato crisps. I reckon any minute it's going to jump out of the bushes and tear us to pieces. It'll probably go for Lizzie first because she's the one who shot at it.'

'Bill's really scaring me, Dad,' I said. 'Is that all right? Or is it only Emma who shouldn't be frightened?'

'Stop being sarcastic, Lizzie,' snapped Dad. He scratched his head. 'I've heard stories that some of the American troops who were stationed here during the Second World War brought in panthers as their mascots. I've heard people say that the animals were left behind when the men went back to the States. The story goes that they brought them in as kittens in their backpacks, and when they were going home, the cats were too big to smuggle out again, or so I heard.'

Dad grinned at me. There was a twinkle in his eye and I could see he didn't really believe what he was saying. I shrugged. I knew what I'd seen last night, although I had no idea where the panther had come from. Or why it had three heads.

He continued his story. 'Most of those stories came from the eastern states of Australia, though, from Victoria, or from New South Wales. There's never been any sightings of big cats in South Australia. The only monster we've ever had here was the Tantanoola tiger down near Mount Gambier. And that turned out to be a wolf that'd escaped from a travelling circus. And although people say they've seen panthers in the forests in Victoria, I've certainly never heard any reports of a three-headed cat. It's physically impossible, Lizzie. It must have been a trick of the light that made you think you saw a three-headed cat.'

'Why?' I asked.

From the corner of my eye I caught a movement in a tree ahead. My heart started thumping. Was it the cat? But it was just a couple of sulphur-crested cockatoos hopping along the branch. One of the birds cocked its head, raised its yellow crest, extended its wings and screeched at me.

Startled, I stumbled over a fallen tree branch. 'Bugger,' I said as I nearly stepped on a small lizard which glared at me before darting away to seek cover.

'Do you have to be so clumsy, Lizzie?' Dad asked.

I shrugged, trying to look as if I wasn't scared. But surely any self-respecting cat lurking in the bushes knew exactly where we were by now. I imagined the three heads disputing about the best way to launch itself on us. I just hoped there wouldn't be a consensus reached before we worked out where the thing was.

Dad still wasn't convinced the cat existed. He continued to expound about the impossibility of a three-headed panther. 'How would its mother give birth to it? You've watched ewes lambing. It's tough enough on a mother to get a normal one-headed baby out, let alone one with three heads. The baby would get stuck in the birth canal and die. I reckon a pack of dogs killed the sheep and when you came out here you saw a couple of feral cats finishing off the carcass and your imagination did the rest. It was a dark night and you did say Emma didn't use the spotlight all that well.'

'I tried hard, Daddy, but Lizzie kept yelling at me. It's her fault I dropped it.'

'We all saw it, Dad,' I said wearily. 'There was one cat with three heads. Long necks like serpents. Lashing around and glaring at us. Snarling and showing their fangs. Enormous fangs at that. Tearing the sheep to shreds.'

Dad shook his head. I knew he thought I was telling fairy stories, but I wasn't going to back down.

I continued. 'The mother probably manages to give birth to it because those heads are on such long necks, and maybe the baby somehow folds a couple of its heads back along its body so that only one head presents at the birth canal and it manages that way. We had a ewe give birth to a two-headed lamb once, remember that? It was just after Mum died.'

'Yes. As I remember it, the poor ewe nearly died giving birth to that monstrosity. I sent her off to market right away, if you remember. If a ewe breeds that sort of thing once, she's likely to do it again.'

I did remember. Dad said we couldn't afford to have genetic defects happening in our flock. Let one weird birth happen and if news of it gets out your whole flock is valueless. He killed that lamb before Bill or Emma saw it and he got rid of the body by burning it. We didn't even eat it, which I thought was a bit of a waste. Only someone must have eaten that ewe's meat, though. Just not us.

I had another idea. 'The babies might be encapsulated,' I said. 'When puppies are born, they're in little individual membranes that the mother has to break. If the kittens were wrapped up, they'd slide out fairly easily. How do giraffes give birth, anyway?'

'I don't know. You're still proposing a monster, Lizzie. You don't often get genetic variations like that. And if you do, they aren't viable. They'd never survive in the wild.'

'It might happen here, though, Dad. And this one must have survived, because we saw it. Maybe there's only one. I really hope there's only one. Because if this thing is breeding, if what we saw is the origin of new animal, then we're in big trouble. Perhaps it's a mutation because of radiation or something. It might be due to the magnetism that makes the cars roll up hill around here. Maybe people are right when they say this place is peculiar.'

Dad shook his head. 'That's crap, Lizzie. There's nothing weird about Magnetic Hill. It's just an optical illusion. It's because of the shape of the hill. There's a false horizon, or so I've heard. People always believe there's a mystical explanation for things they haven't looked at properly. You didn't see a three-headed cat last night, Lizzie, not really. A dark night and shadows cast by headlights can be deceptive. It's easy to see monsters at night when everything's distorted by shadows.'

I shrugged. Dad would believe me when he saw the cat. He wouldn't be able to deny his own eyes, to rationalise his way out of this situation. If we saw it, that is. I was almost hoping that he was right and I was delusional. But the other two kids had seen it too.

Before I could answer, Banjo yelped and so did Bill. The dog froze, his legs rigid, head raised, teeth bared in a snarl, tail held out behind his stiff body. Toby cringed and tried to hide behind me, but Banjo was alert. Bill was pretty alert, too.

'Bill,' Dad ordered, sounding as if he was back in the army again.

I hadn't hear him speak with that much authority since he organised Mum's funeral. Now he fixed a glare on Bill so severe that I thought my brother might salute. 'Hold tight to Banjo's leash. He's acting as if he can smell something up ahead. Keep Toby's leash tight, too. Be careful, Lizzie. Stay back here with me. If there really is an animal, wild dog or panther, it might be hiding in that outcrop of rocks over there. Emma, stay back there with Bill and let Lizzie and me go ahead. Lizzie, cock your rifle!'

'I want to see what's happening, Dad,' said Bill, inching forward and dragging Banjo and Toby behind him.

'And I won't be left behind,' whimpered Emma, grabbing my arm.

'We should have taken her to school, Dad. She would've been safer there.'

'Well, she's here now, Lizzie, so we just have to make the best of it. But we aren't going to take any chances. This might be a bit risky. No noise now.'

'And what about last night, Dad?' I felt like asking. Wasn't that just a bit risky?

It was a pretty silly telling everyone not to make any noise, because just then Banjo started yipping and yodelling and really sounding like the *Hound of the Baskervilles* in pursuit of an escaped criminal across the English moors. Toby, who would have preferred to stay at home with a bone to crunch up in the shade by the chook shed, began to whine. He tried to hide behind me and my legs got tangled in his leash and I fell over.

Emma clung to me and she gasped when I shook her off me. It was a good thing I hadn't taken the safety off the rifle yet. I looked at Dad. He shook his head. I knew that he was disgusted that I'd be clumsy when carrying arms. Because he used to be in the army, he's always impressed on us kids the rules for responsible gun use.

'For goodness sake, Lizzie, stop clowning around,' he hissed. 'What's that moving over there in the shadows under those rocks? Bloody hell, it really is a cat! It's a bloody panther! And it's huge. Oh, Christ, it has got three heads. Get back, Lizzie. Let me deal with this. Take the kids and get back to the ute.'

I resisted the urge to say 'I told you so' but I wasn't about to obey Dad either. I wasn't going anywhere. There was no way I'd let Dad deal with this situation. Not on his own. It didn't matter what sort of army orders he gave. This was mutiny. I was staying put. I cocked the rifle and took a sight along the barrel at the creature.

The cat was lying in the shade of the boulders and its tawny coloured sides speckled with darker coloured spots were heaving, and the eyes on the head that was facing my way were glazed. The animal didn't look at all healthy and even though I knew the thing was dangerous, that it had killed our stock and that it was a threat to our lives and to our livelihood, I felt sorry for it. Bill was right, it is the duty of a hunter to administer a swift and painless death if at all possible. That's another of Dad's rules, too.

Because it was lying on its side, I could see that the animal was a female and also that its breasts were engorged. It must have young at milk.

The other two heads twisted our way and the entire animal looked at us. Then its tail began to move, slowly at first, but then more rapidly. The dust rose as the tail lashed the dry earth. The animal growled and Emma clutched me again. The cat rose to its feet and began to advance wearily towards us as if it had an unpleasant duty to perform, perhaps a task that it was compelled to do even though it was against its will. That was a lot like the way I felt, too.

Emma pushed in ahead of me. She held the digital camera high. Dad grabbed her and tried to push her back behind him, but Emma had made up her mind that she wanted pictures for show and tell. Toby rushed after Emma. He's always been very protective of Emma.

Later, when we looked at the photos, there was one that showed an enormous paw raised towards Toby's head. Toby must have moved much faster than I thought he could to evade that blow.

Emma had only managed to get half the dog's head and half of the cat's paw with the lethal-looking claws extended in the picture, but you could work out what was happening if you'd been there. What I couldn't work out was how Toby had survived. He must have jumped like a kangaroo to escape those claws. I didn't see exactly what happened, because I was trying to shoot the cat. I think my hands were shaking so much that I missed. Dad said later that he couldn't use his gun because he was trying to shove Emma back out of the way.

There was another photo depicting the business end of my rifle just as I pulled the trigger. Emma had managed to capture the smoke coming out of the end of the gun and part of the animal's back but because she'd nudged my arm, my shot went high. But it was an impressive photo, as photos go. There was a third picture of the retreating backside and tail of the creature as it fled towards a small cave that Bill and I used to play in when we were younger.

That cave was halfway up a hill and we used to drag our bags of goodies up there for picnics. Back in the days before Mum died, Bill and I slept there overnight a few times in summer. We had the time of our lives, hauling a bucket of water up the hill from the creek, cooking sausages over a little campfire and lying in our sleeping-bags in the cave, giggling in the darkness and feeling very adventurous. Dad never objected to our camping trips, but Mum wasn't at all happy about them. She said we could be in danger. I remember asking her whether she thought it was spiders, snakes, wombats or possums that she was worried might attack us. I hate to think what she would have said if she was with us when we encountered that cat.

I reloaded my rifle and I looked at Dad, hoping for orders or instructions. But Dad was shaking his head violently as if to clear the sight of the monster from his eyes.

We watched the cat disappear into the cave. I could see the end of its tail protruding, lashing about like a decapitated snake's body. At any minute, I thought, it's going to turn round, charge down the hill and attack us.

Dad must have had the same thought. 'Get back to the car, you kids! I'll save you!' he yelled, pushing Bill back and knocking him over.

Bill lay on the ground clutching Banjo's leash and moaning.

'Sorry, mate,' said Dad, pulling Bill to his feet and hugging him.

Then Dad jumped in front of us kids and extended his arms. He looked like Superman about to take off, though he didn't have his undies outside his pants. I think he'd decided he would defend his family with his bare hands if necessary. Real super hero stuff. I don't think he was trying to stop us from running after the cat. If that was the case, it was a bit unnecessary, because I had no intention of following the panther into its lair. Toby decided he had had enough too. I grabbed his lead again when he ran back and tried to hide behind me.

Seeing that thing in the full glare of the morning sun had scared me even more than seeing it in the spotlight last night had done. At least in the dark I could almost pretend to myself that I was imagining things.

Emma, after her first rash decision to get near enough to photograph the cat, had shrunk back behind Dad. She was clutching her bag. Bill had dropped Banjo's leash when he was knocked over, but he held it now in both hands, afraid that the dog would rush after the cat. Toby was tugging on his leash now, too, but he was facing the other way, back towards the ute and, he hoped, back home and a safe spot under a chair or a bed.

I looked at Dad for guidance. He was, I could see, having problems. I saw doubt, confusion, fear and anger pass over his face. I could understand the doubt and the confusion and the fear, because that's how I had felt when I first saw the cat. But why was he so angry? I could see he was absolutely enraged.

'Don't anyone move,' Dad ordered grimly. 'Just let it get away. Lizzie, check your rifle again in case it decides to come back again. Cats are unpredictable things.'

He re-loaded his rifle and cocked it and I did the same. We stood together like the Spartans waiting for the Persian attack at Thermopylae. But the cat was staying inside the little cave. A strong smell of feline urine wafted down to us on the breeze, and I knew the panther must have been using that cave as a den for some time. Had generations of panthers bred there, their genes mutating over time, producing worse and worse offspring until this beast with three heads was born?

After a while, the animal came out carrying something in each of its three mouths. Three little somethings that wriggled and squirmed. The cat turned one large head in our direction and glared balefully at us. I realised what it was carrying down the hillside. There were three kittens, one in each mouth, held gently in the great jaws, carried by the folds of skin on the kittens' shoulders. Each infant, like the mother cat, had three writhing heads on long necks, clearly visible as they twisted about in the morning sunlight. When I say 'kittens' I should qualify that by saying that these babies were about the size of my friend Zoe's full-grown Burmese cat, Miaou Tse Tung. And Tung is a very big boy. The mother's other two heads were turned away from us. She seemed to be working out her escape route.

'She's got babies,' gasped Emma from her place of safety behind Dad. 'I can hear them crying. And look, there's another little one at the mouth of the cave, trying to follow her, but it can't keep up. Its legs are all shaky. It hasn't learned how to walk properly yet. Look how cute it is.'

'My legs are all shaky too,' I said. 'Keep quiet, Emma. We don't want to distract her. Dad, we'll have to get some help. We can't cope with this on our own. You've seen how big that thing is. If she's got babies, there must be a male somewhere out there. It'll be bigger than she is, and she's big enough to pull down a fully grown sheep.'

'Yes,' said Dad, very quietly. 'And now I know what you must have gone through last night, Lizzie. I failed you. I've failed all you kids. I've failed in my duty as a parent, I've failed in my duty as a human being. Your mother would be disgusted, disappointed in me. She'd be furious if she knew how I've let you down. I just want you to know that I'm never going to fail you again. Not ever again. I swear it on your mother's grave.'

I sighed and nodded. I'd heard Dad make promises like that before. He'd said something like that when we stood beside Mum's grave after the coffin was lowered into the dusty earth. Something like 'It's just us now, kids, and I'll always be here for you. You can count on that.' I hoped he was right this time, but I wouldn't be holding my breath about the odds. But even if he stayed off the drink for as long as it took to do something about the cat, that would be something.

I patted his arm. 'We'll get through this, Dad. We'll have to phone the neighbours, get everyone in on this. We'll have to call the police or the emergency services in. The whole community's at risk from that thing. And from its mate.'

We turned to go back to the car.

'Daddy, Daddy, what about the other baby? Look at it. It's been left behind and it's crying. It'll die if its mummy abandons it. It's so little. We have to help it.'

'You've got to be kidding, Emma,' I said. 'That thing's a monster. If it doesn't die, we'll have to kill it. We can't tolerate creatures like that on our farm. When it grows up, it'll be just as nasty as its mother and it might even eat you.'

But Emma was already running up the hillside towards the dark little cave and was scooping the kitten up in her arms, cradling it and crooning to it, stroking the spotted fur on one of its three heads. As we rushed after her, I heard the thing mewling and then, unbelievably, I heard deep purring begin. The head that Emma had been stroking rubbed against my sister's face.

'The mother will come back in a minute to get it and she'll kill us all,' I gasped. 'Put that thing down and let's get out of here. Fast.'

'She might not be able to count,' said Emma. 'She might think she only has three kittens. She might forget about this one and just think about the other three kittens. See how small this one is. It must be the runt of the litter. Sometimes animals abandon the runt because they think it won't survive. Can I take it home, Daddy?'

'No!' I yelled. 'Definitely, absolutely, no!'

The mewling grew louder. The kitten was distraught. So was Emma. Tears welled in her eyes and ran down her face.

'But it's crying, Lizzie. Listen to it. It's got no one to look after it. I'll take my teddy out of my bag and we can put the little kitty in there to carry it home. Bill can carry Ted. I'll empty the kitty litter tray every morning and I'll feed the kitten and you won't have to do any of the work for it, Lizzie. I promise on my word of honour.'

'You don't have any honour, Emma,' I said. 'Or any words for it either.'

She cradled the kitten and it cuddled into her, rubbing all three heads against her chest. She smiled at us. 'No one at school has a kitten with three heads.'

'I knew you had your rotten bear in that bag,' I said. 'What did you do with those sandwiches I made this morning?'

'I left them on the kitchen table because I needed Ted with me. I was scared of the big pussy cat and I needed my teddy to give me courage,' said Emma, clutching Dad's arm and smiling up at him through wet lashes.

No, I told myself. He's not going to give in this time. He's going to stand up to her. Just because she's looking at him with those eyes that look so much like Mum's eyes, just because the tears are welling up in those eyes, he won't say yes to her. Not about something like this.

Dad sighed. 'We can't do this, Emma. This is really dangerous. Cats always know how many kittens they have in their litter. When the mother has found somewhere to put her other babies, she's going to come looking for this one and she could follow us. She might even track us back to the homestead, and then we'll all be in really big trouble.'

'Please, Daddy.'

3

I felt like screaming when we got home because Dad immediately started pulling six-packs of beer out of the fridge. Three six-packs. There was always more beer than food in our fridge. He put the bottles on the kitchen table and reached for the bottle opener.

'He's going to drink himself silly to forget what he's just seen,' I told Bill, sniffing hard and fighting back my tears.

Bill pulled a face and shrugged as if to say, 'What did you expect?'

'And there I was kidding myself that he was going to be noble and protective of us and fight off the monsters,' I said. 'We'll have to go into town ourselves and call the cops to chase the cat. And then we'll all be put into protective custody and we'll lose the farm and have to live in the city. Probably in an orphanage or something, because Auntie Bet can't take us all in. I suppose she'll take Emma, but she won't want us.'

'Here's the bottle opener. Open all those bottles and pour the beer down the kitchen sink, Lizzie,' ordered Dad. 'I've got phone calls to make.'

I've never moved faster in my life. The beer was gurgling in the sink before Dad picked up the phone. I hoped that for once the phone connection wouldn't be impaired by the magnetism from the hill, or whatever it was that makes communication difficult around here. Usually our home phone works reasonably well, but there are often strange crackles and noises that you don't hear when you ring from some where else. From my friend Zoe's house down in the town, for example.

'Why don't we just go into town to the police station and report that we've got a three-headed panther on the property?' I asked, leaning away from the amber liquid that swirled in among the breakfast dishes I hadn't had time to wash this morning.

I really hate the smell of beer, especially in the morning. I realised that the colour of the beer was the same colour as the six eyes that had glared at us this morning with so much malice in them as the panther had carried away three of her kittens. The same colour as the eyes on the kitten that Emma had insisted we bring back home.

Had we brought evil into our home in the shape of the three-headed kitten? Emma didn't think so, but as I watched her empty the clean washing out of my linen basket and install the monster on top of a towel that she had taken from the bathroom, I knew that we had made a very big mistake in letting her keep the creature. Especially when I recognised the towel as the one I usually used.

Emma caught my eye and shrugged. I threw a bottle top at her and missed. It hit an ear on one of the kitten's three heads and that head bared its fangs and spat at me. The other two heads, apparently oblivious to whatever was happening in their siblings' brain, watched Emma tucking my towel into a more comfortable shape to fit the basket. Then I saw the front paws they all shared begin to knead the cloth to suit their joint body, and the entire animal curled itself up and settled into a comfortable position. The kitten I had assaulted with the bottle top still showed its fangs to me and held its head stiffly erect, even though the other two heads purred as they rubbed against Emma's hands. This is a seriously weird beast, I thought.

'I'll phone first to make sure Sergeant Wylie's on duty today,' said Dad. 'It's useless talking to that young idiot of a constable he's got. What's his name? Perkins?'

Dad listened for a dial tone, shook the phone, put it down and picked it up again. Please make the phone work, God, I prayed. Dad dialled the number again and waited for a response.

'If Jack Wylie's in the station and not out playing golf with the mayor, I'll take the camera with those photos on it with me and go in and see what he suggests we do. If he isn't there, I'll hold off going in until this afternoon.'

'I'll come with you,' I offered, opening another bottle. I wanted to make sure that Dad didn't replace this batch of beer with fresh supplies while he was in town, and I didn't particularly want to stay in a house with a demented kitten and a crazy sister. Let Bill cope with them both. I needed a bit of space.

'You can't come, Lizzie,' said Dad. 'I told the school that you had diarrhoea. I'm stretching my credibility already with a story of a cat attacking my stock without being shown to be lying to the headmaster. Jack Wylie's wife works at the school, remember? And anyway, you need to be here in case the mother cat comes looking for that kitten. Defend the homestead. When you've finished emptying the bottles, load every gun we've got, just in case. Including that old shotgun, the one we haven't used for years. It's out in the shed.'

He listened to the phone again. 'They take their time answering, don't they? What if someone had been murdered or had their house broken into?'

'That sort of thing never happens in Bullyacre, Dad,' I said. 'Nothing ever happens in Bullyacre.'

'It has now,' said Bill. 'Three-headed cats happen here.'

'What a pretty kitty you are,' crooned Emma, stroking one of the kitten's heads.

The kitten arched its back and rubbed a head against her hand.

'The spare ammo's on top of the kitchen cupboard,' said Dad.

'Maybe I could start by shooting that thing,' I said, frowning at my sister and her new pet.

The thing in question stretched luxuriously in the laundry basket while Emma fed it with strips of the stir-fry chicken meat I had intended to cook for our dinner. She had pinched some of the raw mutton that we feed the dogs, too, I noticed. And a bit of leftover meat pie from the day before yesterday.

'Just what do you think we're going to eat tonight if you feed the stir-fry stuff to that monster?' I demanded.

'Cuddles doesn't like the mutton,' Emma said, when she saw me frowning at her. 'But she really likes the chicken. Spotty likes the mutton, though. And Tabby prefers the pie.'

'You've given that ugly, horrible monster three names?' I asked. 'Why don't you just call the whole thing Satan or Lucifer, and then we'll know where we are? You could call it Lucy for short.'

'But all the heads are different,' protested Emma. 'They've all got different personalities. Cuddles always purrs when I touch her, Spotty doesn't like being handled much, although she's improving now and I think she'll be quite sweet soon, and Tabby bites me all the time.

Not very hard,' she added when she saw Dad turn to watch what was happening. 'Just a little nip to tell me to back off.'

I had a sudden inspiration. 'Why don't you take Cuddles with you when you go into town, Dad? There'll be no question of your credibility if you've got an actual specimen with you. I mean, I wouldn't believe a story about a three-headed monster just because someone told it to me. Especially when it's our family and we live on Magnetic Hill. You know about all the things people believe about this place. They'll think we're crazier than they already do unless we have proof. The three-headed kitten is perfect proof. Small enough to be transportable, won't bite Sergeant Wylie too hard, and the mayor could stuff it and put it on exhibition for the tourists.'

'No!' shrieked Emma, lifting the kitten out of its basket and hugging it so tightly that all the six eyes bulged. 'You're not going to take Cuddles away from me. She's my pet and it's not her fault she's got her sisters stuck to her. She's not a monster, and I really love her. And she trusts me. She needs me. And I need her. '

The head that Emma had said was called Tabby – I suppose it was a lighter colour than the other two heads – swished its neck around and nipped Emma on the ear.

'Ow!' she yelled. 'Now see what you've done, Lizzie. You've upset her.'

She put the creature back in the basket. The head called Cuddles extended itself on its serpent-like neck and rubbed itself against Emma. The Spotty head, which, I had to admit, did have more blotches on it than the other two heads, twisted away as far as it could, then turned and regarded Emma and its two sisters' heads with disdain. The Tabby head straightened its neck vertically as high in the air as it could and spat at Emma.

This is one schizophrenic cat, I thought. I wondered if the mother cat had similar problems. If so, how was consensus ever achieved? How did it come to agreement about anything? What if one head wanted to climb a tree at the same time that another brain decided it was time to snooze in the sun, while the other one wanted to go hunting? It would be like having a committee run your life. I almost felt sorry for the monster. Almost, but not quite.

I rapped on my own head with my knuckles. Maybe none of this was actually happening. Maybe I was delirious and dreaming the whole situation. Or maybe I'd fallen over, banged my head and gone totally, absolutely mad and any minute I'd wake up in a nice clean white bed to see a doctor in a white coat asking me what day it was and who the prime minister was and if I could remember who'd won the latest football match.

'Sergeant Jack Wylie?' Dad was saying. 'Hello, Jack. Frank Epsom here. I've got a bit of a problem out here on Epsom Downs. My sheep are getting torn to shreds by a panther. Yes, Jack, that's what I said, a panther. No it's not a bloody bad phone line. It's a panther. A bloody big cat.'

There was a silence, which I took to mean that Sergeant Wylie was absorbing Dad's news and preparing some sort of reply. It was like waiting for an earthquake to strike. He's a pretty explosive sort of bloke, our local copper. He always says he's a very busy man, though if anyone wants him the best place to look for him is on the golf course, but he's not known for his patience on the course, either, if you listen to what the mayor, who's his favourite playing partner, says. Apparently Wylie's been known to throw his best golf stick into the bushes if a ball doesn't go where it's meant to go, and heaven help any hapless kangaroo that wanders onto the fairway when he's hitting a drive. The mayor says the baby kangas hide in their mothers' pouches with their paws over their ears so they can't hear the language the sergeant uses.

I was worried about the response that Dad would get from the sergeant. What if Dad, discouraged in his quest for help, changed his mind about giving up the demon drink and decided to drown his sorrows?

I knew it was time to speed up the alcohol disposal. I grabbed Bill and pushed the opener into his hand. 'You open and I'll pour,' I said. 'Quickly!'

'I'll snap and you glug and gurgle,' agreed Bill.

'No, it's not feral cats,' said Dad. 'Well, OK, it is feral cats. But it's the biggest feral cat I've ever seen. It has to be a panther or a leopard. I saw it in broad daylight, Jack. A huge, tawny-coloured thing with spots. It has to be a panther. The kids saw it too.'

I noted that Dad hadn't made any mention that we kids had seen the thing first in the darkness; that he had allowed us to go out hunting last night on our own while he was drunk and disorderly. That's not the sort of admission that a man makes to the cops, even in a small town like Bullyacre. Probably amounts to child neglect, I reckon. I could hear an agitated voice on the other end of the phone, because Dad had taken the phone away from his ear and was holding it at arm's length. People tend to do that a lot around our copper. The yelling went on for a bit before Dad could get a word in.

'I was stone-cold sober when I saw it, Jack,' Dad protested. 'Lizzie shot the thing in the leg with a .22 last night, and that slowed it down a bit but not much. Yes, I know the average moggie would be more than slowed down by a .22 bullet, but we aren't dealing with the average moggie here. This thing's bloody big. No, I'm not having you on, Jack. I haven't got the DTs. And no, it's not an April Fool's Day joke. It's not even April, for God's sake.'

Dad tugged at his hair, drummed his fingers on the kitchen table and cast longing glances at the remaining bottles on the sink. I nudged my brother. Bill opened, I poured.

'I've got photos,' Dad said. 'Emma took photos of the panther. Well, bits of it. A paw, a backside. Enough to see what we're up against. It's not just my sheep, Jack, it's everyone's bloody sheep. When mine are all gone, the next bloke's sheep will go.'

Dad did some more finger tapping and hair pulling while Bill and I did more bottle opening and more beer pouring. Emma stroked Cuddles's head and tried to avoid Tabby's teeth. Spotty glared at Banjo, who had wandered into the kitchen. Banjo snarled and all three kittens simultaneously spat and arched their collective back. Emma cooed and stroked her pet, and eventually they settled down again, although all three heads swivelled to follow Banjo as he slunk around the kitchen with his tail between his legs and the hackles raised on his neck and shoulders. He glared at the kitten from behind a chair, and the kitten glared back with six angry eyes.

'What if it decides to attack people after that? Do you want that on your conscience? It won't help your career much if the newspapers find out that you sat on your hands and allowed a massacre to happen, will it? That would be classed as criminal negligence, wouldn't it? Don't you have a duty of care as an officer of the law to protect the good citizens of Bullyacre and their livestock?' Dad paused to let those ideas sink in.

There seemed to be silence at the other end of the phone, or at least the splutters that I had heard before had ceased. But of course, the phone connection might have failed, or Sergeant Wylie might have hung up.

'The whole community of Bullyacre could be at risk,' Dad continued. 'What if the monster comes into town at night and eats some of the townspeople?'

Dad put the phone down and grinned. 'I reckon that's the first time anyone's ever got the better of Jack Wylie,' he said. 'Hand me that camera, Lizzie, lock the doors and keep those guns ready in case the mother comes looking for her kitten. I'm going into town.'

4

'We can't let the media get hold of this story!' shouted the mayor. 'We've got tourists coming here because they've heard the legend of Magnetic Hill. Tourism brings a lot of money into our business district. If they get scared off, we'll lose that money and my pub'll go broke. And the caravan park and the bed and breakfasts and the café and the ice cream shop and the newsagent. We've got to keep the lid on this.'

'People won't even stop to refuel here!' said Ted Jenkins. 'I'll be bankrupt if the tourists don't stop for petrol. And let's face it, most of them only do stop for petrol. They drive in, go out to see if their cars really do roll up the hill when they ought to roll down, then they come back into town and refuel and off they go, back to Adelaide, or wherever they came from. Sometimes they don't even go out to the hill. They just stop here because it's far enough from Broken Hill to need gas. Never mind your pub and the caravan park. It's the passing trade that brings the money into this town.'

'What about the safety aspect?' thundered Sergeant Wylie. 'I have a duty of care here. I've got to look after the whole community of Bullyacre. If there really is a big cat out there, we've got to destroy it. And I reckon we'll have to have to call in extra help. We can't do this alone. If that thing really exists, if Frank Epsom is telling the truth about this thing, I'm going to have to file a report to my superiors. And yes, the media will probably hear about it, and yes, there goes the tourist trade and there's nothing we can do about it.' He hammered on the podium with his fist and yelled, 'If you lot don't shut up, I'm arresting the troublemakers!'

The audience shut up immediately.

'So we have to go out there and shoot that thing,' he continued. 'If it's there. I'm not saying that it is out there, and I'm not saying that it's not. I'm keeping an open mind. Just in case.'

'It's out there, Jack, it really does exist. My kids and I saw it and we've got the photos to prove it. I say we work together systematically, track it down and shoot it,' said Dad, standing up to make himself heard. 'The last time we saw it, it wasn't looking too healthy because Lizzie shot it. Once in the gut and once in the upper leg. It was limping away carrying its three kittens, headed deeper into that big gully on my property. It shouldn't be too difficult for a group of us with dogs and guns to track it down and put it out of its misery.'

'How was it carrying three kittens at once?' asked the mayor. 'It'd only carry one at a time, wouldn't it? All the cats I've ever seen carry one kitten at a time. Some of your story doesn't add up. The whole thing sounds more than a bit weird to me, Frank.'

You don't know just how weird it really is, Mr Mayor, I thought. Dad and I had previously decided not to tell the people at the meeting in the town hall that the mother had three heads. 'One step at a time, Lizzie,' Dad had said. 'Just let them take it slowly, or it'll be too much for them to absorb.'

I'd thought it was a mistake to mention about the kittens, and I thought Dad had agreed not to say anything about them. But that's my Dad: you can never be quite sure what he is going to do. Unpredictable; a lot like Bill, actually. That's where Bill gets it from. Genetics again.

'Frank probably doesn't mean the panther took them all at once,' said Ted Jenkins. 'Everyone knows that cats carry one kitten at a time. It must have taken away one kitten, dropped it in the bushes and come back to pick up another one. The whole thing would have been pretty stressful. You can't expect Frank and the kids to remember every detail about the incident.'

Dad just nodded. He wasn't about to offer an opinion about the kitten carrying. 'You're right, Ted, it was very stressful,' Dad said. 'You have no idea how much stress the kids and I suffered out there.'

One of the ladies of the auxiliary who was sitting behind me reached out and patted my back in sympathy. I nearly went through the roof when I felt her touch. I had been drifting off to sleep, perhaps lulled by the heat in the hall or simply because I was totally exhausted. When I felt Mrs Evans touch me, I thought it was the mother cat who'd crept up to claw me.

Dad put his arm around me. 'Best not to complicate matters, Lizzie,' he whispered. 'Let them find out what we're really up against when we actually find the thing. Sometimes you're better dealing with the devil you think you know than the devil you don't know.'

I nodded. It had been hard enough to convince Dad that the cat had three heads. I wasn't going to get into discussion about genetics with a whole hall full of adults. And our town hall was full of adults tonight. Chockers, in fact. Most of the population of Bullyacres was here tonight.

Old Miss Cobbledick wasn't here, but she never goes out any more except when she wants to. She's ninety-eight, after all, and she lives in a huge old house on the edge of town. She says it's too far to drive in at her age. That's a pretty good excuse to keep away from emergency meetings in the hall and stay at home with a cosy cup of tea and the television, even if there was a wild panther at large. And if I know Miss Cobbledick, any cats foolish enough to turn up on her doorstep would probably be beaten to death with her walking stick. And Mr Murchison, who had a heart attack last week, was still down in Adelaide in the hospital, so he had a good reason not to attend too.

But I reckon everyone else was sitting on the edge of the hard wooden seats in the hall, craning forward to hear what Sergeant Wylie, Mayor Murphy and the town councillors had to say. But I reckon they craned forward more to hear what my dad had to say, even more than when Sergeant Wylie was speaking. That made me feel pretty good. No one had ever listened to my dad much before tonight. He had always been dismissed as the town drunk before this.

Amazing how they'd all come along. One phone call from Sergeant Wylie about a panther being on the loose in the area, and the people of Bullyacre had panicked. One citizen phoned the next one, and the news spread faster than a jar of Vegemite spilt on the floor on a hot day.

Of course, it's not every day you get news like that in an Australian country town, so they were all here, young and old. I suppose the parents didn't like the idea of leaving their offspring at home alone in case a marauding big cat came tapping on the door while the kids were sitting in front of their televisions watching *The Simpsons*. Some of the younger kids were in their pyjamas. They'd all brought along their Nintendos and Play Stations and they were busily tapping away at them. There were bleeps and dings and blats all over the row where those kids were sitting. I really hate those machines. Electronic babysitting, I call it. I wouldn't let Emma have one even if we could afford it. They destroy children's brain cells, in my opinion. I believe in kids reading books, not peering at flickering lights on a hand-held electronic toy. Kids should be reading. Reading makes you think. I managed to grow up without those gadgets, and so did Dad. In fact, whole generations of people have lived without them. There's nothing in our genetic make-up that says we should spend hours playing silly games on electronic toys.

As it was, though, Emma was looking over her best friend's shoulder and taking great interest in the little flickering screen. But the older kids appeared to be interested in the current affairs of Bullyacre and tonight's proceedings in the hall. A bit too interested, some of them.

Before the meeting started, while we were waiting outside the hall for the doors to be opened, I'd had a bit of ribbing from my friends. Well, the ones who were doing the ribbing weren't actually my friends. Just kids who attend the same school that I go to. Kids that I usually avoid.

'So you've got a real live monster out there on Magnetic Hill this time, have you, Lizzie?' said Alex. 'Not just your brother Bill dressed up in a Halloween costume?'

'Shouldn't you be at home doing your homework, Alex?' I asked. 'Last time I heard, you weren't doing too well at algebra. Or haven't you learned how to use a calculator yet?'

'Are you sure this panther wasn't just something your dad saw when he was under the influence of whisky or brandy or Flanagan's hooch?' asked another of the kids. It was Matthew this time. 'He's half-tanked most of the time, isn't he? Can't hold his drink, or so I hear.'

'There's no need to say stuff like that, fellers,' said Jake. 'Fun's fun, but you don't have to be rude. It's not Lizzie's fault if her dad tipples a bit. Anyway, apparently it was Lizzie who saw the cat, not her dad. And Lizzie's credibility has never been in question. Ever.'

I resisted the urge to punch Matthew. And Alex, and Jake as well, for good measure. Patronising twit. I suppose he gets it from his dad, the Anglican vicar. Jake's sort of OK really – well, he's not as horrible as the other two – but the way I saw it, if he hung around with them, he'd be tarred with the same brush even if he wasn't quite as bad. Stupidity by association.

'Lizzie, calm down!' My friend Zoe was tugging on my arm.

I hadn't realised how angry I was until I noticed I was shaking. I'd clenched my fist and it was only inches from Matthew's nose. I'd almost lost my cool entirely. It wouldn't be a good look if those boys had gone into the town hall with bloody noses blaming me for beating them up. It wouldn't do my reputation any good at all. The whole town would say I'd been driven mad from living on the hill.

'Leave Lizzie alone, you pack of dim wits,' Zoe said. 'I've seen the photos Emma took of the panther. That's a really scary wild animal. I bet none of you would have had the nerve to stand there and shoot at that cat. You'd have run for the hills, and pissed yourselves while you were running, too.'

'And what would you have done, Zoe?' demanded Alex.

'That's just what I mean. I probably would've run away too. We all would've been scared shitless. Only Lizzie had the guts to stand there and shoot at that thing.'

The mayor stuck his head out of the door. 'I might have known. We can't hear ourselves think inside the hall with all the noise you kids are making. Shut up, get inside and sit down. The meeting's about to start.'

As we walked into the hall, Zoe turned to me. 'Jake's really keen on you, Lizzie.'

'No, he's not,' I said. 'He takes every opportunity to have a go at me. I can't stand him. Anyway, I thought he liked Rebecca Wilson. He hung around with her all last term.'

'They split up ages ago,' Zoe said. 'He said she was boring and she said he was too religious for her taste. He goes to church every Sunday, you know.'

'He has to go to church. His dad's a minister.'

'Nathan told me that Jake wants you to be his girlfriend,' Zoe insisted. 'Apparently he thinks you're really cool. He told Nathan that you're smart and funny and pretty and he wants to take you to the family picnic at the Lions' Park next month. Only he's too scared to ask you.'

No one had ever called me pretty before. I've got this sort of orange-coloured hair. Mum used to call it auburn, but Bill says it's red and it reminds him of over-ripe tomatoes. And I've got the skin to go with it, sort of pale like a fish's belly, and I get freckles all over my nose in summer unless I wear a hat. And I always forget to wear a hat. And my eyes get this sort of greenish tinge especially when I'm angry, which I still was when I sat down next to Dad, even though it was nice to hear that Jake liked me.

'I'll be going with my family,' I called after Zoe as she headed for the row of seats where her family was sitting, 'but if Jake wants to sit on my picnic rug he's welcome. He'll have to put up with my brother Bill and my little sister, though.' I almost said, 'And with my dad who'll probably be half-plastered,' but then I remembered that Dad had given up the booze. And I couldn't have said that out loud anyway, because Dad was sitting there, patting the seat beside him where he'd kept a place for me. I smiled at him and hoped that this time he'd keep his vow.

Inside the hall, it was the adults who were making all the noise. Or the adults who had a vested interest in tourism, anyway. The rest of the townspeople were, as I said, sitting up very straight on the hard wooden slats of their chairs, anxious to hear what the danger was and what was going to be done to protect them. Even the ladies of the auxiliary, who were fussing about at the back of the hall with their tea urn and their cups and scones, stopped work, leant against their table and listened intently.

'We haven't had this much excitement in Bullyacre since we had that plague of mice about ten years ago,' I heard Mrs Mitchell say. 'This business has brought more people into town even than the time when those grasshoppers were swarming and everyone panicked because we thought they'd eat all the crops and our gardens too. And the government sent contractors to spray them. How long ago was that? Five years back? There's nothing like a bit of a scare to unite people, is there?'

'We've got more people here tonight than when we had that line-dancing craze a few years ago when everyone danced down the main street and Ada Smith was hit by that horse,' Mrs Jenkins agreed. 'There's almost as many folk here as we get on New Year's Eve for the fireworks display. But do you think the rumours are true? I mean this business of a panther supposedly wandering about up on Epsom Downs. Near that Magnetic Hill.'

'I wouldn't go out there if you paid me, panthers or not. But I wouldn't trust anything that Frank Epsom said, anyway. He hits the bottle a bit, doesn't he?'

'Anything could happen out there on Epsom Downs. There's a hex on that place. Haunted, it is. Everyone says so. Cars run up hill out there on Magnetic Hill when their engines are turned off. Would you believe that? My Alf saw it happen once.'

'Don't look now, Elsie. That's Frank Epsom's daughter, Lizzie, over there. And there's the whole Epsom family with her.'

My ears were burning. I looked at Dad, and he was going red in the face, too.

'Hush, Lizzie. Don't let them know we heard,' he said softly. 'Don't give them the satisfaction.'

I couldn't resist glancing their way. They were both looking in my direction. I felt like giving the sign of the evil eye to spook them. Silly old things. We wouldn't have overheard their conversation if they hadn't been shouting at the top of their voices. They probably forgot to bring their hearing aids along. Although it was rowdy in here, with everyone talking at once.

'The meeting will come to order,' roared the mayor.

Obediently, the audience fell silent.

Sergeant Wylie waved copies of the photos that Emma had taken. 'Frank's young daughter, Emma, took these pictures. My wife, Ms Wylie from the high school, printed them off for me. Have a look at them. I reckon they'll dispel any lingering doubts that you might have. Pass them around, but don't take too long about it. We have to decide pretty quickly what we're going to do, and who are going to be the ones to do it.'

The photos were passed around. Even Alex, Matthew and Jake

looked impressed when it came their time to peer at the photos. They pointed to various bits of the pictures and whispered amongst themselves.

'Don't hold on to them too long, kids. Keep passing them around. The adults need to see those photos. We don't want to stay here all night gawking,' said the mayor.

'Right,' said the sergeant. 'It looks as if the consensus of opinion is that we, the people of Bullyacre, would rather sort this out ourselves than call in the appropriate authorities. I don't see why we shouldn't have a go at it, to see if we can fix our own problems in the first instance, but unless we have this cat business knocked on the head inside a week, I'm eventually going to have to file an official report, alert the authorities and, to use a pun, let the cat out of the bag.'

The mayor groaned. He ought to be accustomed to the way Sergeant Wylie acts, I thought. They spend hours on that golf course. He probably sees more of the sergeant than the sergeant's wife does.

The police officer waved a piece of paper at the assembled Bullyacrists. 'I've got a list here and I expect every able-bodied man who's capable of bearing arms to write his name on it, and show everyone what you're made of.'

There was an immediate hubbub from the women in the audience, who felt that they were being excluded. The word 'misogynist' was one word that was shouted vehemently and loudly, along with a few cries of 'Just who do you think you are, Jack Wylie?' and 'I can shoot as well as the next man' and 'I can shoot better than the next man.' I'll admit that I was the person who yelled that one out, but I was supported loudly in my boasting by most of the Country Women's Association members. 'We ladies can do more than cook fruit cake and knit, you know,' one of them yelled, and the rest of them grumbled in agreement.

I think it was Jack Wylie's wife, the schoolteacher, who had called Jack a misogynist. When she was appointed as assistant head, Jack's wife had her hair cut really short and told everyone to address her as Ms Wylie. Apparently she's been writing articles on women's lib and conservation and birdwatching, but I don't think any of them have been published yet. I had a feeling that Sergeant Jack Wylie was going to be in big trouble when he got home unless the more militant ladies of Bullyacre were included in the vigilante group.

'When we've got the panther's body, we can get a taxidermist to stuff it and we'll mount it here, in the hall, in a glass case, and we'll charge the tourists admission to see it,' suggested the mayor. 'That's what they did down at Mount Gambier with the Tantanoola tiger. And that isn't even a tiger. It's just a moth-eaten dog. I've seen it. A timber wolf that escaped from a travelling zoo, apparently. If this thing really is a panther, and if it really is as big as Frank Epsom says it is, people will come from all over Australia to see it. This is going to be better than that moose-head they've got hanging in the council chambers at Orroroo.'

'Bloody good idea, Dick,' said the sergeant. 'So now all we have to do is find the cat and shoot it. I reckon this is going to be the making of Bullyacre. It's going to put us on the map! Go home now, everyone. Get your guns, get your dogs and meet back here in an hour's time!'

'What about the women who don't want to go hunting? What about the kiddies?' demanded Rex Jeffries. 'I'm happy to go out looking for the panther, but I'm not leaving my wife and kids alone in my house while I'm away.'

'Bring them back here,' said the sergeant. 'The windows in the hall are high up and not all that big, and nothing can get through that door when it's locked. The wood's six inches thick, whatever that is in centimetres these days. Any schoolteachers who don't want to come out looking for the panther,' he paused and looked in Mr Gonski's and Ms Wylie's direction, 'can stay here and take care of the children. And the Ladies Auxiliary can do the catering. Bring sleeping bags, toothbrushes, that sort of thing back here for the non-combatants.'

The ladies of the auxiliary protested that they had gone to the trouble of baking scones and preparing tea, and no one was going to leave until their efforts had been consumed and enjoyed. No hunters should go out in the field without full bellies, they insisted. It would improve everyone's concentration if there were no tummy rumbles to contend with. There was no telling how long it would be before the next meal.

After a good deal of muttering between themselves, Jack Wylie and the mayor agreed to this short delay, but the scones were gulped down in great haste and with less appreciation than they and the ladies who'd baked them deserved. Then the people of Bullyacre jostled to leave the hall to prepare for battle. Sergeant Wylie stood in the doorway as the citizens filed out and made one final announcement. He always has to have the last word, I thought. Although, of course, sometimes the mayor managed to do that. No wonder they were best friends.

'This will be an alcohol-free excursion. Any man who brings a bottle of anything stronger than lemonade is banned from taking part. Guns and booze don't mix.'

I was insulted that he looked directly at Dad when he said that. My father had promised Bill, Emma and me that he would never drink again. To be perfectly honest, I wasn't all that confident that Dad would keep his word, but that was my private opinion, and I didn't see why our family honour had to be besmirched in front of the whole town. I gave the sergeant a dirty look as I edged past his big beer belly, but he didn't seem to notice.

Now Bullyacre was committed to find the cat and destroy it. The community would be saved from annihilation. But I wondered what would be the reaction of the brave hunters when they actually saw their quarry. Would they stand firm and confront the monster? They might find the three-headed cat of Magnetic Hill more intimidating than they expected, and it might put up more of a fight than the town anticipated.

5

Emma protested that she wanted to bring the kitten back to the hall with her. She had fetched the old cat carry basket from the shed, the one that we used to take Mulligatawny to the vet when he was vaccinated.

'Are you planning to have that thing immunised, Emma?' I asked sarcastically. 'Against feline enteritis, cat flu and the monster gene, perhaps. I don't think the vet would enjoy doing the job.'

'The kitten will have to stay here, Emma,' Dad said firmly.

'We can't leave her here alone. She'll be lonely. She's lost her mum and she hasn't even got a kind big sister to look after her. Not that Lizzie is kind to me, of course. And what if the mother comes back and jumps through the window and takes her away? I'll never see her again and she really wants to stay with me now that she's learned how nicely I look after her.' She cuddled the creature against her chest.

Cuddles twisted her neck around Emma's throat and rubbed her head against Emma's face. Spotty glared at Cuddles as if to protest against the betrayal of feline principles. Tabby bit Cuddles's neck and then nipped at Emma's nose.

'She didn't really hurt me. It was only a little bite,' said Emma hurriedly as Dad rushed over to see if Emma had been hurt. She wiped her nose. 'There's no blood. Well, not much anyway.'

'That damned kitten has got to stay here,' Dad repeated. 'What if she escapes from the cat carrier and attacks the people in the hall?'

'If Mayor Murphy sees her, he'll have her killed and stuffed and mounted as a specimen to put in a glass case in the hall,' said Bill.

'That sounds like a pretty good idea to me,' I said.

'No!' shrieked Emma 'I'd die if I lost my Cuddles. I love her more than I love my teddy even. Can't I smuggle Cuddles into the hall in my sleeping bag? She'll be good if she can feel me holding her. She just needs reassurance because she misses her mummy. The same as

I miss my mummy. Cuddles is the only creature in all the earth that understands how I feel.'

'Rubbish,' I said. 'You're always going on about how you feel. You just don't care about how anyone else feels, that's your problem.'

'No, Emma, someone would hear her mewling or she might get out and bite one of the other children. You heard Mayor Murphy. He wants a stuffed cat so he can charge tourists admission to see it. And he doesn't even know that Cuddles has three heads yet. If he sees how very,' Dad paused for the right word, a word that would describe the monster but not upset Emma when he made that description, 'how very unusual and different Cuddles is, he'll be even more determined to put her on display. Do you want that to happen?'

Emma brushed away her tears and agreed to leave the kitten behind. 'But we have to put her somewhere safe in case the mother comes looking for her.'

'Why don't we lock her in the lavatory again?' suggested Bill. 'That'd be the safest room in the house. The window's small and the mother would never fit through it. She was all right in there when we went to the meeting earlier. Lizzie can put extra newspaper down. It's the safest room in the whole house. I've been planning to sit in there if I hear the mother prowling about outside.'

'You didn't tell me that,' I said. 'Trust you to look after yourself and let everyone else suffer. It's not a bad idea, though.'

'She doesn't like being on her own. She gets lonely and scared in the dark with no one to talk to.'

In the end, we put the kitten and Toby in the lavatory. We fed them both as much as possible, in fact to their full capacity, before we shut them in, in case anyone decided to make a meal of anyone else. Then there was the problem of the kitty litter tray. The kitten was fairly reliable in that regard because Emma had trained it. But Toby was used to going in the backyard. All over the backyard. You had to be careful to check your shoes before you came inside. Not that Bill ever did that, though. I put lots of newspaper on the floor and hoped for the best. I knew I'd be the one who'd get the job of cleaning up any mess. I just hoped that I wouldn't find pieces of Toby spread about the way the ewe's carcass had been distributed in the paddock.

Toby cringed and hid behind the toilet bowl as soon as he saw who his companion for the evening would be. He didn't like any of the three personalities embodied in the kitten, not even Cuddles. I have to admit that Toby seemed to bring out the feral in the kitten.

We tossed Emma's sleeping bag, her toothbrush and her teddy bear into a bag, gathered up our rifles, the shotgun and some lemonade and biscuits for our own use, and set off for Bullyacre.

Most of the parking spots in Main Street were full when we arrived. You could hardly see Hugh Foulkes's statue for illegally parked cars. There were vehicles on both sides of the road, and more of them on the median strip grass between the trees and statues. I wondered whether the sergeant would object to that, but then I thought that, since he had called for a vigilante shooting party, he'd want as many people as he could get and he shouldn't complain about where they parked their cars.

Some of the male Bullyacrists were clustered together under the light from the lamp over the door of the town hall. It looked as if the hunters were reluctant to venture into the darkness lest they meet the panther lurking there.

I saw a bottle being handed around surreptitiously and looked about to see where the sergeant was. His vehicle was directly in front of the door, but he was nowhere to be seen.

'What do you think about all this?' I heard Fred Mudge ask his brother, Jim.

'Those photos were pretty convincing, but I have to admit I always take anything that Frank Epsom says with a grain of salt.'

'They're a funny mob, those Epsoms,' said Fred. 'Funny place, Epsom Downs, if it comes to that. I wouldn't live that close to the hill if you paid me to.'

'Hits the bottle a bit, too,' chimed in Pat Vincent, taking a long swig of the liquor that had been handed to him. 'This homemade hooch is all right if you've got a head for it,' he chuckled as he passed the bottle to his mate, 'but not all of us can handle a drink.'

I walked past them to follow Dad and Bill into the hall. Dad was depositing Emma and her baggage into the corner where her school friends had gathered and were all talking at once.

'This is going to be a really great sleepover!' said little Katie. 'I've got my Nintendo, Emma, and I'll let you have a go at it because I know you haven't got one. What did you bring?'

'Just my teddy,' said Emma, piteously. 'I haven't got any electronic toys. Lizzie says they won't work near Magnetic Hill but I think she's lying just because she doesn't want to spend any money on buying one for me. And they made me leave my new kitten at home. You don't know how I suffer, Katie. I have just got an awful life compared to everyone else. I think I'm probably an abused child.'

Just try changing places with me, Emma, I thought. But I said nothing because I knew it wouldn't accomplish anything. There's no point in complaining when you know there's no solution to your problem.

Jake sidled up to me as I was leaving. I saw him looking around to see if Alex or Matthew or Nathan were around. He looked relieved when he saw that all his friends were on the other side of the room. Coward, I thought. I watched as he checked again that they weren't looking our way before he reached out and touched my arm.

'I just wanted to say that I think you're really terrific, Lizzie. You're really brave. You remind me of Joan of Arc. I wish my dad would let me do just half the stuff you do. That's what you get, though, when your dad's the Anglican vicar. He just told me that I have to stay here and entertain the kids and old ladies with my piano accordion.'

'They also serve who only stand and wait,' I said. 'I think Winston Churchill said that during World War Two.'

He nodded. 'You know absolutely everything about every-thing, Lizzie.' He looked around the hall again and when he was absolutely certain that no one was looking in our direction, he asked, 'Can I give you a kiss?'

I let him peck me on the cheek. This had to be the weirdest thing that had ever happened in my entire life. Even weirder than seeing the three-headed cat, even weirder than knowing that there was a three-headed kitten in my indoor toilet back home.

'Take care, Lizzie,' Jake whispered.

I gave him a gallant little wave to prove my courage, although actually my knees were knocking together so hard I thought they might be making more noise than my chattering teeth. Somehow I managed to walk through the door without falling over.

Constable Perkins was standing in a puddle of light from the lamp outside the town hall, his hand caressing the pistol on his belt. There were moths circling the naked globe and I saw a couple of them come too close to the lamp and burn their wings on it and fall to the ground at the young policeman's feet to join the other corpses there. Constable Perkins didn't see them. He was gazing intently at the shadows under the bronze statue of the bullocks just across the road. He jumped when I touched his arm.

'Oh, Lizzie, it's you,' he said, sounding relieved.

'What are you doing out here, Ian?' I asked. 'Are you coming with us?'

'No, the sarge says I've got to stand here and guard the hall in case the panther attacks,' he said. 'Lizzie, I wouldn't say this to anyone else, but I'm scared stiff. I think I'm going to be sick.'

'Probably too many scones with jam and cream,' I said. 'The ladies of the auxiliary have been shovelling them down every one's throats.'

'Yair, I have had a few of those. Do you reckon this pistol would stop a panther, Lizzie?'

'Of course it would, Ian,' I lied. I was beginning to think nothing would stop the panther. 'But the panther isn't going to come into town. It's got kittens up in the hills and it wouldn't go too far away from them.'

'Thanks, Lizzie. That makes me feel a bit better. It's just that I keep seeing movement in that dark patch under Hugh Foulkes's statue, and it's giving me the willies.'

'I expect it's just possums,' I said. 'Dad says he's often seen possums there at night when he's coming back from the pub.' And probably seen zombies and vampires, too, if he's had enough to drink. 'You'll be fine, Ian. You're doing a great job, defending the women and children of Bullyacre. We're all proud of you.' I gave him a quick hug. 'Don't worry. We won't be long,' I said.

He nodded and seemed a bit happier.

Just then the door opened a crack and a hand belonging to one of the ladies of the auxiliary appeared, holding a plate full of fruit cake.

Constable Perkins took it gratefully, despite the nausea he said he was suffering from. He set the plate on the ground next to him before standing to rigid attention again and surveying the streets for invading panthers. I wondered if I should tell him that it was raining moths. His back seemed to be a bit straighter and I thought he looked a lot like the heroic marble soldier on the plinth just a bit further down the road from the statue of the bullock driver and his team.

I walked back to the car to check that the guns were secure. You should never leave a gun unattended. Especially if you've got the ammunition in the same place. At home we keep the guns locked in one safe (except for the old shotgun we keep out in the shed in case foxes attack the chooks at night) and the ammo locked in another safe or, if we were planning to use it soon, in a tin on top of the kitchen cupboard where theoretically the kids couldn't reach it. Dad said that was an army rule and he sticks to it.

I met Sergeant Wylie, who was inspecting the vehicles in the street. Perhaps he'd had the same thought about leaving the guns unguarded that I'd had.

'It's a pretty silly idea going out at night to look for the cat, Sarge,' I said. 'We ought to wait until the morning and go out and track it from the place Dad and I saw it last time. It was heading up the creek bed towards Fred Mudge's property. I reckon we're just going to blunder about in the dark and find nothing. It could be dangerous, not just for the panther but for the hunters on this trip, too.'

'Don't tell me what to do, young Lizzy Epsom. I've got a bone or two to pick with you. Your father said you took a shot at the panther.' he snapped. 'How old are you? You're a minor, aren't you? Have you got a gun licence?'

'No,' I said. 'Has Ms Wylie got one?'

He ignored my question. 'And you were driving that utility truck when you shot the panther. That vehicle doesn't look to be in very good condition. I don't know what it's like mechanically, but it could stand a visit to a panel beater's shop. In fact, it looks as if it ought to be defected. Have you got a driver's licence?'

'No,' I said. 'You're the local cop. You do the exams for driving licences. You know I haven't got my licence. I'm not sixteen yet and you have to be sixteen in this state to get L-plates, let alone a licence. All of the kids around here drive vehicles on their farms and none of them have licences. We all drive quad bikes, and utes, and four-wheel drive vehicles and even tractors. You know that and you've never worried about it before. So how come you're worrying about it now?'

'Just don't tell us adults how to run things, girlie,' said the sergeant. 'I'm the copper around here and I'm running the show and no teenaged girl is going to interfere with what I say. And just keep a civil tongue in your head or I'll be charging you and your father with multiple offences, including child neglect because he let you get away with driving a car and shooting guns.'

Silly old fool, I thought. I ought to tell him that half of his hunters are passing a bottle of Flanagan's hooch around and most of them are only half sober. But he'd probably accuse my dad of providing the bottle. When you've got a bad reputation, any mud that's around will stick. Better keep quiet, Lizzie, I decided.

'Let's get this wagon train moving!' yelled the sergeant. 'We'll head out to Frank Epsom's property. The criminal always returns to the scene of the crime. If the panther's still in the neighbourhood, that's where we'll find it.'

The hunting party piled into their vehicles. Bill was wedged between me and Dad, who was driving our utility truck. We had three passengers standing on the tray and clutching the roll bar where Emma and I had ridden last night. Pat Vincent carried his shotgun, Mike Young had a .303 rifle and wore a belt full of ammunition hung from his shoulders, and John Harvey had a spotlight in one hand and his .22 rifle in a sling on his back. They were all heroes going into battle, confident of success and believing that they were prepared for anything.

'I'm putting my money on the cat,' said Bill. 'I just hope no one gets hurt tonight. Did you smell the booze on those blokes' breaths? They won't be able to shoot straight even if they can see the target. They're probably more dangerous than the panther is.'

'What do you think they'll do when they see that it's got three heads, Dad?' I asked.

'After the amount they were drinking back there, they'll probably think they're seeing double, if not triple,' said Dad. 'I reckon Jack Wylie should have breathalysed the lot of them before we left. Bill's right. Those hunters are more dangerous than the cat is. I'd like to change my mind about going on this expedition if I could. Only people'd call me chicken if I did. It might be a good idea if you two stayed back here at the hall. It won't be safe out there when they start blazing away at shadows.'

'I'm not staying here, Dad. I said I was coming and I can't go back on my word.'

'Lizzie's right, Dad. We put our names on the list and we'd look like cowards if we backed out now. The name of Epsom is at stake here. We have to go hunting.'

Dad shook his head. 'I doubt that the name Epsom carries much weight in this town, anyway. Stay close to me, and don't get in the way of those idiots' bullets. We're all in the cabin, so we should be safe. If I say to put your heads down, do it. They're a bloody disgrace, those men. I promise you, Lizzie, and you, too, Bill, I'm off the grog for good. We've got enough monsters out in the countryside without me adding to them.'

The convoy roared out of town. I knew we were doing the right thing. We were dealing with a dangerous animal that had to be eliminated. Bullyacre and the farms around the town were in grave danger and our families and friends must be defended. Logically, I knew that we Epsoms could not afford to keep feeding our sheep to the predator or we would lose our farm. So the panther and its children had to die.

But I wondered, despite knowing all this, and even despite my own fear of what lay ahead of us in the darkness, why was I feeling just a little bit sorry for the cat? Perhaps it was the idea of being stuffed and put on display in the hall. Or had being around the baby cat influenced me? Was I becoming as crazy, as schizoid, as Emma's kitten?

6

'Why don't you spend a bit less on beer and a bit more on getting your tracks graded, Frank?' said Mr Vincent, leaning over the side of the ute and into the cabin so he could yell into Dad's ear.

'That's what I'm intending to spend my next wool cheque on, Pat,' said Dad. 'If the cat leaves us any sheep to shear, that is. Just hold on to that roll bar. We're nearly there.'

When we reached the spot where the ewe's bones lay strewn about in the grass, everyone exclaimed at the ferocity of the attack that had demolished the carcass.

'If one panther did this, it must have been a bloody big one,' said Mr Harvey, kicking at the skull. He picked it up and showed everyone the puncture marks of the teeth penetrating deeply into the bone. 'Not the sort of thing you'd want to meet on a dark night, is it?'

I wondered if this was the time to tell them that the panther in question had three heads or that the kids and I had met it on a dark night. I decided it wasn't. The men all looked about them apprehensively. The bravado that had been present back at the town hall seemed to have evaporated with the dregs from the shared bottle.

'It might be a panther,' said Sergeant Wylie. 'But I still think it could have been a pack of wild dogs. A large pack of very big, very wild dogs. We'd still have to do something about it, even if it was dogs,' he added. 'Community initiative, duty of care, et cetera, et cetera. But dogs or cats, they have to go. If it is a panther, we're going to have to be extremely careful.'

'What do you mean, if there is a panther?' demanded Dad. 'You saw the photos. Your wife printed them off the digital photo card on her computer.'

'Photos can be doctored,' said Sergeant Wylie. 'Ms Wylie says that Lizzie is pretty good with a computer. All kids are, these days. You add stuff, take stuff out, impossible to detect that it's been done.'

'How can you doctor a photo card that's just come out of a camera?' I demanded.

The sergeant snarled at me in much the same way as the panther had snarled when she was defending her kittens.

'You would know the answer to that better than I do, young Lizzie. You kids know all about that sort of thing. Hacking, you call it, don't you?'

'I saw the bloody animal, Jack! Are you calling me and my kids liars? Where's your wife, anyway?'

'She's in the car. She'll do her bit, don't you worry about that. I'm not saying that Lizzie is a liar, just saying that it's a pretty weird story to swallow, and that dogs are more likely to have been the culprit than alleged panthers, that's all. Ms Wylie says you should always look for a simple explanation to any problem.'

Occam's razor, I thought. William of Occam back in the fourteenth century who worked out the *Lex Parsimoniae*. If I remember it correctly, it runs *pluralitis non est ponenda sine necesitate*, which roughly translates to the idea that the simplest explanation is usually the correct one. I admit that it was a simpler explanation to believe that a pack of wild dogs had demolished our ewe. But unless you did call the Epsom family liars and you discounted the photographic evidence, you'd have to admit that a cat attack was the actual cause, even if it was a more complicated one.

'There's nothing here apart from a few bones, so we'll head up the hill a bit,' ordered Sergeant Wylie.

There wasn't a lot to see on top of the hill either, apart from a flock of our sheep huddled together near the fence above the hill.

'There it is!' yelled Mayor Murphy, his head sticking out of the window of his Land Cruiser. 'Over there, near the trees!'

For a moment I thought he was right and my heart started thumping. There was a dark shape looming in the middle of the field near the trees. Then I remembered that there was a big tree stump where he was pointing, left over from the time lightning had hit the hill and burned a big gum tree. Dad had salvaged most of the timber for firewood but hadn't gotten around to taking out the whole stump. But it was too late. The vehicles were all following his and they were headed towards the stump. And towards our flock.

A gun blazed, and then another. The sheep, who couldn't have had a lot of sleep the night before and who probably felt as tired as I did, took fright and stampeded.

'Hold your fire. There's nothing there,' Dad shouted at our passengers.

But it was too late. They were caught up in the general hysteria and began discharging their arms too. The lead sheep (there's always one sheep that people call the bellwether in any flock which is the one that does the leading, although you have to study the flock for a long time to work out which one it is) ran like the clappers straight against the side of Sergeant Wylie's police Toyota, which had slowed down so the sergeant could assess the situation.

The old ewe collapsed when she hit the car, and Dad swore. I won't repeat the word he said, because it was a particularly virulent word, but it was appropriate for the situation.

'There's another bloody sheep dead,' he said, as he stopped the ute and jumped out to check the animal. 'Can't you blokes tell the difference between a tree stump and a panther?' he demanded. 'Which one of you shot my poor bloody ewe?'

'What's wrong with your stupid sheep, Epsom?' yelled the sergeant. 'Look at the damage to my vehicle. I'm going to have to put in a report about this. Have you got magic mushrooms growing on your property and you're allowing your stock to graze on them? And maybe swallowing a few yourself, too? Even your sheep are crazy!'

'My sheep are as sane as the next man's sheep,' thundered Dad. 'First you insult me and my kids and now you're insulting my sheep. And killing them too. It's probably your fault or the government's fault that there are wild animals running amok on my property. You're supposed to uphold the law. Didn't you take an oath to defend the peace? There has to be a law against letting panthers run loose in the countryside.'

'It's all due to that Magnetic Hill,' said Mr Young, yelling out of his car window. 'Everyone knows this is a spooky place where anything could happen. You wouldn't get me letting my car roll up that hill. That road ought to be closed, if you ask me. And the whole area put under quarantine. The ground's probably radioactive. We could all get cancer just from standing here. I'm not getting out of my vehicle until we're clear of this accursed place.'

'Geoff's right,' shouted the driver of the car next to him.

He'd raised his voice because the car motors were still running and making a lot of noise. Enough to scare off every cat in the district, I thought.

'There could be all sorts of monsters out here. Things worse than panthers, I'll bet. Really big snakes and creepy crawlies that you wouldn't be able to describe. This place has a hex on it. Evil walks the earth on the hill, my old mother used to say.'

'You're right there,' yelled another voice. '"Never go near Magnet Hill in the moonlight," my mum used to say, "especially on the thirteenth night of the month."'

'Didn't Frank's wife die of cancer?' I heard one of the women say to her friend. 'That was probably due to living on the hill. Radiation, that sort of thing.'

I would have donged her one, but I would have had to get out of the car to do it, and I would have had to explain why I did it, and I didn't want Dad to know what she'd said, so I kept quiet. I suppose Sergeant Wylie would have arrested me on the spot for assault, anyway, and then claimed it was further proof that we Epsoms were mad.

The policeman straightened up from the examination of his car. Dad had discovered that the ewe was not dead, just stunned, and he and Bill helped her to her feet, gave her a reassuring pat on the rump and sent her trotting back to the trees where she'd been standing before the shots were fired. She immediately bent her head and began to graze the dry grass, her previous panic forgotten. Sheep aren't the brightest of animals. The rest of the flock, I noticed, were still running, headed towards the fence that overlooked the hill.

'Dad,' I said, pulling at his arm. 'The fence is pretty wonky over there. The flock could knock it over if they keep going at that rate and we'll lose the lot.'

'Rex,' Dad shouted, 'get your dogs out of the ute and set them to rounding up my sheep. I want them brought back here to the trees. Immediately. In one piece.'

Rex complained that the panther might be lurking out there and he didn't want to risk a valuable dog to save a few demented, flea-bitten, mouldy old sheep. He added a few other adjectives, but I won't repeat them. Eventually his dog and Banjo, demoted from the role of hunting dogs they'd assumed for the night to their usual ones of sheep-minders, scurried over, rounded up the flock and brought the sheep back to join the bellwether. I fancied I saw accusatory looks on the faces of a couple of the animals as they passed me. I'm glad I wasn't born a sheep. It's not much of a life, even without the possibility of being eaten by panthers. Humans are bad enough predators, from a sheep's point of view.

'Whatever killed the sheep isn't hanging about here tonight,' announced Sergeant Wylie. 'It might be a better idea to go over to Fred Mudge's property and take a look around there, seeing that Frank says that's where this putative panther was headed last time he saw it. Is there a track from your place to Fred's property, Frank?'

Dad wasn't too happy about the word 'putative' but he led the convoy out along the barely visible path from our land to Fred Mudge's place. There were a lot of gates to be opened and closed, and I got the job of gatekeeper. I kept my rifle at the ready because I didn't relish the thought of six eyes sizing me up for a meal. Although, would the panther need to eat again already when it'd had a good meal last night? Hadn't I heard David Attenborough on one of his programs say that big cats hunted once a week or so? Or did having three heads alter that fact?

The party paused at the last gate and Fred climbed out of his Land Cruiser and held up his hand. 'Listen here, you blokes,' he said. 'From here on you're on my property, and there's no panthers here. There's definitely nothing weird on my land. I can assure you of that. Over here, everything is plumb normal. Cars don't roll up hills, and I haven't ever had a panther here or even a two-headed lamb like that one Frank had once that he tries to keep quiet about.'

Dad glared at me when he heard that. I shrugged. I knew I hadn't told anyone about that lamb. Bill was the only possible origin of the rumour. We hadn't told Emma in case the idea upset her. I didn't think Bill had seen the corpse, but he could have heard me and Dad talking about it.

'I might have a few kangaroos and foxes, but I don't want any trigger-happy idiots blazing away at them,' Fred continued. 'I've got a herd of valuable cattle over there, most of them in calf, and I don't want any of them spooked the way you just frightened Frank's sheep. Sheep might put up with that sort of thing, but cows can't. They'll either drop their calves or break their legs and I don't need either of those things happening. And my prize bull isn't far from this paddock, either. So watch yourselves.'

It was great to see that the roads on Fred Mudge's land were just as badly in need of grading as our tracks were. I stuck my head out of the ute window and told anyone who was listening that these were the roughest roads I had ever travelled on and that the suspension of our utility truck was being totally destroyed. No one answered me.

'Don't big cats eat only once a week, Dad?' Bill asked. He'd seen that David Attenborough show, too.

His voice sounded a bit drowsy, and I realised that I was sleepy. We had been out for quite a while last night, and no one had slept much when we finally got home. We'd been too excited, too scared. Strangely enough, I didn't feel all that scared now. It made a big difference not having to make decisions, and having Dad with us helped. I wasn't sure whether the company of the sergeant and his gang was reassuring or not, but there was supposed to be safety in numbers. But I certainly felt more relaxed than I had been last night, and I felt that if we were just going to drive about for an hour or two on Fred Mudge's land, I might drift off to sleep the way Emma does when you take her for a long car trip.

'Usually lions feed only once or twice a week,' Dad was saying. 'So, yes, if our panther had a good meal last night, we probably won't see it out tonight. That's a good point, Bill. Although that three-headed kitten of Emma's has a pretty good appetite. So if the mother has to feed her young, she might have to hunt again tonight.'

I sank back against the hard vinyl upholstery and rested my head against Bill's shoulder. My eyes began to close, but I forced them open. They closed once more. Then we hit a particularly bad patch of corrugations and I was half awake again. I could hear the men in the back of the ute muttering together, complaining about the jolting they were receiving. I chuckled at their discomfort, then I glanced through the windscreen and saw movement in the distance. Probably one of Fred Mudge's resident kangaroos, I thought. I hope no one's silly enough to shoot at them.

Then I recognised it. A large, sleek form was streaking across the grass, chasing another similar large shape that was just slightly ahead of it. It's like a movie of the Serengeti, I thought drowsily. Another of those nature movies that Bill and Emma are so fond of. I half expected to see elephants or giraffes looming out of the night.

I came to my senses, wide awake again as I realised that there was more than one monster out hunting tonight. Suddenly I felt nauseous, just as Ian Perkins had felt earlier. There were definitely two panthers out there. Would they attack our convoy of hunters? The men on the ute tray were just as vulnerable as the kids and I had been the other night. Although it was selfish, I was glad that my family was in the cabin of the vehicle. And I really wished there was an unfortunate sheep about the place to divert attention from us humans.

However, the only other animal I could see in the dark paddock was a bulky black shape silhouetted against the moon that was rising over the hill. That must be one of Mr Mudge's cattle, I thought. One of his cows in calf, munching on grass, placid and unsuspecting in the night.

Ill met by moonlight, I thought. That's a line from *A Midsummer Night's Dream*. We did that for Shakespeare last year. Was that quote from the second act or the third one? I couldn't remember whether it was Titania, the queen of the fairies, saying it when she met her husband Oberon wandering about the forest, or vice versa. I did remember that they didn't like each other much, although they were a married couple. Then there was something about a donkey called Bottom…

Wake up Lizzie, I told myself. This isn't a dream, midsummer or not. This is actually happening. Mr Mudge's cow is about to be devoured, as Emma would say. In fact, I was fairly sure that the grazing that Mr Mudge's cow was doing would be the very last act that it performed. The two feline shapes were heading towards it at a rate of knots, if that was an expression one could use on the pastures of Bullyacre, which was a very long way from the sea. This must mean that the mother's mate had joined in her predations. Did panthers do that? Join together to hunt for food for their young? I had no idea. I wished that I'd joined the kids to watch David Attenborough. I'm always doing the dishes at that time, though, or working on my homework.

I shook my head again. No one else could have seen what was happening because there'd been no reaction from any of the other vehicles. I was fully awake now and I knew I had to warn the hunters what I'd seen. 'Look!' I yelled. 'Over there! There's two of them.'

Dad swung the steering wheel and sounded the horn to alert our companions. One of the panthers paused briefly in its stride. One of its three heads swung in our direction. But the pause was for a microsecond. I had a feeling that once that panther had begun its charge it would be almost impossible to halt it, even if all of the creature's heads had agreed to terminate the rush. It was that committee agreement problem again. Or a bit like World War One, when the war's impetus couldn't be slowed or even stopped once the troop trains had started to carry the armies all over Europe, so truce became impossible. I forget who the general was who'd proposed a truce to try to avert the war, but I do remember that he wasn't popular and no one listened to him. Too much patriotic frenzy, my teacher said. He said unless people learned from history, it would repeat itself.

But there wasn't time to try to remember history now, because we had a war of our own to fight. And the first animal, the huge panther that I'd decided was the male, didn't slow down at all. I decided that the second panther must be the mother because she was a bit smaller and I could see she had a problem with one of her back legs. My bullet hadn't done much, obviously, because she could still move pretty well.

The cats hit the cow in unison. The mother leapt onto the cow's back and stood there, tearing pieces from the living flesh with all three sets of jaws. I saw blood spurting from the wounds. The male stood up on his back legs under the poor creature's throat and bit into the jugular vein with one head and snarled at us with the other two. The cow reared up, trying to dislodge the smaller cat from its back, then crouched back down, attempting to defend its throat. But the male had sunk another set of fangs into the throat and the whole animal was intent on a killing frenzy.

This was an instance when the three heads of each panther worked in perfect unison. And the teamwork of the two panthers was impressive as well. The whole attack could have been rehearsed. How often, I wondered, had this pair of panthers hunted together in the past?

The cow tossed its horns, bellowed with the last of its breath, and kicked frantically, but it had no idea how to defend itself. How could it, born and bred to peace, and suddenly confronted by predators which it had never dreamed existed? It was like watching a scene from that horror film about dinosaurs when the raptors jumped on their prey.

One of our passengers shone his spotlight across the field and I could see dark blood spurting from the jugular vein, flowing on to the ground, and one of the panthers lapping it up with one of its heads while five other heads ripped into the cow, which had now fallen to its knees and, despite its injuries, was still bellowing and turning its head this way and that, futilely trying to cling to life. I heard the agonised lowing of the doomed beast as well as the snarling from six panther throats, but Fred Mudge's screams were even louder than the rest of the cacophony.

'Shoot, you damned fools, shoot!' Fred yelled. 'That's my prize bull those devils are killing!'

All of us fired our guns at once. It sounded like New Year's Eve in the Lions' Park at Bullyacre when Mayor Murphy spends more than half our rates and taxes on a fireworks show. Dad says that's the only reason the mayor is re-elected every year. The whole town enjoys those fireworks.

No one was enjoying this show, though. Fred's bull was long past enjoying anything. Fred was anguished at the loss of his bull. I was horrified to see that my worst fears had been realised. The mother had a mate and they were roaming the hills of Bullyacre, hunting together. There really were two panthers loose. And they had expanded their horizons as well as their family and had lifted their menu from mutton to beef.

But the worst thing of all was the fact that the panthers got away. I still don't know whether it was the alcohol that the hunters had consumed before we left Bullyacre, the horror of seeing actual panthers in the flesh, or general hysteria that made us all miss our targets. You would have thought that at least some of our firing squad would have slain at least one of the cats. But there it was: panthers, victory; Bullyacrists, total defeat.

Sergeant Wylie was not happy. 'I'm going to have put in an official report about this,' he said. 'It doesn't look good. We're going to get the big boys,' he paused and looked at his wife, 'and the big girls from the city up here on this one. You're all going to have to stand witness to these incidents. Affidavits will have to be sworn. We need the army, I reckon. These monsters have to be wiped out. All six of them. Are we agreed on how many of them there were?'

'There were more than six. I reckon there were at least a dozen of them, Jack,' said Rex. 'They were coming out of the bushes like a plague of mice. I've never seen anything like that in my life.'

'I know I'm going to get nightmares about this forever,' said Mike Young. 'I can feel post-traumatic stress disorder coming already. I need a stiff drink.'

'But none of them mentioned anything about the panthers having three heads,' I told Dad and Bill when we were back in the ute and on our way home after we'd collected a very sleepy Emma from the hall.

'Either they saw what they expected to see or none of them have the courage to admit what they actually saw,' said Dad. 'No one wants to be thought to be crazy.'

Poor Toby had nearly been driven crazy, we decided, when we got back to the homestead. He was still cringing behind the toilet bowl trying to hide from the kitten, which was prowling up and down the confines of the loo, jaws wide open and sharp little teeth gleaming in the electric light, glaring at Toby with all three heads.

The kitten's tail was held high and stiff, but Toby's was tightly tucked between his legs. There were deep scratch marks all over the toilet door and on the window frame. The kitten must have jumped up and stood on the cistern in its efforts to escape.

'What if it attacks Emma?' I asked. 'This thing's crazy.'

'Cuddles would never hurt me,' said my sleepy little sister, embracing her pet, which rubbed its heads against her legs and then rolled over on the lino so she could tickle its tummy.

We settled Emma down in her bed and tucked the kitten in beside her. It curled up immediately and began to purr loudly, then dropped off into sleep, all three heads floppy on the pillow beside my sister's head.

7

Sergeant Wylie phoned to say that Dad would be required in the town on Sunday in the early afternoon. The big boys and big girls from Adelaide, including, the sergeant said, trepidation making his voice shaky, the head superintendent of police, would be arriving about then and they would expect to interview and take statements from everyone involved in the Incident of Magnetic Hill.

But there's always work to do on a farm, no matter how many incidents have occurred or how many superintendents of police are arriving from Adelaide. The chooks still needed feeding, the eggs had to be gathered, and someone has to make sure that the windmills are working and pumping out bore water for the sheep to drink. Also, towards the end of summer the pasture is a bit thin and you have to supplement the grass with the occasional feed or your sheep tend to lose condition and die.

'I'll go and check the windmills today, Dad, so we'll be free to go into Bullyacre tomorrow.'

Dad had a bad headache. It might have been stress, I surmised, but it could equally well be alcohol withdrawal symptoms. I dosed him with aspirin and coffee and insisted that Bill and I would do the rounds of the windmills so he could have a bit of a rest at home. Sometimes I wonder who the parent is around here.

'I don't want you kids driving around the property alone,' protested Dad weakly. 'Those panthers might still be hanging about. I can't let you endanger your lives again.'

'I thought we agreed that lions and panthers don't feed every day,' I said.

'We don't know anything about these things,' said Dad, wiping beads of perspiration from his forehead. 'We don't even know how many of them there are out there.'

'Still,' said Bill, 'those cats must have had enough to munch on from Fred Mudge's prize bull to last them for a while.'

'Yes,' I agreed. 'I bet they went back last night after we all left and finished off the carcass at their leisure. They probably chewed off great lumps of prime beef and took meat home for the kittens to enjoy as well. Come to think of it, those cats are eating better than we do.'

'It's still risky, Lizzie,' said Dad. 'Oh God, my head is pounding. I must have developed migraine or something.'

'Have some more coffee and chill out for a bit. Listen to some soothing music, Dad. None of that stuff that Bill likes, though. That would blow your head away. Try some of Mum's classical stuff. What about Beethoven's Sixth Symphony?'

Dad shook his head.

'Well, maybe not,' I said. 'That's the Pastoral one, isn't it? A spot of Vivaldi perhaps. Bill and I'll take the guns with us in case there's anything nasty lurking in the undergrowth. We'll be fine. The panthers are probably lying in the sun somewhere with bloated bellies so full that they're completely unable to move.'

'I wouldn't bet on it, Lizzie,' said Dad, sinking into an armchair and allowing me to put a wet cloth on his head and a disc in the player. 'That kitten of Emma's spends all day every day eating all of its heads off, but it still manages to dance about pretty well.'

We watched Emma playing with the kitten. She had tied a piece of paper on the end of a string and was pulling the string across the floor. The kitten crouched on its belly and slunk after the paper, sliding across the linoleum. I polished that lino last week, I thought. And now its going to be covered with kitten claw scratches. It's always a waste of time polishing anything around here. I don't know why I bother. It's just that sometimes I look around and wonder what Mum would think of the way this place looks, and then I get an attack of the guilts and try to bring it up to her standards.

The Cuddles head extended itself on its long neck and sank its little fangs into the white paper just as the Spotty head arrived at the same goal. There was a brief tussle as the two heads fought over the prize. Then the Tabby head spat at the other two and snatched the paper away, using the front paw on its side of the body to bat at the Cuddles head. Cuddles hissed and lunged at Tabby but her fangs made contact with Spotty and the battle resumed. The entire kitten rolled over and over, paws, heads and tail going this way and that. Fur rose into the air and glistened in the sunlight coming through the window. The animal was screeching at the top of all three of its voices simultaneously. The din was horrible. Vivaldi didn't stand a chance against it.

Dad put his hands over his ears and looked sick. Emma shrieked and tried to retrieve her pet. I picked up the glass of water that I'd used to administer Dad's aspirin and tipped it over the brawling mass of kitten. The whole animal leapt up, turned in mid-air, hissed loudly and faced me, pure malevolence written all over the three small faces.

'I wouldn't play games like that with the kitten if I were you, Emma,' I said. 'What was the big idea, anyway?'

'I wanted to teach her to hunt,' said Emma.

I've often wondered about Emma's IQ level. Shaking my head, I told Bill we were leaving. It might be safer out in the paddocks.

'We'll do the bottom windmills first and work our way up to the one on Magnetic Hill,' I said.

Bill pleaded to be allowed to drive, but I was still feeling a bit shaky after last night and the night before last as well, so I refused to let him take the wheel. There's a limit to how much stress a body can take, and the thought of Bill careering all over the shop was more than I could bear this morning.

Fortunately there were no problems with any of the windmills, which was great because I didn't fancy climbing up to do anything to them while Bill held the shotgun under the tower. They were all pumping bore water out nicely and the sheep near them looked happy enough, or as happy as sheep usually look. We tossed out a bit of hay to supplement the dry feed in the fields and went on to the next trough.

The last windmill we visited was the one on top of Magnetic Hill. There was a small flock of sheep here, the same flock that had stampeded last night. Their heads were hanging and they looked dejected, but I told Bill that after all they'd been through recently they were entitled to look a bit miserable. I felt pretty miserable myself and

I hadn't had to spend the night in the fields being chased by panthers and mad drunken hunters. Some people say that sheep don't show emotion, but if you look at the face of a sheep that has just been shorn on a cold day you'll know what I mean by ovine misery.

When we got to the windmill on Magnetic Hill, we were surprised to see a bus on the road at the base of the hill. I think I mentioned previously that we get tourists in cars out here all the time, but I don't believe I've ever seen a bus there before.

This bus had 'Geology Survey Society' emblazoned on its sides and there were people wandering about all over the road. Some of them were looking up at the hill, and some of them were gazing down the hill. A few people were scribbling notes on clipboards, and others were holding up big brightly coloured geological maps that flapped in the wind, and studying them carefully. I know what a geological map looks like because my class did a full semester of geology back in term one. We learned how to use clinometers, too, and I noticed a couple of these people were carrying them. One man was rolling a tennis ball down the hill while another man stood at the base of the hill with a stopwatch. Others were photographing the scene and the bus and each other. There must have been about thirty of them, and they were all totally immersed in what they were doing and oblivious to anything other than their fascination with Magnetic Hill.

'They've got a nice day for it,' said Bill. 'They look as if they're enjoying themselves, whatever they're up to.'

I smiled. It was good to see people doing normal-looking stuff, leading ordinary-looking lives. Maybe, I thought, one day I might lead a normal sort of life. It would be nice to experience boredom again. I toyed with the idea of going down and having a chat with them. It would be interesting to know what the official geological explanation for the phenomenon of Magnetic Hill was. What they were doing looked so scientific and rational and I would really welcome a little rationality in my life.

Then I realised that today was not destined to remain rational. Out of the bushes on top of Magnetic Hill slunk a sleek tawny body that gleamed in the sun. It crept slowly along the ridge of the hill and then it raised itself on its back legs, the better to survey the road below. I didn't know that panthers could stand up like that. It actually looked more like a meerkat than a panther. Its three heads on their impossibly long necks snaked upwards, and six golden eyes glistened with malice.

'God help us,' I said softly. 'It's seen them. I think this one's the male cat.'

'You mean, God help them,' said Bill. 'Quick, Lizzie, honk the horn and then shoot at the cat. You might get lucky this time. You can't miss from this angle.'

'I'll sound the horn first to attract their attention and I'll point at the cat and see if they get the message,' I said. 'If I fire the gun, they might think we're shooting at them. The panther's well out of range, anyway.'

I honked the car horn. The geologists looked up at me and some waved hesitantly.

I pointed at the big cat, which was advancing rapidly down the hill. I yelled, 'Look out!' and 'Danger!'

The people below smiled and waved their maps at me cheerily.

'They can't hear you, Lizzie. It's too far away,' said Bill.

I fired the gun in the air and the geologists stood as if frozen, gazing at me in total disbelief.

'They think I'm an assassin like the American ones you see on the television and read about in the newspaper. You know, those idiots who do mass murders in schools with firearms,' I told Bill. 'Get on your bus and get out of here!' I yelled.

They just stood there looking like stunned chooks. They were as helpless as sheep bound for the abattoir. I took a sight along the barrel and fired at the panther. I had no expectation of hitting it because I'd lost faith in the power of bullets to stop this thing. I was beginning to believe that we were dealing with some sort of supernatural cat, an animal invincible to normal weaponry. Maybe you needed a silver bullet or something. It was still too far away to hit, although it was advancing towards the bus quickly now. I knew that the only chance the geologists had was to pile back on their bus and drive away.

Now the panther had slowed and was creeping down the side of the hill, implacably stalking prey that appeared totally vulnerable. And these prey, although smaller than the bull that been on the menu last night, were very numerous. A whole flock of scientists for the taking. All three heads must have been summing them up and deciding which one to choose first. Maybe the decision was already made, because the animal moved in perfect unity. And now it had sped up again and was closing the gap rapidly.

I fired at it again. I thought, hoped, that I might have hit it in the flank. At that distance, my bullet was unlikely to do much harm, but perhaps the animal might change its mind about springing on the people below.

'You got it, Lizzie!' Bill was yelling. 'You've hit the cat!'

The panther was down, rolling in the dust. Heads were colliding with heads as the animal gyrated on the ground. The panther seemed disorientated, confused. The club members were also confused, milling about on the road and bumping into each other. There was a lot of shouting and some screaming. Geological maps and notepads were lying in the road. I watched as the wind caught one map and carried it up and over the hill.

The people didn't know what to do. I didn't know what to do, either. All I could think of was that Sergeant Wylie was going to be mad as hell if I'd succeeded where he and his mates had failed. And tomorrow was the day when the superintendent of police was coming up from Adelaide, too. I had a feeling that no amount of affidavits was going to help Jack Wylie's career now. It would break his heart if a teenaged girl had stopped the cat, had succeeded where he had failed. It wasn't very nice of me, but I really wanted to do that.

I took another sight along the barrel of the rifle. Of course, this was only one of the pair of panthers. It must be the male, because it had looked much bigger and stronger than the female had that last time I saw it up close. Or were there actually more than the one pair roaming the hills, more than one couple like the panthers we had met last night? Had there been previous litters of kittens before the litter that we knew about? Could this be another panther entirely, one that we hadn't encountered before? Was the country around Bullyacre infested with these monsters? Where had they come from? And how long had they been here?

If I'd been ambivalent in my resolve to destroy the panther and all the members of its family last night, that ambivalence was gone. Now I realised that the threat to human life was real.

The panther was up again and limping away from the bus, going up the hill, its three heads hanging low. It looked quite despondent. I fired once more. I saw the spurt of white dust on the hillside just behind the beast, and I knew that I'd missed. I was disgusted with myself. I can shoot rabbits, but I couldn't kill the panther. And the panther presented a much bigger target area than a rabbit. I must be losing my skill. Was there something wrong with the rifle? A bad workman blames his tools, I remember Dad saying. Still, I decided I would check the sights when I got home.

'I knew it was too good to be true,' I told Bill. 'It's still alive.'

Suddenly we were surrounded by people. Well, by five or six of the younger, braver, more physically able of the geologists who had climbed the hill where Bill and I stood. The rest had taken refuge in the bus; the door was shut tightly and the engine was revving up. My back was slapped and my hand shaken. I had a number of hugs from people I had never laid eyes on before.

'Congratulations, young lady, you saved the day,' said a man who wore clothes that looked as if they had come from the army surplus store. 'Great shooting. Unfortunate that the animal got away. We were in enormous peril. You've saved a number of lives. I would venture to say that you've earned the eternal thanks of the entire club.'

'What was that thing?' asked a tall man with a wide-brimmed hat. 'I would've put it in the feline genus, but there was something deformed about it. It didn't look quite right from where we were standing.'

'The body looked like a leopard or a panther, but there was something very wrong with its head,' ventured a tall lady. 'In fact, I'm almost certain that there were more heads than there ought to have been on that creature. I know it sounds impossible, but I really believe I saw at least two heads on long necks.'

'You're imagining it, Barbara. No animal has more than one head,' snapped the man in the clothes from the army surplus stores. 'Absolute impossibility. Against all the laws of nature.'

'You were playing with your clinometer at the time. You wouldn't have seen the animal until it was at your throat.'

'I saw three heads,' ventured a small lady with grey hair. 'And they were very big. The animal looked ferocious. This girl saved all our lives with her intervention.'

'I do wish I'd been able to get a photo of it,' another lady said, 'but my hands were shaking dreadfully and I actually dropped the camera. It seems to be all right, but one never knows until one tries to use it again.' She looked at her camera and then at me and I saw what looked like envy appear on her face. 'You've got some extraordinary fauna and flora around here. It must be something to do with radiation from uranium, although there's no apparent uranium deposit marked on the geological map.'

I was horrified when she took a photo of me. I hoped that her camera really was broken. I didn't want this story to get out.

'In recognition of your bravery, my dear, we would like to award you honorary membership of our club,' interrupted a stout, rather imperious lady who wore the sort of hat the Queen wears, trimmed with blue roses. She seemed to be in command. 'Here's my card. Please contact me and we'll arrange for you to come down to Adelaide and be presented with a certificate. Ronald, please take the young lady's name and address and also that of her brother. I also intend to commend them both to the Governor for a gallantry award.'

'At once, Muriel,' the man said, pulling out a notebook from the voluminous pockets of his baggy pants.

'But all I did was shoot at the cat,' I protested. 'I don't think I actually did it any real damage. They're big animals and a .22 bullet doesn't seem to kill them. Anyway, I was too far away. I probably just scared it off. We've been having a few problems with cats around here lately.'

I suddenly remembered what Sergeant Wylie had said about underage driving of vehicles and the use of guns by minors and the absence of licences for either of those activities. I didn't want any publicity. Dad might get into trouble with the authorities, and we kids might be taken into protective care by the powers that be. For all I knew, these scientist people might be members of the Powers That Be Association as well as of a geology club. They all looked like the sort of people who would sit on multiple committees and even enjoy doing that. A bit like Ms Wylie, though not as aggressive.

'I'm sorry. I would really prefer not to give my name and address. Please respect my privacy.'

'Come on, Lizzie, Dad's going to go ballistic if we don't get home soon.'

A few days later, when the newspapers had got hold of the story and the tale of the three-headed cat of Magnetic Hill was being sensationalised out of all proportion, I read an account of what happened from the point of view of the Geology Survey Society. I must say I sounded quite the heroine, although Bill gave me heaps over it, and so did most of the kids at school, except Zoe.

Jake got into a fight with Matthew because Matthew and his friend Andrew said I was big-noting myself and I ought to come down to earth a bit. They were all hauled up to the headmaster's office and got suspended for a couple of days. Jake's father, the Anglican minister, was furious with Jake and sternly reminded him that it was a Christian's duty to turn the other cheek, but Jake whispered to me that it was worth the suspension and the tongue-lashing from his dad and the black eye that Andrew had given him. Jake, Andrew and Matthew are best mates again now, though.

8

I'd never seen so much traffic in Bullyacre. There were cars ranked all the way along Main Street, all the way from the bronze statue of Hugh Foulkes and his bullocks down to the white statue of the Anzac soldier on his plinth with his rifle reversed and the names of the Bullyacre soldiers who had died in two world wars on plaques on the base. When Dad turned the ute into First and then Second Street, we found that they were full too.

'Who do these cars belong to?' Bill asked. 'I've never seen any of them before, and I thought I knew every car in the town and for miles around. No one in Bullyacre owns a brand-new Range Rover like that black one, or a Prado like that silver one over there. There's not a dent or a scratch on any of them. Not even much dust, either. Look, there's a van with Channel 6 written on the side. And there's another van from the *News of the World*. That van over there's got *The Advertiser* written on its side. There must be something really big happening. Do you think the bank's been held up?'

'No, the bank's shut, it's Sunday. It must be city folk come up to Bullyacre because of Sergeant Wylie's Incident at Magnetic Hill report,' said Dad. 'I don't know where I'm going to park. Can anyone see an empty spot?'

In desperation we drove all the way down to Third Street and parked under the trees outside the tall sandstone Anglican church. It would be cooler there for the dogs, because today was going to be a real scorcher. I sniffed back a couple of tears when I looked at the church. We hadn't been back here since Mum's funeral because it brought back too many memories.

We left the dogs tied to a tree with a bucket of water to drink from because we didn't know how long we'd be away. The four of us walked down to Main Street, where the police station is.

Emma was fretting because we'd had to leave the kitten behind at home and she was worried about it. This morning it apparently hadn't eaten as much as she considered it ought to have. 'I think Cuddles is missing her mum,' she whispered to me, looking back over her shoulder at the big church buildings behind us. 'Perhaps we did the wrong thing when we rescued her. We probably should have left her back in that cave so her mother could come back and get her. I know how she feels. I still miss my mum, you know.'

'I miss Mum too, Emma. We all do, but Mum wouldn't want us to be unhappy. When she was dying she told me to look after you, and I am trying to do that.' I gave her a hug. 'I'm sure Cuddles will be all right. Didn't I see you giving her some of your cornflakes this morning? She seemed to be eating them pretty well.'

'Yes, but I don't think cornflakes are really good for kittens. And Tabby and Spotty wouldn't eat anything. They don't like cornflakes and they don't like toast and jam and they wouldn't even eat any of Banjo's dog food.'

'Well, they do all share the same stomach, so as long as one of the heads ate breakfast, then they all ate, didn't they? I'm sure Cuddles will be sitting in her basket in the loo waiting for you when we get back.'

'I left teddy there to keep her company because Dad wanted to bring the dogs with us in the back of the ute this morning. I told Dad we should leave Toby with Cuddles. I don't see why the dogs had to come. Cuddles likes Banjo.'

'The dogs always enjoy coming to town, Emma. They like standing on the back of the ute with the wind blowing past their ears. Dad said it wasn't fair to leave them home. And poor Banjo doesn't like Cuddles at all. He whines every time she comes near him. Toby can't stand her either.'

'But Cuddles has been left at home on her own,' she whined.

My patience was running out. 'Shut up, Emma,' I said. 'We're at the police station now. And don't tell anyone about your kitten. Not anyone, not ever. Not even your best friends. Not unless you want her taken away from you and stuffed and mounted and displayed in the hall for tourists to see.'

'Do I have to come into the police station, Lizzie?' asked Emma.

'There's Anthea and Amy over there playing on the bullock statue. Can I wait out here with them while you're inside?'

'Only if you promise you won't slide off the bullocks' backs and fall on their horns,' I said.

'Those horns have been filed smooth, Lizzie,' said Bill. 'The mayor did that after his kid Tommy got hurt on them last year, remember?'

I knew that the horns weren't dangerous now, but I still had to warn Emma. My mother had warned me about falling on Hugh Foulkes's bullocks' horns when I was little, just as every mother in Bullyacre does. Bullyacre mums have done it for generations, ever since the town council erected the statue on the median strip in Main Street back in the dark ages. It was a fitting place for the memorial to stand because we wouldn't have had a median strip or such a wide street if it hadn't been for bullocks, because bullocks needed a wide area to turn around in. The statue of Hugh has only got four of them, harnessed two by two and lined up behind each other, but some of the real bullock teams had six or eight animals in them. It must have taken a powerful man to control a team like that, using just a whip that he cracked over their heads and a few choice swear words occasionally. There's a saying 'Swear like a bullocky' but the history book about Bullyacres's founding fathers says that Hugh never swore at his team so he was the exception to the rule. The book says he was a really good man as well as being an intrepid explorer. Ms Wylie gets angry when people talk about the founding fathers because she says that the founding mothers and also the founding spinsters were just as important.

People were lined up much like bullocks in a team at the counter of the police station and more people sat on the hard wooden benches that lined the walls. Constable Perkins stood behind the counter and handed out documents to the waiting multitude. The phone was ringing constantly but no one was answering it. There was no sign of Sergeant Wylie.

'Where's Jack Wylie?' Dad asked Pat Vincent, who was leaning against the door frame. 'I was supposed to see him at two o'clock. He phoned and made an appointment. He said to bring Lizzie in as well.'

'I had an appointment at one o'clock, Frank. I haven't seen hide nor hair of Jack. Constable Perkins says the boss is locked up in the back of the station with that superintendent from Adelaide. In conference, apparently. Fred Mudge is in there with them and young Perkins says the way Fred's been carrying on about his bull, even the superintendent can't get a word in edgewise. Fred wants compensation from the police and the premier and probably from the prime minister and the Queen of England. Apparently that bull was worth zillions.'

'According to Fred, his bull won prizes at the Royal Adelaide Agricultural Show,' interrupted Mike Young. 'A whole sheaf of blue ribbons, Fred says. Nobody's ever seen any of them, but Fred says he's got them in his office at home.'

Rex sniggered, but Mike continued complaining. 'I've been waiting here for a couple of hours, too. We've all got to make statements. Constable Perkins is handing out the forms. You'd better get in the queue and start filling out your affidavit, Frank. The mayor's in the interview room and he's witnessing the signatures because he's a JP.'

'My wife's across the road in the café having lunch,' complained Rex Jamieson. 'She wanted to come into town to go to church this morning. She said we needed to pray for deliverance from the panther. The church service ended hours ago, even though the vicar went on for about three-quarters of an hour about the dangers of losing your soul to sin being worse than facing the ferocity of wild beasts.'

'Yair, I got dragged in to sit through that too,' said Pat, shaking his head.

'The sermon made her feel quite crook, and she's been wanting to go home and have a cup of tea and a nice lie down ever since. She's not too happy about having to wait, and neither am I. I haven't had as much as a cup of tea since breakfast time.'

'None of us have, Rex. If we don't get called in for an interview soon, I'm going home and Jack can stick his enquiries where the sun doesn't shine.'

Constable Perkins handed Dad a copy of the affidavit to fill in and sign. 'Just fill in the details where there are blank spaces and take it in to the mayor so he can witness it, Frank,' he instructed.

Dad looked about for a space to use to fill the form in, and told me to turn round so he could use my back to lean the paper on.

'Are you going to say that the cat's got three heads?' I whispered over my shoulder.

'There's nowhere to put any details about the cat. They just want us to say that we saw a panther and that we were present when it attacked Fred Mudge's bull,' said Dad, scrawling on the form. 'Funny how it's not an alleged panther any more. Jack Wylie must believe the cat exists now.'

Dad carried the document towards the door to the interview room, where Mayor Murphy sat in state with a large pot of tea and plate of homemade biscuits from the Ladies' Auxiliary in front of him.

'Blimey, look at the queue just to get the mayor to use his JP stamp! And then I have to be interviewed by Wylie and his boss. We're going to be here all day, Lizzie. My headache is starting up again.'

'It's stress, Dad. I brought some aspirin with me in case you had problems. I'll ask Constable Perkins for a glass of water for you.'

'Sorry, Lizzie,' said the constable, who was gathering up a pile of paper and stuffing it into his bag. 'I don't have time to fetch water. I have to go out and put parking stickers on cars.'

'What do you mean, parking stickers? We've never used parking stickers in Bullyacre. That's something that only happens down in Adelaide.'

'It's happening here today. Mayor Murphy says this is the opportunity of a lifetime. A real revenue raiser. Tell you what, Lizzie, we're going to have an amazing fireworks display this New Year's Eve with all the money that'll be in the kitty. The mayor said we can charge fifty dollars for a parking fine if people don't move their cars every two hours.'

'But there's nowhere to move the cars to. All the parking spots are full. And everyone's stuck in town because of this stupid Incident inquiry. You can't do it.'

'The town council had an emergency meeting this morning and they passed a motion to say that we can. Altered the constitution, apparently. Here, take this glass and fill it from that tap over there if you need water for your Dad. I'll be back as soon as I've slapped a few tickets on windscreens. Some of the cars have got three notices on them already. It's a real joke, isn't it?'

'Don't you dare put one on our car, Constable Perkins,' I said, too cross to call him Ian.

'Sorry, Lizzie, I have to be impartial. And I've got to get out there right now, or the sarge will crucify me. Orders are orders.'

I was about to make an announcement to the crowd that they had better go outside and move their cars before the constable reached them, when Dick Hunt from the newsagency walked in carrying a pile of newspapers.

'I know you blokes are stuck in here with nothing to do, so I thought I'd bring a few papers over in case anyone wanted to buy them.'

'There's never anything in the paper, Dick,' said Rex. 'Nothing worth looking at. No one down in Adelaide knows Bullyacre exists. We only get yesterday's newspaper, anyway.'

'There's plenty about us in it this time. It just came in on a special delivery truck up from Adelaide. I've never known that to happen, not even when we had that hung parliament. You take a look at the headlines, mate. I reckon you'll change your mind and buy one real quick. There's actually some local news for a change.' He held up one of the papers. It had a big red sticker across the front of it –

STOP PRESS – SPECIAL EDITION

Emblazoned across the first page were the words

Mid-north of South Australia Terrorised by Panther. Local
Girl Saves Scientists, But Modestly Declines All Publicity.

The papers were snatched from Mr Hunt's hands. Money was thrust at him. Coins were flung across from the desk where the lucky people who had managed to obtain an affidavit to fill in and a seat to use while they did it were sitting. The affidavits were forgotten in the rush, and I had a feeling that the original forms might end up started by one person and completed by another. Since most of the swearers of affidavits had compared notes about what they had witnessed, it probably wouldn't make a lot of difference to the final report when Sergeant Wylie lodged it, though. Lots of coins fell on the floor and rolled under the desk.

Dick Hunt scrambled for the money, attempted half-heartedly to give change to those whose requested it, and tried much harder to keep track of who had taken a paper and who had taken one but hadn't paid. 'Steady on, fellers,' he protested. 'Honesty's the best policy. I hope I can trust you to do the right thing in the police station, but it would be nice if there was a copper here to keep an eye on you blokes. I suppose Jack Wylie's busy with that superintendent from Adelaide, but where's young Perkins?'

'No one knows,' Rex replied.

I knew where the constable was, but I thought it might cause a riot if the townspeople found out about the parking tickets, and anyway I was busy reading what the Geology Society had said about me, and at the same time thinking Dick Hunt stood to make almost as much money from this business as the mayor intended to make from the parking tickets. Well, on second thoughts, not nearly as much, but he was certainly selling more papers than he usually did.

There was a sub-headline titled 'Lizzie Get Your Gun'. The story under the headlines identified the local girl as a heroine, a latter-day Annie Oakley, a brave teenager who had saved an entire busload of eminent scientists from certain death as they investigated the puzzling phenomena of Magnetic Hill. The girl was known only as Lizzie, but journalists would be travelling to Bullyacre today to seek her out for interview, the article stated. Her bravery and her prowess with a rifle were truly miraculous, the journalist observed, and the young girl, who was a credit to her family and to South Australia, deserved recognition. It was suggested that the Young Australian of the Year Award might be appropriate.

The lady whose hands had been shaking too much to photograph the panther had managed to take a snap of me. It was a bit blurry, but there I was, with my rifle in my hand, my image plastered on the front of the paper.

Everyone in the police station turned and looked at me. I was blushing all over. I was famous. Maybe that was infamous. And all I had ever wanted to do was blend into the crowd and get my homework done. How could I ever go back to school? I'd never live this one down. Probably even Zoe and Jake would say I was getting too big for my boots and that I'd need a bigger hat soon because of my head swelling.

I didn't like to think what Ms Wylie might say when I landed back in her English class. Probably talk about Macbeth and overwhelming ambition bringing about one's downfall. Or about ancient Greeks and hubris.

The clamour in the police station reception area was so great that Sergeant Wylie came out and gave us all a filthy look. You'd have thought that we'd jointly tortured and murdered old Miss Cobbledick the way he looked.

'What the hell is going on out here?' he demanded. 'Do you want me to read the Riot Act? I've got an important meeting happening back there. The bloody superintendent is going to think I've lost all control of you people.'

Dick Hunt thrust a newspaper into the sergeant's hand. 'You can pay me later, Sarge,' he said generously.

'I haven't got time to read this rubbish,' snapped the sergeant, crumpling the paper and thrusting it back at Dick's hands. 'Just simmer down, you lot. You'll all get your turn to see the super soon. Where's young Perkins? Is he skiving off again? Lazy little bugger, he is.'

'He's out slapping parking tickets on all the cars in Bullyacre,' I said, 'because you ordered him to do it. And it's nothing but a dirty money-grabbing exercise that you and the mayor have set up. It's not the constable's fault at all.'

Everyone in the police station turned to look at me again. I probably should have blushed, but I'd decided it didn't matter if I drew attention to myself now. I was already notorious in the eyes of everyone in our town, and probably in the eyes of most of South Australia. A bit more infamy couldn't make much difference. This must be how Ned Kelly felt when he said 'Such is life' as the hangman put the noose around his neck and what Joan of Arc felt like when she talked King Louis into fighting the English and got the attention of everyone in France. She was burned at the stake for her trouble, I suddenly remembered.

The uproar worsened. Fists were shaken and the counter got banged a few times. Some of the men ripped up their affidavits, threw them on the floor and jumped on them.

'Stuff you, Wylie!' yelled Geoff Mason and stalked out. He slammed the door behind him.

The superintendent and Fred Mudge poked their heads out of Sergeant Wylie's office, with puzzled expressions on their faces. I decided that there was more noise and fireworks in that police station than there was going to be next New Year's Eve in the Lions Park when Mayor Murphy put on his parking ticket financed so-called free show.

'I could put quite a few of you in the cells!' thundered the sergeant. 'The cells are empty right now. A full cell is a happy cell, that's my motto. Who wants to be the first one to try out the lock-up?'

9

To pacify the crowd, Sergeant Wylie told us all to go and have lunch and said he'd send Constable Perkins to fetch us from the café or the pub when the superintendent was ready to see us.

'He didn't offer to pay for our lunch, though,' whined Rex. 'The town council could afford it with all the revenue from those parking tickets.'

'There's no such thing as a free lunch,' said Dad. 'Unless you're a panther.'

Soon the sweating queue outside the café reached all the way down the road to the white marble statue of the dejected-looking World War One soldier with his white marble rifle on the plinth where we place wreaths on Anzac Day. It was so hot that even the soldier seemed to be wilting.

Emma and her friends had tired of sliding down the shiny rumps of the bronze bullocks and were sitting in the shade underneath the animals. Hugh Foulkes was OK; his wide-brimmed hat would keep the sun off him forever. And being made of bronze, he already had a suntan.

Dad had the bright idea of going for a pub meal, so we walked over the road to the shade of the hotel. The wide verandas kept the sun out, and the electric fans turned lazily. Even though it was cooler in there, I didn't like Dad's idea at all, and I said we were better off waiting outside in the heat, but Dad promised that he'd only drink lemon squash. I felt really proud of him when he kept his word, especially when I saw the other men of Bullyacre sinking pints.

Fred Mudge turned up, looking very smug. 'The superintendent reckons I'm entitled to compensation for my bull,' he told Dad. 'I'm going to add a few thousand bucks to what they offer me and say I've been stressed and can't sleep. I'll say my wife can't sleep either.'

'Is that true?' I demanded. 'It's only been one night since the bull was killed, and I don't think anyone in Bullyacre got much sleep last night. We were all high on adrenalin.'

'How is anyone going to prove that it isn't true?' said Fred. 'They're not going to sit next to my bed and watch me all night, are they? Well, of course I'm not the only one who didn't sleep last night. I'd be surprised if anyone in the district is sleeping with all these panthers on the loose. The entire population of Bullyacre ought to be getting stress compo. It's just that I thought of it first. Anyway, the super says they're going to take drastic measures.'

'What sort of drastic measures?' Dad asked, sipping his lemon squash and looking longingly at Fred's beer.

'Very drastic ones. They're sending in the army, for starters,' said Fred. 'Can I get you another drink, Frank? Something a bit more sustaining, perhaps? I can afford it now with all that money coming my way.'

'I'll stick to the lemon squash, thanks, Fred,' said Dad.

I felt like kissing him. That's Dad, not Fred Mudge. I wouldn't kiss Fred Mudge if you paid me. I never could stand Mr Mudge and now that I knew he was plotting to swindle the government, I liked him even less.

Fred returned to our table with the drinks. 'On the wagon, are you, Frank?' he asked. 'It's not like you to turn down a beer.'

'Yes, I've decided to join AA,' said Dad. 'I don't need the grog any longer. I've got better things to do with my life. I'm not sure if there's a branch of Alcoholics Anonymous in Bullyacre, but if there isn't one, I'll start one up. I even intend to stamp out the illicit homemade booze trade. Flanagan's days are numbered.'

'Good on yer,' said Fred, taking a deep draft of his beer and ignoring most of what Dad had said. 'The air force or the army, I forget which, is sending up helicopters with heat-seeking devices that'll locate those panthers, and when they find them, they're going to blast them off the face of the earth. Use flame-throwers, I expect. Or cannon. Or even napalm like in Vietnam. That wouldn't do the stock much good, though. Anyway, the super says he can solve the whole problem in a day or two.'

Emma began to whimper. I moved my chair a bit closer to hers and patted her gently on the back.

'Will they detect Cuddles?' she whispered to me.

'You're real scared of them big panthers, are you, love?' asked Fred, his voice full of beery concern. 'Don't you worry none. The super is going to sort it out. There won't be a panther to be found anywhere in the area quicker than you can say Jack Robinson. Or Jack Wylie either, for that matter.'

Emma burst into tears. 'I want to go home,' she sobbed. 'My poor little Cuddles is all on her own in the toilet.'

'What's the army going to do when they discover that the panthers have got three heads?' asked Bill.

Dad and I kicked Bill under the table, but he'd stuck his chin out and had that 'you're not going to shut me up' expression on his face that he gets occasionally when he's annoyed about something.

'What's the kid talking about?' Fred Mudge asked. 'Panthers with three heads? That's crap. Those panthers haven't got three heads. I watched those panthers tearing my bull apart last night. I will admit there were a lot of panthers there, but I didn't see any three-headed panthers. Is your kid a few sheep short in the top paddock, Frank?' He looked at us all suspiciously, took another swig of his beer, and went on, doing his best to sound sympathetic. 'I mean, I know your family's been through a lot lately, what with your wife dying and you drinking to drown your sorrows, and I know young Lizzie's a bit on the unusual side, but I always thought young Bill was fairly sane. Only normal member of your family, I would've said. Of course, I don't know anything about the little girl with the kitten. Maybe she's all right. So far, anyway. So what's going on?'

'I know what I'm talking about,' said Bill stubbornly. 'What I don't understand is how could everyone else watch what was happening last night and not actually see it.'

'Bill, people see what they expect to see,' I began. 'There's this famous experiment where people are asked to watch a group of men throwing a ball at each other and count how many times it happens, and no one who watches the film clip notices a man in a gorilla suit.'

'Lizzie, be quiet,' remonstrated my father, who could see Fred

Mudge getting hot under the collar despite the condensation on the beer glass he clutched.

'Now see here, young Lizzie, if you think for a moment that I wanted to see my prize bull torn to shreds by a gang of ferocious bloody panthers, you have got another think coming. And there weren't any gorillas there last night, either.' He shook his head in disgust. 'I wish I hadn't bought you that lemon squash, Frank. It's just as well you've stopped drinking. You need to control these kids of yours. Lizzie's trigger-happy and going around shooting at geologists and now Bill's talking about three-headed panthers. I'm finding someone else to sit with.' He thrust back his chair and stalked away.

He joined another group of men who were drinking beer at another table. I saw their heads turn our way and I knew the Epsom family was under discussion.

'Why did you say that, Bill?' I asked. 'I thought we agreed that we weren't going to mention that the cats have got three heads. Now it's going to be all over town. They'll think we're crazier than they already think we are. They'll say it's because of Magnetic Hill affecting our brains.'

'Well, it's about time they faced up to how things really are,' said Bill, sticking his chin out the way he does when he's decided he's in the right. 'Mr Mudge got up my nose when he said he's going to rip the country off about the cost of his bull and everything. I've had about enough of being in town, Dad. When can we go home?'

'Yes, Daddy, I have to save Cuddles from those heat-detection helicopters. I'm going to hide her under every blanket in the house.'

Just then we heard the sound of rotors as the first of the helicopters flew over the hotel. Emma shrieked. Dad stood up.

'I thought we were going to order lunch,' I protested.

'I'm not hungry,' said Bill.

'It's the first time I've ever heard you say that,' I replied. I'd been looking forward to steak and fried potato chips and helping myself from the salad bar and, just for once, not having to wash the dishes after we'd eaten.

'I want a sandwich at home,' said Bill stubbornly. 'This pub food isn't healthy. Full of cholesterol and stuff.'

'I'll just go and move the car before Constable Perkins puts a sticker on it, and then I'll see if Sergeant Wylie will let me make my statement. We'll go home as soon as we can,' Dad said. 'Maybe you kids would be more comfortable sitting in the car out of public view while you're waiting. I know it's hot, but there's more than one sort of hot seat.'

We walked back to the church where we had parked the truck and untied the dogs. It was just as well that we'd left the hotel when we did, because they'd managed to knock over their bucket of water and they were lying next to the empty container, their sides heaving, tongues hanging out, panting in the heat. Both dogs managed to wag their tails slowly when they saw us, but there wasn't a lot of effort in it, and I could see the accusation in their eyes. When I filled the bucket from the tap outside the church, their tail wags increased in velocity and after they'd lapped up half a bucket, they both jumped up against us and sniffed and licked us enthusiastically.

Dad drove us back to Main Street and found a park not far from the police station. The crowd had thinned out a bit, because people had left in disgust when they found parking notices on their windscreens. The ones who were still standing around were saying things like 'Sergeant Wylie can go jump in the lake.'

I nearly reminded them that the only lake in Bullyacre was out at the Lions' Park and the water in it was pretty low because of the drought, but Dad dragged us kids away from the men, and pushed us towards the car. Some of the men were saying worse things than that and Dad didn't want us to hear their comments.

'Wait out here, you kids,' he told us, 'and I'll see if Jack's ready for me. Lizzie, you stay here with Emma and Bill. If you're needed to make a statement, I'll come back and get you.'

It was unpleasant waiting in the vehicle partly because there was no shade and we were all very hot, but mainly because everyone who walked past the vehicle stared at me. Fame is not a comfortable thing. I was relieved when Dad finally came back to the car.

'Lizzie, Sergeant Wylie said you don't need to make a statement because you're a minor,' he said. 'Actually, he's not happy about that newspaper article, and he said I'd better get you out of town before the television people spot you. Apparently they're pestering him to tell them where we live because they want to film the young heroine. How would you like to be on the Channel 6 six o'clock news, Lizzie? You'd better work out what you're going to wear for the occasion. Those jeans are a bit grubby.'

I didn't want to be on the news at six o'clock or any other time. It was bad enough being on the front page of the newspaper. Suddenly I understood how Princess Di must have felt with the paparazzi after her. I sank down in the seat to avoid the public glare, and Dad started the engine and drove back down Main Street towards Fourth Street so we could head for home.

10

As we passed the café, I noticed Ms Wylie standing on the footpath outside it, talking intently with a group of people. They weren't locals and I wondered how she knew them.

Ms Wylie looked as if she had been waiting for us, because as soon as she recognised our utility truck, she leaped out on to the road and waved us down. 'Frank, I have to talk to you. Have you got Lizzie there?' Ms Wylie peered through the window of our vehicle and discovered me trying to hide between Dad and Bill. 'Why are you slumped down like that, Lizzie? I keep telling you not to slouch. You should maintain good posture at your age. Otherwise you'll develop a scoliosis in later life. Just park the car here, Frank. Yes, it's all right to double park, no one's going anywhere for a while. If necessary, I'll clear it with my husband.'

Reluctantly, Dad pulled the ute over towards the kerb. Ms Wylie smiled. I recognised it as the smile she used when she'd won a small victory.

'I'll have a word with young Perkins if he comes along and annoys us,' she said. 'I really must introduce you. These people are founding members of the Save the South Australian Marsupial Panther Movement. Or SSAMPM for short.'

She grasped the arm of a young man with dreadlocks and jeans that were even grubbier than the ones I was wearing, and propelled him towards our ute. He stuck out his hand and pumped Dad's hand enthusiastically. Dad retrieved his hand, glanced down at it, and wiped it on the car upholstery next to me. I looked down and saw a puddle of sweat and oil on the already murky seat cover.

'This is Simon. And this,' as she pointed to a thin, bearded, intense-looking fellow with a stained white T-shirt and a shaven head, 'is Jeremy. This is Sarah and this is Jenny.'

Sarah and Jenny looked almost identical. They were both dressed in long gowns that looked as if they were made from my grandmother's old red velvet curtains and they both had long straggly hair. All of them, male and female, wore sandals and smelled of something vaguely herbal.

'Of course, we don't actually know for certain yet if the panther is marsupial,' said Jeremy earnestly. 'But as an Australian animal, the probability is that it is of marsupial origin.'

'More than a probability, it's almost a certainty,' said Jenny indignantly.

'The whole point is, as ecologists, we have to establish beyond doubt that this panther is definitely a marsupial,' Simon said. 'Because if it is a marsupial, it's a newly discovered, very rare native animal and as such it must be protected. At all costs.'

'And the army intends to blast it out of existence,' Sarah said angrily. 'We can't allow that to happen. It would be a tragedy.'

'It would be criminal,' said Simon. 'An act of ecological vandalism.'

'We should have a demonstration,' Jenny interrupted. 'I can make the placards, and we'll all march up and down this street. We could chain ourselves to that statue over there with the bullocks and stage a hunger strike.'

'That statue ought to be removed, though. You shouldn't be celebrating the harnessing and exploitation of bullocks like that,' observed Sarah. 'It's an archaic custom, and it was extremely cruel to the poor animals.'

'The bullock drovers worked those unfortunate animals to death,' agreed Jeremy. 'And then they ate the corpses. People should be vegetarians like us.'

'That's Hugh Foulkes's monument,' I snapped. 'He's a local hero. And he wasn't cruel to his bullocks. His life depended on them. He looked after them extremely well. It's in the history books.'

'I'm not going on a hunger strike,' said Bill defiantly. 'I'm going home now to have one of Lizzie's sandwiches. She makes great sandwiches. Ham and cold mutton or beef when we can afford it. Nothing vegetarian. Not even lettuce or grated carrot or tomato. Anyway, what makes you think the panther is a marsupial? Kangaroos are marsupials and they hop. The panther doesn't hop. It pounces. It's not vegetarian either. It eats sheep and cows. And what about the three heads?'

I punched Bill on the arm.

'Stop that, Lizzie,' said Bill. He punched me back.

'Stop it, both of you,' said Dad.

'It could be related to the thylacine,' said Simon. 'There are no native panthers in Australia, but there used to be thylacines, not that long ago. They were carnivores, unfortunately. The last one died in Tasmania last century.'

'They were murdered. It was genocide,' said Sarah.

'Thylacines looked like big dogs with stripes and this doesn't look anything like a dog,' I said. 'It looks like a cat.'

'A very big cat,' said Emma.

'With three heads,' said Bill.

'Shut up, Bill,' I said and punched him again.

'That's right, Bill, shut up this minute,' said Dad.

'There was a marsupial lion back in the Pliocene era,' Simon insisted. '*Thylacoleo crassidentatus*. It was the size of a leopard. That could easily be mistaken by a lay person for a panther.'

'Did that crassy thingy have three heads?' asked Bill. 'Was it vegetarian or carnivorous?'

'Stop being facetious, William,' snapped Ms Wylie. 'Of course it didn't have three heads. And it was carnivorous. That's natural for some animals.'

'It's only unnatural for humans,' interjected Jenny.

'Your marsupial lion from the Pliocene era would be extinct by now,' I said, beginning to feel a bit hysterical. 'I think it's far more likely that we've got panthers roaming about here, panthers that escaped from a circus or a zoo. Or were left behind, as my dad says, by the American troops who brought them in as mascots during the Second World War when they were stationed in Victoria.'

'With three heads,' said Bill wickedly. 'The panthers, not the Yanks.'

'The fossils of *crassidentatus* have been found extensively at Riverslea,' said Jeremy. 'It's not beyond possibility that some could have survived in a micro-environment and be living here.'

'There could be a micro-environment on Magnetic Hill,' said Ms Wylie. 'It is an extremely unusual sort of place. One feels the supercharged vibes out there. The ambience is most peculiar. One feels it when one breathes in the air on the hill.'

And I wish I was breathing that air right now, I thought. The air here was a bit thick, particularly around Simon.

'It's very easy to believe that there could be a remnant population of marsupial lions on Magnetic Hill,' continued Ms Wylie dreamily, 'just as there could well be a Loch Ness monster in the wilds of Scotland.'

The ecologists nodded their agreement.

'The Loch Ness monster is probably a plesiosaur,' said Sarah.

'I've applied for a grant to go to Scotland to study it,' said Jenny. 'But I haven't got it yet, and Bullyacre is closer so we'll have a smaller carbon footprint by coming here. Also, it's our patriotic duty to investigate the marsupial panther and save it for posterity.'

'I wanted you to meet Lizzie,' Ms Wylie told her friends, 'because, of all the inhabitants of Bullyacre, Lizzie has had the most contact with the panther. Or, as you say, Simon, contact with *Thylacoleo crassidentatus*. I thought perhaps you might compare notes. Perhaps Lizzie could give you a detailed description of the actual animal and the habitat in which she has observed it. I've already shown you the photographs. Lizzie could take you to the actual area.'

'What we need to do,' Jeremy said, 'is to capture a live specimen. Trap it, if necessary. Humanely, of course.'

'Are you going to use carrots or lettuce as bait in your trap?' asked Bill. 'Maybe you could put three heads of lettuce in it.'

Jeremy ignored the interjection. 'Or even,' he continued, 'we could just take more photographs that show whether it is in fact a marsupial.'

'We could set up night vision cameras to record movement in the fields,' suggested Jenny. 'We must establish whether the pouch faces the front or the back, for instance.'

'Why?' I asked. And regretted asking the question as soon as had I posed it. These people really didn't need encouraging and I could see that Dad was growing more and more impatient. His teeth were clenched and he'd turned the engine back on and was pressing the accelerator pedal occasionally, probably hoping that Ms Wylie and her ecologists would get the hint he wanted to leave. Dad was certainly increasing our carbon footprint. That didn't worry me too much, but was I worried that this encounter might be enough to drive him back to the drink if it didn't end soon.

'Because,' said Jeremy as though he was explaining calculus to a five-year-old, 'that would indicate whether the animal was a burrowing creature or not. Wombats, for example, have pouches that face towards the back so that the mother doesn't get soil in the pouch while she's excavating her burrow, whereas koalas and kangaroos have forward-facing pouches. Soil in the pouch would be detrimental to the young marsupial.'

'Very interesting point,' said Dad. 'I'll tell you what, next time I see one of those panthers out attacking one of my sheep, I'll take a good hard look at it and I'll let you know if it has a pouch, and which way the pouch faces if it does have one. Of course, if it turns out that the panther that's eating my sheep is a male specimen, the whole exercise will be in vain. Unfortunately, we really have to go now because we have lots of things to do back at the farm. I wish you good luck with your investigations.'

He revved up the engine and we drove off at a higher speed than was legal in the township. Hopefully Constable Perkins would not have seen the offence committed if he was still patrolling the streets attaching parking infringement notices to windscreens.

I glanced back at the group beside the road. Ms Wylie did not look pleased. She and the ecologists huddled together deep in discussion. I was reminded of the three witches in Macbeth, although, of course there were four people involved in this particular coven.

'We ought to let them have a good look at Cuddles,' said Bill. 'Or better still, at Cuddles's parents.'

'Is Cuddles grown-up enough to have a pouch if she's a marsupial?' asked Emma. 'We should've asked those people how old a kitten has to be before the pouch appears. She hasn't got one at the moment. I'd have noticed it when she lies on her back waving her legs in the air so I can tickle her tummy.'

'What we ought to do is donate Cuddles to science,' I said grimly.

'It would solve a lot of problems. What are we going to do when that cat grows up? It isn't going to stay little and cute forever, you know. It's going to be dangerous later on.'

'We'll cross that bridge when we come to it, Lizzie,' said Dad. 'Right now it's dangerous for us to stay in Bullyacre with Ms Wylie and her tame ecologists on the rampage, so we're going home.'

11

Emma burst into tears when we opened the toilet door. Cuddles was fine, but Emma's teddy bear had been reduced to a pile of plush fabric and stuffing. I was very glad that we'd decided to take Toby to town with us instead of leaving him or Banjo in the loo with the kitten or they might have met a similar fate.

'You'll have to mend him, Lizzie,' Emma wept. 'Why did she do it? It's that horrible Tabby cat, that's who did it. I expect Cuddles tried to stop her, but Tabby's really nasty sometimes. I've had my teddy since I was a baby. Mum gave him to me. Lizzie, get the needle and cotton and make him better.'

I spent the evening trying to patch the bear together. He ended up looking a shadow of his former self, although eventually he did have two ears and four legs. I wouldn't have gotten more than a D minus in domestic science for the job, but Emma was happy. Well, she was happier than she'd been when the bear was totally dismembered.

'Why don't you give him three heads like the cats?' asked Bill. 'Then he'll match Cuddles and she mightn't tear him to shreds next time she's alone with him.'

We heard the helicopters going over the farmhouse at about eight o'clock, just as I was putting Emma to bed. She screamed and tried to hide the kitten under her bedclothes. The animal rebelled and all three heads on their long necks thrashed about on the bed. I tried to calm the thing down and was bitten and scratched for my trouble.

I decided to concentrate on soothing Emma. 'It's all right, Emma, they aren't looking for panthers in people's houses,' I said.

Then I wondered whether the devices were in fact sensitive enough to differentiate a cat-shaped object from a person-shaped object or a dog- or sheep-shaped object. You never knew just how advanced technology was, these days. But surely there was no way any military technology could determine that a little girl had a three-headed kitten in her bed. Or was there? Were we committing some sort of offence against the realm by harbouring a panther kitten? If so, what was the actual law and how would it be worded? Surely the lawmakers would have to know about three-headed cats before they formulated such a law? Was there perhaps even a Mosaic law written in the Bible, a 'Thou Shalt Not' that said you couldn't nurture something that the rest of the world considered a monster? Perhaps Jake's dad, the vicar, would be able to explain it to me.

How did a culture determine what was a monster and what was not a monster? Morality changes from society to society, I knew that from history. I mean, the ancient Babylonians used to sacrifice their firstborn children to their god, Baal. They used to toss babies into fiery furnaces. Their priests commanded it and their community expected it. The gods would have sent droughts or flooding rains if the babies weren't thrown into the fire. These days, that sort of thing would be considered child abuse.

So even if the community decided we were doing the wrong thing by keeping Cuddles and her sisters as a pet, in a few years' time they might change their collective mind and decide that we were doing the right thing by saving a species from extinction. Jeremy and Ms Wylie would agree with that. Maybe they were ahead of their time. Sergeant Wylie and the superintendent had other ideas about the cats.

I decided that if the military did detect the presence of Cuddles in Emma's bed, I might appeal to Ms Wylie. Perhaps I could stitch or stick a pouch on to Cuddles's belly. I doubted that Cuddles would cooperate. But it could mean her salvation if she looked like a marsupial – Ms Wylie and her gang of ecologists would fight to the death on Cuddles's behalf.

A backward-facing pouch or a frontward-facing pouch? Personally I favoured a frontward-facing pouch because cats don't usually dig burrows, although of course they did dig in their cat trays if they were domestic cats. I could use a bit of skin from a dead sheep if I shaved the wool from it, and then I could stick on some of the hair that the dogs shed constantly to make it look more authentic You can do wonders with superglue.

My planning was interrupted by Banjo and Toby barking loudly when they heard loud knocking on the door.

Dad turned on the outside light and peered through the curtains to see who was there. 'Lizzie, if Emma's still awake, tell her to keep herself and the kitten very quiet. Shut her door. And Bill, if you say one word about three-headed cats, I'll thrash hell out of you, child protection agency not withstanding.'

'Who is it, Dad? Is it the army?'

'No, it's worse than that. It's a television crew. There's a whole crowd of people out there and they've got lights and microphones and cameras.'

'Just say we're not interested, the way you do when those religious people come calling,' suggested Bill. 'Or just don't open the door and they'll get sick of knocking eventually and go away.'

We let our uninvited guests hammer at the door for a while, but they didn't give up or go away. Perhaps they were used to that sort of reception. Then the screaming began.

Dad opened the curtains again just in time to see a dark panther-shaped creature dragging a man by the legs into our orchard. Well, we refer to it as our orchard, but it's actually a dead apple tree that Dad keeps saying he's going to cut down for firewood, a couple of fig trees covered with mistletoe, and a lemon tree that hasn't had a lemon on it for years because Dad never prunes, fertilises or even waters it. And two almond trees that the cockies eat all the almonds off before they can be eaten by us.

To be exact, two of the heads were working in unison so two sets of fangs were embedded in the unfortunate man's leg – one leg to a head. The other head was snarling at the remaining camera crew, who had scattered. Most of them had climbed into their van and they appeared to be trying to use their mobile phones. Which, as I could have told them, wouldn't work here in the proximity of Magnetic Hill. One brave soul was hitting at the cat with the end of a camera tripod. That's not something I would have done. It's a gun or nothing for me where three-headed cats are concerned. Another chap, either possessing nerves of titanium or stainless steel or else determined to get an award as Cameraman of the Year, was standing on the roof of the van filming the whole sequence and talking rapidly into one of those furry things that reporters thrust at people. The furry thing was held by a young chap who was crying.

'Get the guns, Lizzie!' Dad ordered. 'Get that .303 that I borrowed from old Miss Cobbledick. It's in the laundry. Ammo's on the shelf next to the fly spray.'

I've never obeyed an order so quickly in my life. I loaded the gun while I was running back to Dad's side, which is something Dad always says not to do, but I figured that this was a special occasion. I ran back and grabbed the .22 and the shotgun as well. Dad used the butt of the rifle to knock the glass out of the window nearest the front door. He began firing into the darkness.

'Try not to hit the man that the cat's taken,' I said. 'Or the chap on the van.' I stood beside Dad and loaded guns for him as fast as he emptied them. There was only room for one person at that window. It felt like being Ned Kelly at the siege of that hotel in Glenrowan when he tried unsuccessfully to keep the entire Victorian police force at bay. Well, most of it, anyway.

Much later, when we were pretty sure the panther was dead, we ventured outside. Bill was instructed to keep Emma and the kitten in her room at all costs. For once, he obeyed. I think he was in shock.

The television people were hysterical. I sat them down on the grass and Dad found a bottle of whisky that I hadn't known was in the back of the wardrobe and fed it to them, never once taking a swig himself. I got the first aid box and bandaged the people who needed it (the man who'd wielded the tripod had received a nasty slash from the panther's claws and he reminded me a bit of Emma's teddy before it'd had surgery) and a couple of the others had what looked like minor scratches on their arms. The panther must have been too preoccupied to give them its full attention. They were going to need tetanus shots and quite a few stitches too.

The camera man filmed me giving the first aid. The man who'd been dragged into the orchard was dead and there wasn't anything we could do about him. Dad got a tarp and covered the body but one bloody foot protruded and I couldn't bring myself to go near him to pull the tarp down, in case I saw his face with the awful staring eyes looking at me again. I don't think I'll ever forget the expression on his face.

The only other dead person I'd seen before that night was Mum, and she looked peaceful, albeit a bit disappointed and worried because she didn't want to leave us, even though I'd given her my word that nothing awful would happen to us after she was gone. I suddenly realised that I'd lied to Mum. But of course there was no way I could have known that there was stuff like this in the offing. Just as well, really.

The dead man's friends filmed him lying on the ground under the tarp although they said they'd probably have to cut that out before it went to air because someone would be bound to object to that particular bit of footage. They said it was politically incorrect. I don't know why they filmed something that they couldn't use, unless it was for private viewing. I decided they were sick people but maybe journalists are like that.

Dad phoned Sergeant Wylie and asked him to send an ambulance. Dad was filmed making the calls. The cameraman helped Dad to drag the panther's body out into the open. I had to hold the camera while they were doing it so they'd have a record of that, too.

Now there was no hiding the fact that the panther had three heads. The dead cat would be on national television as soon as the crew could get the film back to their studio.

I looked and I could find no sign of a pouch, but then the panther we'd killed was a male.

12

'Hurry up, Lizzie, it's starting,' shouted Dad.

I carried the two mugs of tea into the lounge room and put them on the coffee table beside the bowl of popcorn I'd just taken out of the microwave. Cuddles, who was sitting on Emma's knee, stretched her neck out as far as it would go and began helping herself to corn straight from the bowl. Emma tried to persuade Spotty to take a piece, but after mouthing the morsel for a moment or two, she spat it out. It landed on the edge of the lounge chair and Bill absent-mindedly picked it up and had it halfway to his mouth before I knocked it out of his fingers.

'Don't let the kitten eat that stuff, Emma,' I said. 'It's not hygienic to have an animal eat from a dish we're eating from, and popcorn's probably not good for her either.'

'Shut up, Lizzie. The commercials are over and the show's begun,' said Bill.

The television screen showed footage filmed in the Hobart zoo a long time ago. The last known thylacine in captivity paced up and down a small concrete enclosure, yawning with boredom, opening its incredibly wide jaws.

'Doesn't look anything like the cat,' said Bill.

'We all want to hear this, Bill,' said Dad sternly.

'That film was taken just before the demise of this animal and, indeed, the demise of an entire species,' said the announcer.

'Look, it's got stripes, so how can that dill Jeremy say that the panther's a thylacine? The panther's got spots. Even Emma's kitten's got spots. The Spotty head's just got more than the rest of it.'

'Quiet, Bill,' said Dad. 'I want to hear what Terry Furphy has to say.'

'And that thylacine's only got one head,' said Bill with satisfaction, reaching for the popcorn.

I punched him on the arm. He glared at me but he knew Dad was sitting next to me, so he didn't punch back.

'We will hear shortly from Superintendent McCormick, who is leading this investigation, but first we will play film taken by the intrepid crew involved in the incident at Epsom Downs last week. We also have an exclusive interview with the schoolgirl who has been acclaimed as the bravest girl in Australia. My crew and I flew to Adelaide yesterday to record my meeting with Miss Lizzie Epsom, who has been recommended as Young Australian of Year and also for various bravery awards.'

The photo of me taken by the geologist lady flashed up on the screen and Bill groaned.

'You will recall that this was the young lady who rescued the party of geologists on Magnetic Hill recently from certain death. Now Lizzie has been involved in yet another, even more horrific incident. I know you will enjoy this delightful young lady with her refreshing ideas and bubbly personality just as much as I did.'

Bill groaned and took another handful of popcorn. 'Can I have your autograph, Lizzie?' he asked. 'Or do you charge for that? How long has your personality been bubbly? You didn't fart on camera, did you?'

'Shut up, William,' ordered my father in his army voice.

We watched as our front door appeared on the screen.

'I wish I'd mown the lawn before all this happened,' said Dad. 'And I should've pruned that rose bush. That heap of beer bottles definitely gives the wrong impression. The whole place looks neglected. I'll clean it up tomorrow. I'll take the bottles to the recycle centre.'

'Can I have the money from the bottles, Dad?' Bill asked.

'I'll give it to Lizzie and she can buy the week's groceries with it,' said Dad. 'Now keep your mouth closed, Bill, unless you're putting popcorn into it.'

The film had been heavily edited, which was just as well, but I have to admit that even the remaining events were dramatic. They'd cut out a lot of the screaming and put bleeps over the swearing. At the time, I hadn't noticed how much the film crew were swearing, so when the incident was over and the cameraman was sitting in our kitchen running the film back to check it, I was amazed and even a little shocked. Jake's dad, Miss Cobbledick, and in fact the entire Ladies' Auxiliary would not have been at all impressed if they'd seen the first draft of this film.

'That was horrible,' said Emma, feeding popcorn to Tabby and pushing Spotty's head out of the way as she tried to steal the food from Cuddles's mouth. 'It wasn't at all suitable for children to watch. It ought to have an R rating at least. You shouldn't have subjected Cuddles and me to this, Lizzie.'

Cuddles didn't seem affected by the film. Her head was darting towards the popcorn bowl again. I pushed it away and it showed me its fangs. They seemed to get longer and sharper every day. Popcorn must be an acquired taste for three-headed kittens, I thought. Although Spotty had refused it at first, she seemed to like it now, and Tabby was on the way to becoming a popcorn addict. She was snapping and snarling at both Spotty and Cuddles in her efforts to gulp down the corn. The salt must be bad for them, I thought. It wasn't good for us, either, come to think of it, but since we could die at any moment if the mother launched herself through one of the windows, why was I worrying? I gave up trying to prevent the kitten from scoffing corn. I'd make a fresh bowl for us humans when the ad break came on and toss the kitten into the toilet while we ate it.

'I'm so glad the kitten and I didn't see it happen. Tabby would have gone berserk if she'd seen her daddy getting shot. I put my hand over her face just now so she wouldn't see the worst bits of that film. And she bit me, the ungrateful pussy. Spotty is angry too, and Cuddles is feeling sad.'

I thought any feline depression was more likely caused because the bottom of the bowl was now visible.

'How do you know it was Cuddles, Tabby and Spotty's daddy who got shot? There might be hundreds of those things out there,' said Bill, filling his mouth with popcorn, uncaring that three cat mouths had been at it. 'We'll need another bowl of this soon, Lizzie.'

'Will you please shut up, Bill?' said Dad. 'We're getting to the good part of the program now.'

'We will now play the pre-recorded interview with Lizzie Epsom, girl extraordinaire,' said Terry Furphy, tossing his head so that the quiff of dark hair which was his trademark bounced.

Zoe's mum thinks Terry Furphy's wonderful and she wanted me to get his autograph for her but I conveniently forgot to ask him. I said I was too nervous to ask him, but I wasn't really. I was just disgusted with him and didn't want to boost his ego by asking for his autograph. You wouldn't believe how big that man's ego is.

I would have liked to ask him one thing, though. I couldn't understand why he used the name Furphy. If that was my name, and I was a journalist, I'd change it. Surely he must know that a furphy means a rumour and that the term comes from the water carts used at Gallipoli because they were manufactured by a firm called Furphy. The soldiers used to gather around the carts and swap news and gossip and the stories often got changed in the telling. Furphy is a rotten name for a reporter to have.

On the subject of nomenclature, Ms Wylie, who was waiting outside the studio before I went in for my interview, reminded me that it was both my privilege and my duty to choose the official scientific name for the marsupial panther. She had already called me into her office at school and suggested that I might call it *Pantheris marsupialis wyliensis*, both in homage to the excellent education I had received at her hands and the unstinting care and protection given to the community of Bullyacre by her husband, Sergeant Wylie, our police officer of many years standing. She also took the opportunity to warn me about Mr Furphy.

'He's reduced many prime ministers to tears,' she warned me. 'Just one glance from those steely green eyes and people melt.'

I nodded.

'By the way,' she said, 'your frock is very pretty. I don't believe I've ever seen you in a dress before. Did you buy a new one for the occasion so you'd feel better about appearing on television?' She fingered the cloth and I could see she was estimating its value. 'It looks expensive. I wouldn't have thought your father could afford anything like that. I've heard that he spends all his money on alcohol.'

'Dad insisted that I get a new dress. My Auntie Bett down here in Adelaide chose it. But I didn't need it. Even without the window dressing I'd be all right,' I said.

'How can you be so confident?' she asked.

'I'm a kid,' I said. 'Mr Furphy's not going to upset a kid on national TV, is he? He wouldn't get the Logie this year if he did that. Besides, I'm famous and very popular and you can't be nasty to a national celebrity who's been featured in the *Women's Weekly*. It would ruin his image.'

'You should watch out that you don't become arrogant, Lizzie Epson. You mustn't let this momentary fame go to your head. Now remember to be respectful to Mr Furphy in every way. Say please and thank you and only speak when spoken to. Remember that both Mr Furphy's image and that of the township of Bullyacre are at stake here.'

Terry Furphy's image did come close to ruin during my interview, though. I still don't accept it was really my fault. Thinking back, it was just as well that my interview was pre-recorded. That way, they managed to cut out the worst bits.

'Lizzie,' Mr Furphy said, after my hair had been tidied and my nose powdered, and I'd been told what to do and where to sit. 'Lizzie,' he repeated gently, bending forward in a paternal sort of way and patting my knee, 'you were the first person to have actually seen the Panther of Magnetic Hill. That gives you the right to name the creature, did you know that?' He smiled indulgently.

I realised he was trying to look like my favourite uncle. It wasn't working. I sat there wondering if his famous hairdo was actually a wig. Close up, that's how it looked.

He continued, dividing his attention between smiling at me and smiling into the camera. 'It isn't really correct protocol to name it after yourself, although you could, of course, name it after your father. Or you could decide to call it after another person. The dinosaur that was discovered in western Queensland, for example, is called *Muttaburrasaurus langdonii*, after a man called Langdon, who was one of its discoverers. The *Muttaburrasaurus* means that is a dinosaur from Muttaburra, which is where it was found.'

'Yes,' I said. 'I know that.'

'I believe one of your schoolteachers, Ms Wylie, who is here with us tonight and who is going to appear later with the panel of ecologists who support the conservation of the marsupial panther, is putting pressure on you to name it after her. Is that true?'

'Yes,' I said. 'But I'm not going to do that.'

'So will the panther be called after your family, Lizzie? Perhaps *Pantheris australis epsomii*, as I believe was suggested to you by both the University of Adelaide and the South Australian Museum? Or if you wanted to pay tribute to someone you truly admired, you might name it *Pantheris australis furphii*.'

'No,' I said. 'I'm going to call it Cuddles. My sister suggested that name. It's the name of her pet kitten. Maybe I'll choose *Pantheris australis cuddlii*. But the name ought to have something about it having three heads in it, because that's what makes it unique. So I want to put something about that in it too. There's a nice man at the museum who's going to help me work out the name because I'm not all that good at Latin – I only got a C in it last term.'

Mr Furphy frowned and tapped me on the knee to shut me up. I ignored him. He looked to see if the cameras were on him. They were on me. He looked furious.

I was beginning to enjoy myself so I kept waffling. 'Mr Gonski was quite cross when I got a C because I usually get A. I do know that the Latin for three is tri so I might put that in. And maybe something about the heads, like cephalus, as well.'

Terry Furphy's eyes opened wide. I thought I saw tears in them. The left eye seemed somehow different to the right eye. I was mesmerised. No wonder people talked about his gaze. It reminded me of the basilisk that we learned about in Greek mythology. One of his pupils detached itself from the eye and began to ooze slowly down his face. I was horrified. I clutched wildly at his shoulder.

'Mr Furphy, what's happening? Your face has gone all funny! Your left eye is sliding down your cheek.'

I don't believe it was the sight of Mr Furphy's eyeball apparently travelling down his cheek that did it. I've seen far worse things when Dad slaughters a sheep to feed us, and of course it wasn't pretty when the panther attacked the camera crew a couple of nights ago. I suppose my nausea could have been caused by nerves because I knew that I was on national television, but I really thought I'd psyched myself up pretty well.

Personally, I blame the lasagne and roast beef and vegies followed by strawberry and cream covered pavlova that Auntie Bett had insisted I eat before I went to the TV studio. She said I needed to keep my strength up, but I'm just not used to rich food like that. That frock was a bit tight, too. I told Auntie Bett I'd rather wear my jeans, but she insisted on the dress. And the lights in the studio were very hot.

I clutched at my mouth. 'I think I'm going to be sick.'

'Shit,' said Mr Furphy, ignoring me. He grabbed at his face and tried to put his eye back in, then he flinched as I vomited all over his expensive shirt, tie and suit.

'Stop the cameras,' yelled the director. 'Terry's contact lens has come loose.'

They made me swear I'd never mention what I'd seen to anyone. I haven't breathed a word about what Terry Furphy called our little secret. Well, I haven't breathed many words to many people at least. The only person I have told was Zoe, and of course she told her mum. Zoe never keeps anything from her mum. Zoe's mum still thinks Mr Furphy is marvellous, though, contact lenses or not. And probably all Zoe's mum's friends still like him, too. His ratings haven't suffered yet. Apparently most of Australia planned to watch tonight's show.

I was sent off the set after that. They said that I 'd had enough television exposure for a child and that the child protection laws precluded further on-screen time. One of the production team pressed an envelope into my hand and I thought at first it was the fee that they'd promised me for appearing. Only there was three hundred dollars in the envelope and the producer lady whispered that it was just a little extra for being cooperative and keeping Mr Furphy's little secret. My actual cheque would come in the mail.

I saw the superintendent waiting outside the studio while the make-up people completed their adjustments to Mr Furphy's appearance. I don't know how long he waited there, because I was being ushered out the back door but I have a feeling it must have been quite a while, because neither of them looked happy in the latter part of the film clip we watched tonight, but I will admit it all looked quite seamless, and even the tie that Mr Furphy wore when he was talking to the superintendant was almost identical to the one I'd vomited on. They must keep extra ties and suits in the dressing room in case of accidents.

It's amazing what you can do with film. My school is going to run a semester on film production next term, and I'm thinking about enrolling for it.

'Superintendent McCormick, you are the police officer who has been in charge of the investigation of the tragic and dramatic events that have taken place recently in South Australia's mid-north,' began Terry Furphy, with a grim expression on his face.

The superintendent nodded glumly. 'Yes, that is correct,' he said. 'I do have that honour.'

'Can you give us an estimate of just how many of these animals are lurking around Magnetic Hill?' asked Terry Furphy, now smiling his famous sardonic smile and stroking his fresh immaculate tie. 'Strolling, or should one say skulking, the green and pleasant pastures around Bullyacre? Terrorising the unfortunate inhabitants of the area and killing their valuable stock?' He leant closer to his guest in a rather threatening manner. 'How many of these monsters, Superintendent, how many?'

The superintendent shook his head. 'No one knows,' he responded gloomily. 'We are receiving different accounts from different sources. With all due respect to the people of Bullyacre, there appear to be a lot of unreliable witnesses in that general area. A lot of conflicting evidence is coming in.'

'And do you personally believe, Mr Superintendant of Police, that this creature is an animal that has allegedly escaped from a travelling circus at some time in the past? Or is it perhaps even a mutation caused by radiation in the local area as some experts are saying, or possibly even a feral cat grown to enormous proportions and mutated horribly, and, in fact, grown an additional couple of heads?'

'No comment, Mr Furphy,' said the police officer, squirming a little in his chair.

Mr Furphy smiled again at the superintendent and continued his interrogation. I had a feeling that Machiavelli would have smiled just like that. 'Or do you believe, as our ecological friends do, that this is a native Australian species, albeit one whose existence was hitherto unsuspected? Possibly even a native marsupial animal? I am referring, of course, to the bizarre appearance of the animal. An animal that has been reported to have three heads. The panther definitely does have three heads, does it not, astounding though that is?'

'I have no expertise in this area,' said the superintendent firmly. 'No comment.'

'But if it is an endangered Australian species, perhaps a variation on the so-called marsupial lion or…I've got the name here…'

There was a great rustling of papers at this point, although I don't for a moment think that Mr Furphy would not have had the name ready and in fact would have rehearsed the pronunciation because that's the sort of fellow he is

'…*Thylacoleo carnifex*…

'The name I heard put forward was *Thylacoleo crassidentatus*,' said the superintendent smoothly. He, or his department, had done their homework. He seemed to grow in confidence now that the cat was, so to speak, out of the bag. 'They are similar animals, I believe. But different epochs, I suspect. I have been advised by experts that both of them became extinct a very long time ago. *Crassidentatus* is the more likely culprit, however. It fits most of the descriptions received. Apart, of course, from the three heads.' He put his hand over his mouth then shrugged and continued. 'If indeed, the creature does possess three heads. But, I reiterate, definitely both species have definitely gone extinct. I believe that the South Australian population has nothing to fear from either of those two species.'

'But what if they didn't!' said the interviewer triumphantly. 'What if this is a last remnant or vestige of those animals and what if they are now driven into final extinction by the actions of a foolish and short-sighted, heavy-handed police action? Is the crass behaviour of the past, and here I refer to the sad extinction of the Tasmanian tiger, more correctly called the thylacine, to be repeated in our own time?'

'There was definitely no pouch on the specimen recovered,' said the superintendent triumphantly. 'It was unlikely to be marsupial, and therefore not a native Australian species.'

'The specimen was a male. A male marsupial would not have a pouch! And are you certain that those marsupial lions did actually have pouches? Does the fossil evidence support that theory? Would a pouch fossilise? Apparently the thylacine had a pouch.'

'I have no expertise in this area,' said the superintendent wearily. 'No comment.'

'But the body of the animal that you recovered and that you are holding in so-called protective custody definitely has three heads,' said Mr Furphy triumphantly.

'Yes,' admitted the superintendent a little reluctantly. 'There are three heads on the body of the animal we are holding in protective custody.'

Terry Furphy was now firing a mix of questions and statements at the unfortunate superintendent with the machine gun velocity for which he was famous. 'You are refusing to release that body for examination and investigation into the care of the group Save the Marsupial Panther. Do you not believe that full identification of the specimen is vital to this investigation? Why are you impeding that investigation? Do you have any social, environmental conscience at all? Are you aware that there is a strong lobby put forward to Parliament by a group of eminent ecologists who are determined to resist this species being driven into extermination?' demanded Mr Furphy, his voice positively booming in triumph.

You would never think this man had just been vomited on by a girl heroine, I thought.

'Yes,' said the superintendent weakly. 'I have no further comment.'

'We will now invite comment from the panel of expert ecologists who have formed an action group with the aim of preventing the extinction of the marsupial panther.' Terry Furphy sat back in his chair triumphantly as the superintendent rose from his seat, following an invisible command from above.

I thought I saw Terry Furphy dabbing at his left eye as if to reassure himself that it was intact. I wondered whether the contact lens was still troubling him, but then I forgot all about that. We were about to see Ms Wylie and her panel of experts. But there'd be a commercial break soon, so the make-up people would have time to work on Mr Furphy before he came back on camera.

'Can you make some more popcorn, Lizzie?' asked Emma. 'Tabby really likes it and I'm trying to make her more docile.'

'You'll never make Tabby docile,' I said. 'She's feral. Can't you wait until this finishes? I want to see what Ms Wylie says. Feed Tabby some of that chocolate in the dish, and then chuck her in the bathroom. Or the toilet.'

'She doesn't like chocolate. Spotty does, though. Dad says chocolate's not good for them. Apparently it can kill dogs. It might kill her.'

Good idea, I thought. I went to make more popcorn.

'Cuddles was dreadfully upset, so I couldn't possibly leave her in the bathroom,' said Emma when I came back and saw the monster still installed on her knee.

I put the bowl on the table and sighed.

'Emma, quiet,' said Dad. 'Please.'

To the panel of expert ecologists, which consisted of Ms Wylie and her associates, Jeremy, Simon, Sarah and Jenny, Mr Furphy, whose face seemed to be fully functional again, said, 'The first thing we have to establish is whether you believe that the creature killed at the siege of Epsom Downs belongs to a native Australian species. I consider, and you will no doubt agree, that the whole discussion hangs on that point.'

'Of course it's a native Australian,' said Ms Wylie. 'Have you ever heard of a three-headed cat or indeed any three-headed animal living anywhere else in the world? This is a truly unique form. Australia has many truly unique forms. When the first platypus was taken to Britain it was at first judged to be a hoax. The British thought that someone had constructed the platypus as a joke. Are you suggesting that someone sewed the extra heads onto the marsupial panther of Magnetic Hill in jest, as was supposed by the British back then? By the way, we really are going to have to find a better name for the animal.'

'Lizzie Epsom has proposed that it be called Cuddles,' said Mr Furphy.

'Ridiculous,' said Ms Wylie. 'Just the sort of frivolous idea I'd expect from Lizzie Epsom. She's an under-aged child, no judgement at all. Typical teenaged thinking.'

'Teenager or not, Lizzie Epsom has rights of nomenclature as the primary discoverer of the species,' insisted Mr Furphy. 'I disagree with her choice, but I don't think anyone has the right to overturn her decision. Perhaps we might call it, for this evening at least, the Beast of Magnetic Hill.'

The panel nodded their assent.

Mr Furphy continued. 'Do you, or the panel of ecologists, have proof of the origins of the Beast of Magnetic Hill, Ms Wylie?'

Simon spoke up. 'If and when we gain access to the cadaver, we're going to have DNA testing done which will ascertain the actual genetic origin of the beast. That will prove whether it is a marsupial or not. However, I'd like to point out that dingos are not marsupials, but they are accepted as part of the Australian ecology. No one is suggesting that dingos be exterminated.'

'It has been established that dingos were brought to Australia when the first humans arrived here. Probably about fifty or sixty thousand years ago, depending on which anthropologist to whom you speak. They were companion animals to the indigenous people and therefore they have a right to be here, even though they're neither marsupials nor actually native to the country,' said Jenny.

'But dingos are shot and baited and kept away from human activity as much as possible,' interjected Mr Furphy. 'There have been problems on Fraser Island, and, dare I say it, central Australia. Farmers don't tolerate stock losses due to dingo predation. We have a dingo fence to keep them away from sheep grazing areas.'

'We might need to establish designated beast zones,' suggested Sarah. 'But it would be absolutely criminal to wipe the creatures out entirely. Just as you showed at the beginning of this presentation, we would be repeating the mistakes of the past if we allow the beast to be exterminated. This is exactly the same scenario as wiping out the Tasmanian tiger. Our protest movement aims to protect the beast in its native habitat. If that means putting a big fence around Bullyacre to save the beast, so be it.'

'It would have to be an extremely high fence. Panthers, I'm told, can climb and leap with ease. What about human activity in the Bullyacre area, though?' asked Mr Furphy. 'Surely you don't advocate moving the entire population, farmers, graziers, even the town. Bullyacre, I surely don't need to remind you, is an historic town, settled soon after the explorer Hugh Foulkes passed through the area back in the 1800s. You cannot propose to move the town away from its present site for the sake of a few putative beasts?'

I was astounded when I heard Mr Furphy mention Hugh Foulkes. I didn't think that anyone outside of South Australia or, really, outside of Bullyacre, would have heard of him. In Bullyacre we think that Hugh was a great man because of what he did back in the days when there was so much of Australia's arid outback to explore, and I was thrilled to hear his name mentioned by someone of Mr Furphy's calibre. Well, 'putative' calibre since he had used that word. Of course, we Bullyacrists have that statue of Hugh and his bullocks in Main Street, but as well as that, Hugh's name is written on the plinth of the statue of the explorer Charles Sturt in Victoria Square down in Adelaide, although I'm sure the city people all walk past and never read the inscription. It just lists Hugh Foulkes as Sturt's bullock driver, but he's a lot more than that to us.

'I bet it was Mr Furphy's research team who came up with that information about Hugh,' I said, 'because I don't think Mr Furphy would have known anything about Bullyacre. He comes from Sydney, doesn't he?'

Dad nodded. 'He'd have people checking things out so that he looks as if he's well informed. Just like the superintendent with that fossil thing.'

'Lizzie, Bill just ate the last bit of popcorn,' whinged Emma.

We all ignored her.

'That is exactly what we do propose,' said Ms Wylie. 'People can live anywhere. The beast has only a small chosen habitat left to it, an ecological niche it has selected as a sanctuary. It must be free to roam that habitat, protected from the ferocity of the police and the army and from all interference by human intervention.'

'But at least two people have died at the hands, or rather the teeth, of the Beast,' said Mr Furphy. 'The first death, as we all witnessed tonight, was that of the unfortunate cameraman, Bill Jenkins, who was killed at the siege of Epsom Downs.' The newsman paused and regarded the panel gravely. 'We have just had breaking news that today there has been another casualty, Constable Ian Perkins of Bullyacre, who was taken by the panther in the performance of his duties. He died late this afternoon while putting traffic infringement notices on cars illegally parked in the main street of Bullyacre.'

There were gasps of disbelief and horror from the panel. Ms Wylie, in particular, covered her face with her hands and her body shook with emotion.

Mr Furphy, ever the consummate journalist, continued. 'The Beast has moved into the actual town where you live, Ms Wylie. The Beast of Magnetic Hill is striding the streets of your home town. No citizen of the mid-north is safe. As the wife of the serving police officer at Bullyacre, Ms Wylie, surely this gives you pause?'

Ms Wylie and the rest of the panel were not given the opportunity to respond. The camera cut to a full face shot of Mr Furphy.

'This is Terry Furphy, bringing you, the people of Australia, the very latest stories behind the news. Stay tuned now for an episode of *The Simpsons* which will follow a short commercial break in our program.'

Dad reached for the remote controller.

'Hold on,' said Bill, 'I really like *The Simpsons*.'

13

We stood silently in the cemetery, all our heads bowed in respect, and listened to Jake's dad, the Anglican vicar, as he read the burial service for Constable Ian Perkins. Around the edges of the cemetery, the army stood ready in our defence. There was even a machine gun with a gunner crouched beside it pointed at the trees that lined the path to the grave site.

Surely that's overkill, I thought. The only panther left should be the mother, because her mate's body was down in Adelaide in the morgue or where ever animal corpses were stored, while the civil authorities from Australia-wide universities and museums fought tooth and nail with the conservationists for the right to dissect it. Unless, of course, we Epsoms, and indeed some of the people of Bullyacre, had made a terrible mistake and there were more panthers out there than we had at first estimated. The mother had borne one successful litter, why should she not have reared other ones before that?

It was a bit disappointing that there weren't more people here, I thought. A lot of the people of Bullyacre were too scared to go out of their doors now. Miss Cobbledick wasn't afraid, though. It took a lot to scare her. She stood opposite us, leaning on her umbrella. It wasn't going to rain, but she probably intended to use it on any stray panthers that turned up at the cemetery.

The whole town thought there were hordes of cats roaming the place and expected panthers to spring out of nowhere and devour them, to use Emma's favourite word. Which, when you think about it, is exactly what happened to Constable Perkins. Maybe the people were right. The authorities certainly thought so, which was why you couldn't move any more without seeing a soldier patrolling the streets.

And Ian had found out the hard way. There he was, lying there in that wooden box in several pieces, about to be lowered into the waiting grave. He didn't deserve this. He was only five years older than I was.

He had just turned twenty. As the vicar said, Constable Ian Perkins's life had been cut short.

'Man that is born of woman is full of woe,' said Jake's dad.

Girl that is born of woman isn't much better off, I thought. I'd had a battle with Emma this morning because she wanted to bring Cuddles along with her to the funeral. Emma was pretty woeful at the moment, and so was I.

'She hates being left alone, Lizzie,' Emma lamented. 'And I want to take her to Mum's grave to show Mum what Cuddles looks like. Mum doesn't know anything about the stuff that's been happening in our family. You and Dad never take me to see her grave because you say I cry too much when I go there, so I can't even tell her my news.'

'Emma,' said Dad in a voice that revealed even he was sick of hearing Emma whinge. 'It would be in extremely poor taste to take the offspring of the creature that killed poor Constable Perkins to the man's funeral. Surely even you can understand that?'

In the end Emma had settled for carrying her battered teddy bear so that she could show that to Mum. I had to promise that we'd go and visit Mum's grave as soon as the funeral for Constable Perkins was over. I hoped that Mum couldn't see the teddy through her granite slab. She wouldn't be all that happy if she saw what the teddy looked like now; I knew Mum had paid a fortune for it when she bought it for Emma's third birthday.

'The wages of sin is death,' said the vicar. I almost tapped him on the shoulder to ask shouldn't that be 'the wages of sin *are* death?' 'Wages' being plural, or so I would have thought. But the vicar should know. I decided to keep quiet.

Bill nudged me. 'What sort of sin did Constable Perkins do?' he whispered. 'I mean, I didn't really know him all that well, but I'm sure he wasn't that bad. He shouldn't have been decapitated and chewed up like that. Does putting parking stickers on cars to raise extra revenue for the council qualify as sin?'

'Not in my theology. It was the mayor who told him to do it,' I answered. 'And Sergeant Wylie. They both sent poor Ian Perkins out alone to walk the streets when it was getting dark. They're the ones who committed the sin.'

Perhaps Sergeant Wylie was being punished, I thought, as I looked around at the faces of the other mourners. The sergeant stood to rigid attention with his police cap under his arm at one end of the open grave, and Ms Wylie stood some distance away at the other end of the hole. I noticed that they ignored each other completely.

Rumour had it that they were estranged since Ms Wylie had joined the lobby group for the preservation of the marsupial panther. They had split up, everyone said, because the sergeant was all for destroying the panther, whatever its designation. He'd been overheard in the pub saying that he didn't care if the bloody thing was marsupial, monotreme or placental, that animal and all its sisters, brothers, cousins and aunts was going to be removed from his patch, and that was all there was to that. And he'd use napalm or flame-throwers or atom bombs to do the job if necessary.

There was a story going around Bullyacre that Ms Wylie had become an item with one of the ecologists. There were bets being laid which one of them it was. I couldn't imagine that Jeremy would be Ms Wylie's type, so maybe it was Simon who was her new boyfriend, although Simon was no prize either. Zoe said not to be too certain about Ms Wylie's romantic inclinations, though. She said I'd be surprised if I knew which ecologist Ms Wylie was ultra-friendly with. Zoe says some strange things at times.

But Zoe was right about Jake. He and I were quickly becoming an item. Perhaps not quite items as intense as Ms Wylie and her ecologist friend had become, because we were both fifteen and there was plenty of opportunity for intensity in the time to come. For now it was just nice holding hands with him when no one was looking and walking to the school bus together. I think it's called a platonic relationship, although I don't know what Plato had to do with anything. That's just those ancient Greeks getting into the picture again.

A couple of times Jake has even asked if he could carry my school bag for me, but I told him that was just plain silly. I'm sure my muscles are better developed than his are. We all have bags full of books that are so heavy you can hardly carry one, let alone two bags. And I'm not exactly a shrinking violet when it comes to hefting stuff about. I can lift a reasonably big lamb without help, and I've had to carry Emma a few times, back when Dad was still drinking and my sister had fallen asleep on the lounge watching her favourite David Attenborough documentary about Siberian tigers and she needed putting to bed.

Jake doesn't have to do stuff like that. A minister's son doesn't have to do farm work the way I do. All Jake does is school work, homework and music lessons. And sweep the church out occasionally when they can't find anyone from the Ladies' Auxiliary to volunteer. He even gets stuck doing the flower arranging at times too, although he doesn't want anyone to know that.

Jake was really nice about me being on television. I thought he might be jealous or say I was getting stuck up but he just said he was really proud of me and the way I'd stood my ground so well against that awful Mr Furphy. Apparently his mum and dad aren't all that impressed by Mr Furphy's style of journalism, whatever that means. Furphy's probably too ruthless and too flamboyant for their taste, I expect. The vicar did a good burial service, though, I had to admit.

'The Lord is my Shepherd, I shall not want,' he was intoning.

I wish the Lord would do something about our sheep. Dad kept them in the home paddock as much as we could, but they ate out all the pasture there and that meant we had to carry supplementary feed to them every day. It was a nuisance and it was getting expensive. But if we put them back in the top paddocks, there was a real risk that they'd become panther food. That free lunch for felines that Dad had mentioned.

I wondered whether prayer might help. Nothing else was helping. Would God prefer to help the human inhabitants of Bullyacre over the panther inhabitants? That hymn 'All creatures great and small' says that 'The Lord God made them all'. So why should he be more concerned about people than cats?

The people of Bullyacre were becoming pretty desperate. The army was sending up their helicopters, everyone had soldiers staying in their shearing sheds, and there were patrols wandering about all over everyone's land, but no panthers had been found, which made me hope that the mother and her litter were the only ones left..

However, people were upset in varying degrees. Fred Mudge looked smug because he knew he was going to get inflated compensation from the government for the loss of his bull. He was standing on the other side of the grave from me and, although he was trying to look serious, he didn't look all that sad. Not sad enough in my opinion, anyway. I wondered if he'd only come along for the refreshments that would be served up in the hall after the funeral, which were being provided by the Ladies' Auxiliary. Most of them had said they couldn't come to the funeral because they were preparing the tea urn.

Of course, the people who were really devastated were Constable Perkins's parents. Their family and friends were clustered about them for support, but what sort of support can you give people who've lost their son? No one expects to have their child die before they die; it just isn't natural.

I remembered how awful it was when Mum died, and then I felt guilty because I knew that my attention had been wandering all over the shop while poor Constable Perkins was dead and lying in the coffin that had been lowered into the dry earth of the cemetery. Well, most of him was being buried. There'd be no funeral service for the bit the panther had devoured. I sniffed back tears as I watched the coffin lowered into the waiting grave and the first sods of earth cover it.

I felt guilty. I should at least have given Ian Perkins the respect due to another human being by concentrating better on his funeral service. That was when I found the tears running down my cheeks. Constable Perkins's mum came over to my side while the flowers, including a big wreath from the mayor that was probably paid for out of the parking stickers, were being piled up on the mound of earth that was all that was left of her son. She hugged me and said that she and her husband were comforted to know that her boy had had friends in the community who really cared about him. That made me feel even worse so I cried some more.

14

Most of us were used to hearing helicopters buzzing overhead. The noise merged into our usual background sounds of sheep bleating, magpies carolling, windmills turning, dogs barking and Emma and her kitten making unpleasant noises. My sister always panicked, though, whenever she heard the helicopters, and usually hid under her bed with the kitten an unwilling fugitive beside her. Emma usually emerged with a few more cuts and scratches on her afterwards.

The other thing that we'd learned to accept was the regular discovery of a new carcass out in the paddocks when we did the rounds of the property. You would hear the crows fighting over the corpse even before you saw them gathered together on the ground, and then you'd know another sheep was down. The crows' laments would rise in crescendo when you approached the pathetic pile of wool and bones, and then the birds would fly off together in an evil black cloud. I despise crows. I'd hate to die out in the fields and have my body torn to shreds by those creatures. They tear the eyes out first, sometimes before their victim's dead.

It couldn't have been just the mother; we were losing too many sheep for one cat. There must be lots of panthers out there.

'It's better to lose a sheep or two than to hear that another person has been taken, Lizzie,' said Dad when I complained about the latest massacre.

'But we can't afford these loses,' I said, pausing from tidying up the pantry. I really hate it if the labels on the tins aren't facing to the front. Bill and Emma just pull stuff out and don't care what the cupboard looks like. They never replace the videos alphabetically, either, but I always do. And my school books have to go in my bag in a certain order. Ms Wylie noticed that and told Dad I have Asperger's syndrome, but I think she's just trying to get at me.

'I'm beginning to think the sergeant's right,' I said, putting all the tins of baked beans together. 'Well, I agree that it's wrong to wipe out a species, but why can't the panthers be trapped and kept in a zoo? I don't mean in a horrible little pen like the one the Tasmanian tiger died in, but those free-range zoos like Monarto give the animals plenty of room to roam in. They could even have a breeding program for the panther and study its habits and stuff. It'd be better all round. Especially for us farmers.'

'Apparently that's what the conservationists are suggesting,' said Dad. 'I heard that your Ms Wylie's been in Canberra having a chat with the prime minister to see if an open-range zoo could be established near Magnetic Hill. The only thing that worries me is, what if they decide to compulsorily acquire Epsom Downs to put the zoo on? Of course, Fred Mudge feels the same about his property, and so do all the other farmers.'

I was aghast. I dropped a couple of tins of tuna on the floor and bent to pick them up. Fortunately they weren't dented, because I hate dented cans. 'They couldn't do that, could they? Not our property. I mean, we Epsoms have been here for hundreds of years. Well, a hundred and fifty years, anyway. This is our land. You were born here, and so were your father and your grandfather. They can't throw us off.'

'But our family took it away from the original owners, Lizzie. They'd been here for thousands of years. About forty or fifty thousand years, didn't you tell me once? They probably thought they couldn't be thrown off, either. But they were. So if we have to move on to give space to the panther, we just might have to do that.'

'But where would we go? I don't want to leave Bullyacre, Dad. I go to school here, and all my friends are here.' I almost said 'And Jake is here' but I wasn't ready to admit to Dad that I had a boyfriend. If Mum was alive I probably would have told her, but it's different when it's your dad. 'Why does the zoo have to be here? There are plenty of other places in Australia where it could go.'

'Everyone says that, Lizzie: not in my backyard. People always campaign against rubbish dumps or prisons or public housing or roads going through their land. No one wants to lose their property, but sometimes we have to consider the greater good for the whole community.'

'But it'd break my heart to leave our farm, Dad. And your heart too, and Bill's and even Emma's. Besides, what would we do with Cuddles if we had to move into a house in town? Emma would never forgive us if we shot her pet.'

'There's nothing definite yet, Lizzie, but I thought I ought to warn you. Don't say anything to Bill or Emma yet, though. I don't want to upset them.'

So how come it was all right to upset me, I felt like asking. But it probably just meant that Dad respected my opinion, and he knew I was on the edge of growing up. It's still tough having to bear an adult's burden when you're a kid, though.

I finished putting all the tins of tomato soup together and stood back to admire my work.

15

'Cheer up, Lizzie, the family picnic at the Lions' Park is next week. You've been looking miserable for days. It's just not like you.'

'I'd forgotten all about the picnic, Jake. So much has happened lately. Are you sure it's going to go ahead, though? What if there are panthers lurking in the bushes down by the creek and they leap out and murder everyone?'

'Try to be optimistic, Lizzie,' said Jake. 'Try to look on the bright side. Dad keeps telling people that God will protect us.'

I was unconvinced by Jake's encouragement. I kept on wingeing. 'I know it's called the Lions' Park because it was the Lions' Club people who set it up, but maybe we ought to call it Panther Park now. Maybe we ought to change the town's name to Pantheryacre instead of Bullyacre. Or Beastyacre.'

'Or maybe Cuddlesacre after what you suggested on the television,' said Jake with a grin. 'Don't worry, Lizzie, we'll all be quite safe on the day. My dad said the army's going to be there with their machine gun in case the Beast appears. They're even going to have tanks there. Well, the tanks aren't there to fight panthers. The army's going to use them as a public relations exercise. They're hoping it might inspire a few of us lads to join up when we're old enough.'

'Yuk,' I said.

'There's going to be helicopter joy rides, and the army careers advisory people will be there with a stall. Andrew says he wants to have a look at what they've got to offer. He's thinking of going to Duntroon.'

'You're not thinking about joining the army, are you, Jake? My dad was in the army. That's where he learned to shoot. That's why I'm so good with a gun, because he taught me. But he said that's where he learned to drink too, although of course he only did it in earnest after

Mum died, because he felt he didn't have anything to live for any more. I wouldn't want you to have problems with drinking, Jake. Your mum and dad wouldn't like it, anyway. And I'd really miss you if you went away.'

He patted me on the back. 'No, I'm not joining the army. I told you, I want to be an accountant. What I've been thinking was if I was an accountant I could help you do the books for your farm later on.'

'That's a great idea, Jake. Being a soldier sucks. I mean you get shot at and sometimes you get sent overseas and sometimes you're even sent to places like Bullyacre and you have to tramp about the fields all day searching for three-headed panthers and hoping you don't find them. Those soldiers we've got in our shearing quarters are terrified. I can see they're more scared than we are, only they're too scared to admit they're frightened.'

'We've had time to get used to the idea of panthers. They haven't. Dad's going to remind the people at church on Sunday about the picnic. He's given me all these posters to put up around town. Do you want to give me a hand with them?'

We stuck posters on trees and poles and the occasional fence. Running around the town with posters and glue cheered me up. Feeling a bit reckless, I decided it might be a good idea to put one on the wall outside the police station.

'Are you sure Sergeant Wylie won't mind?' asked Jake. 'He's a bit narky about that sort of thing. He's been even more short-tempered than usual since his wife went off with that ecologist.'

'Are you kidding? This is the annual Bullyacre family picnic in the Lions' Park. Sergeant Wylie is a member of the Lions' Club, isn't he? The whole idea of the family picnic is to raise public awareness of family values and develop community spirit, stuff like that. The only thing around here that's a bigger event than the family picnic is the mayor's firework display. The sergeant ought to be all for us putting a poster on the police station wall. Come on, just hand me the glue and I'll stick the poster up.'

'Maybe we ought to ask permission first,' said Jake hesitantly.

'Just pass the glue, Jake.'

'What are you two up to?' demanded the sergeant, who had suddenly appeared behind us. 'Did that wall ask for graffiti all over it?'

'I didn't see you coming, Sergeant,' I said.

'No, of course you didn't,' he snapped. 'Because if you had seen me, you wouldn't have been defacing the wall of the police station, would you? And who's this with you, Lizzie? Young Jake Jeffries, isn't it? So now you're corrupting the vicar's son, are you, Lizzie Epsom?'

'She's not corrupting me, Sergeant,' protested Jake.

'No, because she's already done the job!' said the sergeant triumphantly. 'You've been corrupted already. You've been taught her evil ways. Does your father know who you're keeping company with, young Jeffries? You shouldn't hang around with the Epsoms, they're a bad lot. The father's a drunk, the brother's mad, and this girl's a gun-toting illegal driver and an attention-seeking, precocious little devil. My wife says the youngest kid ought to be taken into protective care, fostered out before she's infected with the Epsom craziness too.'

'How dare you say those things, Sergeant Wylie? You've got no right. That's slander and libel. I could have you charged with spreading lies about the Epsom family,' I yelled. 'Jake, you're a witness to this.'

The sergeant sneered at me and then turned back to Jake. 'Did you see her on national television the other night? Looked like butter wouldn't melt in her mouth, "Yes, Mr Furphy, no, Mr Furphy." I'm surprised she came back to Bullyacre after that. And that brother of hers'll be in my cells before he's much older, too.'

'That's not fair!' said Jake. 'Lizzie did really well on that program. Even the teachers at school said she was great. Just because she didn't agree to name the Beast of Magnetic Hill after you and your wife, you've got it in for her. You're a bad-tempered old fool, Sergeant Wylie. It's probably your fault that Constable Perkins got killed.'

'Right,' said Sergeant Wylie. Grabbing Jake by the collar, he recited, 'A full cell is a happy cell,' as he marched him into the police station, pulling the keys from his pocket and waving them at me.

We all knew that was his mantra. The whole town recited it behind the sergeant's back. Now he was hauling Jake towards the cells. That was Jake he was thrusting through the door, Jake who stood paralysed at the entrance of the cell as the door was slammed on him, Jake who stood clinging to the bars looking like a hardened criminal.

I couldn't believe it. Jake was innocent. If a crime had been committed, although I didn't believe one had been, I was the one who had done it. I flung the bundle of posters and the pot of glue at Sergeant Wylie and rushed to Jake's cell door. I shook it in rage but it wouldn't open. Sergeant Wylie had locked it.

The lid of the glue pot had come off when it hit the officer's tunic.

He snarled at me, looking a lot like Tabby in a bad mood, and tried to wipe the glue off of his uniform with the crumpled posters. 'That's assaulting an officer of the law, Lizzie Epsom,' he said grimly. 'You do not need to say anything, but anything you do say…'

'And just what is the charge against Jake?' I interrupted. 'You can't go around arresting people like this. You're exceeding and abusing your authority. Especially pushing kids around. That's assault and wrongful arrest and preventing people carrying out a civic duty and infringement of liberty and ill-treatment of kids and lots of other stuff I can't think of right now. But I will think of it later on. We did legal studies and social studies and political science in year seven and I know there are limits to how far cops can go. *Caveat emptor*! *Habeas corpus*! What about Magna Carta?'

'Don't you swear at me in German, girlie. I'll give you Magna bloody Carta, Lizzie Epsom,' said the officer. He grabbed me by the collar and pushed me into the cell next to the one that he had shoved Jake into.

'That's assault!' I yelled. 'I want my lawyer! I want my dad! I'm a female and you touched me. Why is there no female police officer here?'

'Because I don't have a female police officer. I haven't had any help at all since young Perkins got himself killed by that panther that came off your farm. This whole bloody business is you and your family's fault.'

The door slammed and the keys jangled.

'I want Ms Wylie here now!'

'I don't know where she is or what she's doing or who she's with.'

'I want my parents,' shouted Jake. 'They've got a right to know what's going on.'

'I'll ring your parents and they can bail you out if they want you. Your father won't be too pleased, Jake. I don't know if Lizzie's dad will be sober enough to come and get her. He probably wouldn't give a damn about one of his kids going missing, anyway. He might decide one of his infernal cats ate her. She'll have to stay here overnight. And you can tell your precious Mr Furphy all about this next time you talk to him, Lizzie Epsom.' He left, smirking.

'What are we going to do?' I asked Jake.

'There's not a lot we can do except sit here and wait for our parents to come and get us. I don't think the sergeant's very well somehow, Lizzie. He looks as if he's in shock or something. Did you see how his eyes are bulging?'

'He looks a bit like Mr Furphy before his contact lens came loose.'

Jake nodded. 'Overcome with emotion, I think. Not that that's any excuse for his behaviour.'

'I reckon the sergeant's angry because his wife has left him for one of those ecologists, then Constable Perkins was killed by the beast and the beast still hasn't been caught and now it's terrorising Bullyacre, and as if that wasn't bad enough, Dad says he's heard that the superintendent's furious with Sergeant Wylie because the original report wasn't filed immediately. It still doesn't excuse the sergeant from manhandling kids, though.'

We could hear the sergeant apparently yelling into the telephone. There was a loud crash. Then there was silence. Absolute dead, stony silence.

'What's going on, Jake?' I asked. 'Can you see into the office from your cell? You're bit closer to the door than I am.'

'Sergeant Wylie's just sitting on his chair, staring into space,' said Jake. 'His face looks completely blank. He hasn't even hung the phone up. It's dangling by the cord. That must have been the crash when he dropped the phone. That means no one can phone the station. This is scary, Lizzie. I hope no one needs the police tonight. What if the panthers attack? If Sergeant Wylie's out of action, Bullyacre hasn't got any defence.'

'There's the army,' I said. 'The helicopters are still patrolling and there's a whole company of soldiers stationed here. We've got ten of them in our shearers' quarters and the rest of them are scattered around on the other farms. But of course, Sergeant Wylie is supposed to be running the nerve centre of Operation Panther from here. If anyone sees anything, they've been told to contact the police station and the sergeant contacts the various farms so all the soldiers can converge on the problem area. If he's got the phone off the hook, that's not going to happen.'

'No wonder he's spaced out,' said Jake. 'I expect he's cracked under the strain. That's a lot of responsibility for one man to carry. Why on earth was the operation set up like that? Shouldn't the army have been in charge?'

'Dad said that Wylie insisted on it being done like that. Dad says the sergeant's a control freak and he insisted on running the whole show. The army didn't like it, and police headquarters in Adelaide weren't happy either, but Jack Wylie said this was his patch and he was needed to control Bullyacre because we're all hillbillies out here and he was the only one who understood how to deal with us. The army captain who's staying in our shearers' quarters told Dad all about it.'

We waited. There isn't a lot to do in a cell. I expect boredom's part of the punishment that prisoners have to bear. I tried to pass the time by recalling stuff I could remember about prison life, but apart from the poem 'Stone walls do not a prison make, nor iron bars a cell', which between you and me is a lot of crap, because they really do make a cell, there wasn't a lot I knew. Then I remembered about the two little princes in the Tower of London who were murdered by evil King Richard. And Anne Boleyn was locked in the Tower, too, before she was beheaded by Henry VIII.

After that I recalled that Oscar Wilde, who wrote *The Portrait of Dorian Gray* was imprisoned in Redding Gaol for the Love That Dare Not Speak Its Name. They actually used to put gay people in prison in those days! And of course there were those poor convicts locked up in Port Arthur in Tasmania for stuff like stealing a loaf of bread when they were starving. They were deported from England for the term of their natural life. There's a book about that, too, but I couldn't remember the title. Our headmaster, Mr Gonski, wouldn't have been pleased if he knew I'd forgotten that one.

Jake suddenly interrupted me in what sounded like a very relieved voice. When I looked at him, his eyes seemed to have glazed over. If

I didn't know Jake better, I'd have thought he was sick of listening to me.

'I can hear a car outside, Lizzie. It's probably my dad. It'll take longer for your father to get here because he's got further to drive.'

'Sergeant Wylie, Jack, are you all right?' The vicar's voice sounded anxious. 'Mary, I think you'd best send for Dr Jones. And perhaps an ambulance might be in order. Use this telephone. Wait, there's someone on the line. Oh, hello, Frank. Were you trying to reach the sergeant? Do you have a problem? Jack Wylie can't speak to you right now. He seems to be incapacitated at the moment. He told us to come and get Jake. I believe your daughter Lizzie's here somewhere, too.'

'Where's Jake? We have to find Jake,' whimpered the vicar's wife.

'Yes, dear, we will find him. I'm sure he's all right. Sorry, Frank. Yes, I'm still here. Yes, the sergeant's here too, but he can't speak to you at the moment. He's not very well. I haven't seen Lizzie, but the sergeant told me she's here. I expect we'll find her in the cells with Jacob. The unfortunate sergeant appears to have suffered some sort of crisis. What one would colloquially refer to as a nervous breakdown, perhaps. Or even a stroke. He needs medical attention immediately. Perhaps you should come over here and collect Lizzie. Yes, that's right. We'll see you shortly, then.'

'Where's Jake?' demanded the vicar's wife. 'Where is my son? Has this awful man really locked my baby in the cells? And where's poor little Lizzie Epsom? Didn't that man said the children were together? They'll be terribly traumatised. What a horrid, cruel man that policeman is!'

'Don't be uncharitable, Mary,' said the vicar. 'Quickly, you take the phone and ring for an ambulance. Say it's an emergency.'

'Why not just throw a bucket of cold water over him? That would wake him up. I've heard that he drinks quite heavily. He drinks much more than poor Mr Epsom does. I've watched him at social functions at the golf club.'

'Mary, it's our Christian duty to turn the other cheek and all that sort of thing. I'll find the children.'

'Jacob, Jake, are you in the cells?' called the vicar.

'Yes, Dad, we're both here. Lizzie and me. Can you let us out?

We're both hungry and thirsty and there's only a bucket for a loo and neither of us want to have to use it.'

'Good grief, Jacob, you seem to be getting into one scrape after another these days,' said the vicar. 'And you, Lizzie, what on earth happened? I've always thought of you as a very responsible sort of girl. Surely you didn't really put graffiti all over the police station, did you? I didn't see any graffiti at all out there. Just a poster advertising the family picnic at the Lions' Park.'

'The ambulance is on its way, Tony,' said Jake's mum. 'Oh, my goodness, I never expected to see my child holding onto the bars of a cell. And little Lizzie too. You poor, dear children. This is appalling. Where are the keys? Would those be the keys to the cells on the floor next to the sergeant, Tony?'

It took a while for the vicar and his wife to work out which keys opened our cells. When we were freed, we tiptoed past the sergeant, who was sprawled in his office chair, his legs spread wide, displaying his big belly, his hands hanging to the ground, his face a mask, still the captive of his own demons.

Dr Jones was bent solicitously over the limp police officer, murmuring something into Jack Wylie's deaf ear. There was no response from the sergeant. The doctor held a hypodermic syringe which I thought probably contained a sedative, although the policeman already looked fairly sedated to me.

'Do you think Ms Wylie will come back to look after her husband?' I asked Jake's mum.

'I would like to suppose that she would, Lizzie, but I fear that Ms Wylie is relishing her political activities and her friendship with those peculiar ecological people. We can only hope and pray that she and the sergeant will be reconciled.'

'Did you manage to contact my dad, Vicar?' I asked.

'Yes, the phone at your home went to the answering machine, but we spoke to him on his mobile when he rang here. He said he wasn't far away and would be here soon.'

'Bill and Emma never hear the phone ring when they're watching TV,' I explained.

'Lizzie, Lizzie, what the hell have you been up to now?'

Thank goodness, Dad was here. Through the window, I saw his ute parked outside the police station. He must have driven like the clappers to have got here as quickly as that, I thought, and then I saw Dad looking around at the scene inside the police station with a puzzled expression on his face, and I ran to him and flung myself into his arms and I sobbed the way Emma does when she's frustrated and frightened. And I wasn't ashamed to do it, either.

'How did you get here so fast, Dad?' I asked.

'I drove fast. I was just on the edge of town, checking on Miss Cobbledick. What did you do to Jack Wylie, Lizzie?' Dad asked with a cheeky grin on his face.

But I wasn't in the mood for humour. 'It was horrible being locked up, Dad, really horrible. All we were doing was putting up posters about the family picnic at the Lions' Park, and Sergeant Wylie just flipped.' I had a sudden thought and looked up at Dad. 'What are we going to do about a police officer for Bullyacre now? Who's going to run Operation Panther?'

'The army will take over for a bit until we get the problem of the Beast under control. I phoned the shearers' quarters and told the captain what had happened and he's coming down to sit in this office and hold stuff together until Adelaide sends up another copper or two or until Jack recovers. Only it doesn't look as if that will be any time soon, does it?'

We watched as the ambulance men hefted the stretcher with the comatose body of Sergeant Wylie on it and, staggering a little under the weight, carried it out to their waiting ambulance.

'Do you think he'll ever get over this, Tony?' Dad asked the vicar softly.

I heard him, though, and when he glanced furtively in my direction, I wondered if Dad thought the policeman's collapse was all my fault.

'Time will tell, Frank,' said the vicar. 'We must all pray for him. And indeed, for all of the unfortunate people of Bullyacre faced with the ravening Beast that comes in the night.'

I thought that was probably a quote from something, but I was too exhausted and upset to work out its origin.

16

The Lions' Park was ringed by soldiers who faced outwards with their rifles at the ready. They reminded me of the statue of the marble soldier in the main street of Bullyacre, although their rifles weren't reversed and they were slightly more colourful and perhaps a little more animated.

Officially they were on duty, but they did look as if they were relishing the chance of relaxing in the park, enjoying being plied with food by the Ladies' Auxiliary, and of course having a break from their constant patrols through the hilly country around Bullyacre in search of the elusive Beast. Or even Beasts, if they, like everyone else in the area, read the newspapers that said the place was swarming with them.

We were also guarded by a machine gun today, but the gunner was sitting on a white plastic chair with his hat pushed back on his head and a glass of lemon squash in his hands. He kept looking longingly in the direction of the beer keg which was set up under a shady gum tree, but the steely eye of the captain kept him from approaching it.

In the centre of the park, beside the rotunda, a helicopter, its rotors lazily turning like the windmill back on Epsom Downs when there's not much breeze, took pride of place. The local boys, including my brother Bill, were fascinated by it.

Everyone had seen the 'copters flying over Bullyacre, but no one had actually been near enough to touch one before. I saw Bill run his hands appreciatively over the helicopter, and I had a sudden fear that he might decide to join the air force or the army. I made up my mind to give him some more interesting jobs to do on the farm so that he'd decide to stay on the land. Perhaps it was time to let him start making decisions about where to put the sheep and when to service the windmills.

Some of the more enterprising boys climbed on top of the

pair of tanks which were parked beside the helicopter on the grass, and a few of the older kids, boys and girls, wandered into the army recruiting tent, where a couple of soldiers whose uniforms were more immaculate that the ones manning the guns, handed out pamphlets, which most of the kids glanced at briefly before chucking them into the nearest bin.

Tom Evans, the municipal gardener, wasn't at all happy about the tanks or about the helicopter. 'It's taken me a lot of work to get that lawn into the condition that you see it,' he complained to Dad. 'It's bad enough having all these feet walk over it, without having dirty great tanks squashing the turf down and digging their tracks into the soil and bloody helicopters breaking branches off with all those wind currents. It'll take me weeks to get the place looking right again after today.'

Tom Evans complains every year when the whole population of Bullyacre invades the Lions' Park for the family picnic, but Dad agreed with him that this year it seemed the place was taking a worse bashing than usual.

Like Tom, the ladies of the auxiliary had also gone to a lot of trouble for today's event. They'd fried so many chickens that I wondered whether anyone would awake to the sound of roosters crowing or whether we'd eat any eggs in Bullyacre for a long time. Our own chooks were safe enough unless the panthers developed a taste for smaller prey than the mutton which had been their staple fare lately.

Somehow, despite the Beast's best efforts, enough lamb had been found to provide chops for the barbecue as well as the mandatory sausages and onions. The smell of those onions had even lured some of the men folk of Bullyacre away from the keg of beer that the military kept eyeing.

'We have been blessed with a glorious day,' said the vicar, beaming his appreciation of the weather. 'The Lord has been good to us. And, for once, we enjoy perfect peace in Bullyacre.'

He, his wife and Jake had spread their picnic rug next to ours, and Dad and the vicar clinked their glasses together in a toast. When I realised that both their glasses contained lemon squash, I too, agreed that it was a perfect day. I could see the vicar would be an excellent drinking companion for Dad.

The Bullyacre Brass Band, clad in their red uniforms with gleaming brass buttons, played in the rotunda, the sun glistening on their newly polished instruments and on the gleaming white wrought iron that surrounded them. The paint on that iron was so fresh I could smell it, and I hoped it was dry enough that none of the musicians would get paint on their jackets.

It was a bit unfortunate that the tune they were playing was 'The Lion Sleeps Tonight', but probably the program had been chosen before the Beast of Magnetic Hill had made its first appearance. It was, I supposed, an appropriate tune for the venue.

The music ended and Mayor Murphy picked up the microphone. I was amused to hear the vicar groaning. The mayor was renowned for his speeches, which were more protracted than the vicar's sermons.

'Distinguished guests, ladies and gentlemen, boys and girls of Bullyacre,' he began.

I wondered who the distinguished guests were. Perhaps he meant the army captain. And probably himself, if I knew Mayor Murphy.

'I welcome you all today to the Bullyacre Lions' Park and to our annual family picnic held under the auspices of the Lions' Club. Unfortunately, our well respected and much loved Sergeant Wylie is unable to be with us today, due to stress incurred in performing his constabulary duties, but I have a large card here on which I know you will all wish to inscribe your good wishes for his speedy recovery...' The mayor droned on for his usual half an hour.

'It almost makes one wish that a panther would appear to interrupt him,' whispered the vicar's wife. 'Just a very small panther,' she added hastily.

'Be careful what you wish for,' said Dad.

'Nothing like that is going to disrupt our celebration today,' said the vicar. 'But I think perhaps his worship has come to the end of his oration. Perhaps he requires further liquid refreshment.'

As predicted, the mayor headed for the beer keg. The band resumed playing. This time it was the theme from *The Pink Panther*. Another bad choice, I thought.

Jake and I did the rounds of the park and had a couple of rides on the ferris wheel while Bill kept an eye on Emma. Then it was our turn to look after my sister while Bill enjoyed being lifted high above the park. Emma didn't like the idea of the ferris wheel, but she did want a ride on the pony.

I looked around for Bill after his ferris ride trip and saw him disappearing back in the direction of the helicopter, closely followed by a crowd of his mates.

'You have to look after my shopping trolley while I'm on the pony, Lizzie. Don't drop it or open it, and don't walk away and leave it. I hope I can trust you,' Emma said.

'What's in the trolley?' Jake asked. 'It seems very important to her. Where did she get it anyway? It looks pretty old and rusty.'

'It's my gran's old shopping trolley,' I said. 'Emma dragged it out of the shed and insisted on bringing it along today. She gets these funny ideas sometimes. I suppose she's put her teddy bear in it. I can't think of anything else she values all that much. Only, the bag seems too full to be just the bear. Maybe she's brought a jumper along in case she feels cold later on.'

I bent over the bag and opened the zip just a fraction. Spotty stuck her head out and bit me on the finger.

'Shit,' I said.

I pushed the Spotty head back. Tabby thrust her head out through the opening. I dragged my hand away and thumped on the vinyl with my fist. There was a muffled screech from within.

'Don't let my dad hear you say that sort of thing,' said Jake. 'He doesn't approve of coarse language. Shit, Lizzie, you're bleeding. How did you cut yourself?'

'Sharp edge on the zip,' I said, pushing Tabby's head back down inside.

I zipped the bag quickly. There was a loud miaow and the bag began to convulse. It looked a lot like my Auntie Bett's tummy did when she was pregnant with her twin boys. There were lumps appearing and disappearing and reappearing again all over the bag.

'Funny sort of teddy bear,' said Jake.

'It's one of those bears with a battery inside,' I lied. 'A Japanese bear or maybe Chinese. You press the buttons and it jumps about and makes noises. I'll be glad when the battery goes flat.'

'Let's take a look at it. Maybe I can turn it off if I can find the right button.'

'No, Jake, it's makes horrible noises when it's in the light. Photovoltaic or something. It'll upset everyone for miles around. Miss Cobbledick is just over there. She wouldn't like it all. She might even have one of her bad turns.'

Emma came back and retrieved her property. She checked the zip and gave me a suspicious look. 'Did you open the zip?' she asked. 'That looks like blood on the strap.'

'It must be something Gran spilled on it,' I said. 'Ice cream, how would you like some ice cream, Emma? Jake would like a nice ice cream, wouldn't you, Jake? And when Bill comes back, he'd probably like two cones. He's always hungry.'

'If Bill's having two cones, I want two cones too. Otherwise it isn't fair, Lizzie. I'm a growing girl, you know.'

I bought the ice cream cones and handed them out. There goes most of my pocket money for the week, I thought. At least Bill hadn't come back, so I didn't have to buy one or two for him. I saw Emma open the zip just a fraction. She thrust one of the cones inside the bag. The bag shook violently and I could hear soft growls. I imagined the scene within as three kitten heads fought over the delicacy, and I shuddered.

'I can see my friends over there by the water slide,' Emma announced. 'I think I'd like to spend some time with my friends, because I have some important stuff to talk to them about. And it's private. So you and Jake will have to find something else to do.'

Jake and I looked at each other. I shrugged. 'I think we've been told,' I said.

Emma walked off, dragging the bulging shopping trolley with one hand and balancing the remaining ice cream cone very carefully in the other hand. I watched her go. I knew she intended to feed the other ice cream to the kitten as well as soon as she thought I couldn't see her, and I wondered whether two ice creams would be enough to sate the monster's hunger. That kitten had grown a lot in the last few weeks.

What was more disturbing, the disputes between the three heads had become more vicious as the animal grew. Cuddles's ears were the only ones that I dared to touch now.

'It takes up a lot of space. It's about the size of a two-month-old lamb now,' Bill had remarked the other night when the kitten jumped up and sat on the lounge between us.

Neither of us had the courage to push it onto the floor because the Tabby head was likely to deliver a nasty nip.

'A pretty solid lamb, at that. It grew fast, didn't it? I reckon Emma's over-feeding it. They probably don't grow that quickly in the wild.'

'They probably grow faster if they have a proper carnivore diet,' I'd said.

Dad and I had been wondering just how long we'd be able to allow Emma to keep the creature. We both agreed that it would pose a danger, not only to Emma but to the rest of the family, indeed to all of Bullyacre, when it was full-grown. But Emma loved the thing to distraction, and most of the kitten seemed to love Emma, too. Even Tabby rarely bit Emma, although she was not averse to snapping at the rest of us.

'We'll have to consider keeping it in some sort of cage soon,' Dad had warned me last night as we watched the kitten rolling about on the living room floor, swan-like necks writhing, heads snapping at each other, paws batting at the heads, tail lashing the carpet. Sometimes the caterwauling was so bad you couldn't hear the television.

'Ever since I was shut up in that cell, I can't stand the thought of cages of any sort, Dad,' I'd answered. 'I feel guilty about shutting up the chooks at night now, even though I know it's for their own safety. Like the hens, that kitten is free-range. I should think the poor thing would die if it was locked up. It's used to sleeping in Emma's bed, not in a cat run.'

'Do you want to have a look at the careers advisory stall?' Jake asked me, taking me away from past and present problems to future ones. 'We'll be sixteen next year, time to start thinking about what we'll do with our lives.'

'I used to know what I wanted to do with mine,' I said. 'Until the panthers came, anyway. I always wanted to be a farmer, but I'll admit now I'm more interested in going to university and studying genetics. I'd be surprised if the careers advisory people have got anything about that sort of thing, though. Do you still want to be an accountant?'

We began to stroll over to the careers stand, where most of our school friends had gathered. There's not a lot of jobs available in Bullyacre, so kids have to go away to study and usually look outside the town for work. I saw Zoe there with Andrew. They're always together now. I think she's really nuts about him. I can't work out what she sees in Andrew, though. He's got awful acne.

'Lizzie! Lizzie! Where's Emma?' Dad grabbed me. He was shaking me frantically. His eyes were wild and he was trembling and breathless as if he had run very fast from the other side of the Lions' Park.

Oh no, he's had a drink and he's got delirium tremens, I thought. It's that keg of beer. He couldn't resist the smell of it.

'Where's Bill? Oh, thank God, Bill, you're here. But where's Emma? We have to find Emma. Is that her over there with the shopping trolley? Why did you let her go so far away?'

'What's wrong, Dad?'

'Didn't you hear the helicopter going up? Didn't you hear the announcement from the army captain? We're being attacked, Lizzie. Quick, we have to get hold of Emma.'

Dad was racing across the oval, running towards Emma. He grabbed her and swept her up into his arms. She dropped the handle of the shopping trolley and shrieked. Dad dragged Emma back towards Bill, Jake and me, back towards the rotunda, but Emma broke free and ran back to the trolley. Both her hands grasped the handle and when Dad tried to prise them free she kicked at his legs and screamed. In the end, Dad dragged Emma by one arm and pulled the trolley, which was convulsing with movement, with the other.

'Emma's really fond of that teddy bear, isn't she?' said Jake. 'What's happening, Mr Epsom?'

'The helicopter went up to take some of the kids on a joyride, and the pilot spotted panthers on the hillside above the park. A whole pack of them. He was too upset to be able to count how many. We've been told there's no time to evacuate. We have to gather by the rotunda and the army's going to defend us.'

The civilians stood in the centre of the square formed by the soldiers. It's exactly the same strategy that the Romans used when their armies made a stand, I thought. Except that the Romans held their shields up to cover their heads, and their formation was called a turtle. The British army used to do the same sort of thing, which isn't surprising because of course the British originally learned most of their military skills from the Romans. The Brits didn't have shields, of course. Just red coats so you couldn't tell when one of them was wounded, which was good thinking, because the blood might upset their comrades. But Roman tactics were taught to the officers until the twentieth century, when it became less popular to have a little Latin and less Greek. And of course until aircraft made that sort of manoeuvre redundant.

The band, who of course also wore red coats although I don't know why they did, had been told to play as loudly as they could, in an effort to frighten away the beasts. I recalled that that was the same rationale used when Scottish pipers played their bagpipes as their armies marched into war. Bagpipes probably worked better than brass bands, when you thought about it. Bagpipes can be quite intimidating. Almost weapons of mass destruction.

I wondered who'd chosen this piece that the bandsmen were playing, though. Was it the vicar's choice? It seemed a little discouraging to hear the strains of 'Abide with Me'. I glanced over at the vicar. His hands were folded beneath his chin and his lips moved soundlessly. Was he singing along with the hymn under his breath? Then I heard him. Actually, he was singing quite loudly, but the brass band was louder.

'O Grave, where is thy victory, Death where is thy sting?'

There won't be enough bits to fill a grave when the beast and its companions have finished with us, I thought.

'Isn't that what the band played when the *Titanic* sank?' I whispered to Dad.

'Yes, so they say. Personally, I'd have preferred "Waltzing Matilda",' Dad said, pushing Emma, who still held tight to the handle of her shopping trolley, back behind us.

There were muffled growls coming from the trolley and I hoped no one else in the close packed crowd would hear them. The trolley was convulsing as if it contained an epileptic animal. Might the approaching panthers realise that we held one of their own captive and therefore single us out of the crowd?

The grim-faced young captain stood in front of his platoon, or whatever a group of soldiers is called, pistol in hand, field glasses hanging from his neck. I hoped the cats wouldn't come closer than his binoculars could show them, but I had an unpleasant feeling that they would. He turned and said a few words to his men, words that were lost to me as the band reached a crescendo. But the soldiers must have heard his instructions because they straightened their backs, pushed their hats out of their way and aimed their rifles at the approaching enemy.

Bill pulled at my arm. 'I was in that helicopter when the pilot went up,' he told me. 'At first it was great, all of the country spread out under us, but then I saw the panthers coming. There's heaps of them, Lizzie. And we thought only the mother and her mate were out there. I picked out the mother and her kittens. Those kittens are lots bigger than Emma's Cuddles is now. About the size of a wether, I reckon.'

'They probably have had a better diet than the stuff Emma feeds her pet,' I said. 'More meat, of course. And less popcorn. Those cats must have really strange genes to have grown that much that quickly, though. It must go with having three heads.'

'You didn't ask my permission before you went up in the helicopter, Bill,' said Dad. 'Never mind, it's too late to worry about that now. How many panthers did you see?'

'I reckon there were at least eight of them, Dad. There wasn't time to ask you about going on the joyride. I was over there looking at the tanks and I heard the pilot say he'd take some kids up, so I just jumped in. Sorry.'

'Never mind about that now. If we're still alive later on, we might discuss it. So we've got the mother, her kittens and four other full-grown animals, have we?' Dad said, looking at the soldiers surrounding us and at the machine gunner who had been moved in front of our defensive square.

An overturned plastic chair marked the original position where he'd sat earlier in the morning. The man was crouched over his gun now, on full alert for any movement. I should have felt reassured, but I didn't.

'We've got about twenty army blokes,' said Dad slowly, 'although some of them are pretty young and have never seen any action except shooting at targets on a rifle range. The tanks won't be any use. They're only here for the army display and they couldn't be deployed with all these people here. I wonder if the captain will have the wit to put a sniper in the helicopter. That's what I'd do, but of course, that might be risky with all these civilians about.'

'Daddy, I'm really frightened,' said Emma, pulling on Dad's sleeve.

'I'm pretty scared, too,' said Bill. 'I saw those things coming. They looked like they meant business. Do you reckon they smelled the barbecue cooking and that's what brought them down out of the hills? Are they going to kill us, Dad?'

'Perhaps we'll be all right, but some of those army blokes look pretty scared. I hope they won't break formation. I wonder how long before the attack comes? The waiting's always the worst part of a battle.'

The band was playing 'Onward Christian Soldiers' when it began. The first three-headed panther, which I thought was an adult male, leapt out of the rhododendron bushes and sped through the archway covered with climbing roses that was a favourite place for wedding photographs in Bullyacre.

The cat stood up on its hind legs in the same way the beast that had attacked the geologists on Magnetic Hill had done. If it hadn't been so big and so angry, and if it hadn't had three heads twisting and turning to get a good look at us, it would have looked a lot like a meerkat on one of those David Attenborough shows. Its three necks were fully extended, its three great mouths open, displaying three sets of gleaming fangs. The panther growled, and the deep sound that came from those three throats working in perfect unison rumbled around the garden and caused the band to falter in mid-chord. The conductor dropped his baton and swore.

One of the bandsmen, the chap who clashed the cymbals together, yelled, 'We're not scared of you, you ugly great tomcat.' He began to bang the cymbals rhythmically.

The conductor, inspired by his example, picked up his baton, and yelled, 'From the top. Vivace!' and the band resumed the tune, but with the fastest, most upbeat rendition of 'Onward Christian Soldiers' that I had ever heard.

The vicar and his wife sang along. They were shouting the words, so I could hear them above the cacophony of the hysterical bandsmen who bravely kept playing in the rotunda – 'OnwardChristian SoldiersMarchingAsToWarWithTheCrossOf JesusGoingOnBefore.'

This is how the Christians in the Colosseum must have felt, I thought.

The panther gathered itself and pounced at the machine gunner in front of us. The man screamed as three heads grasped various parts of his body and three sets of teeth dragged him towards the bushes. Around us, the soldiers were opening fire with their rifles, the blasts almost but not quite covering the shrieks from the people around us and the noise of the brass band, which continued to play.

Although the panther that had killed the machine gunner had headed unhesitatingly to his target, most of the younger animals seemed to lack direction. I watched as their heads swivelled this way and that, each animal fighting their different heads' desire to pounce on which prey.

'They aren't really coordinated. They're confused. And there's a lot of us to choose from. I think each brain is giving different instructions to their bodies, and they can't make up their minds which way to go,' I shouted to Dad. 'That big cat was the only one that knew what it was doing.'

'I thought that too, Lizzie. They seem to be as mixed up as Emma's kitten gets at times. But there must be a dominant head for each creature, and when the dominant head makes a decision it'll set the entire animal in motion, and then we're going to be in really big trouble. All we can do is stay calm and hope the army can save us.'

'The army looks a bit confused too, Dad.'

'The captain will hold them together, Lizzie. He's young, but he's no fool.'

I watched as the eyes in one of the heads of the nearest panther narrowed. It was looking directly at the captain, who still stood in front of his cowering men, urging them to stand their ground. Then the beast began its charge, all three heads held low in order to give the beast more impetus. The doomed captain looked back briefly at his men and shouted something that I couldn't hear over the brass band and the panther's growls.

The animal was almost on the man, gathering its muscles to spring on him. The young officer fired his pistol. A small round hole appeared in one of the animal's heads. The panther faltered just a little. The eyes in the wounded head glazed and hung low. For a brief moment, the two undamaged heads turned towards the dead one. One head sniffed it and the other licked gently at the unseeing eyes. Then the two living heads turned and snarled savagely in unison at the captain.

To my horror, the beast crouched and lunged at the officer. The slack-jawed head swung, but that didn't seem to affect the creature unduly. The panther still had two brains to direct its motion. I knew that the monster would eventually die, but how long would that take?

The captain was down, blood seeping through his khaki uniform. He lay on his side, the hand holding the pistol still extended towards his target. But he was absolutely still. Gradually the hand relaxed and the gun slipped aside. The soldiers, shock and horror showing on their faces when they saw their officer was dead, wavered. The rifle fire faltered. More panthers of assorted sizes were coming at them and at us. They were attacking from all directions. This time the panthers had purpose. All the heads were decided on one goal, and that goal was the annihilation of the people of Bullyacre.

'Now we do have a problem,' Dad muttered. 'If,' he paused and looked at me, 'if anything happens to me, take care of your brother and your sister, Lizzie.'

There's a poem by Rudyard Kipling called 'If'. The memory of it flashed through my mind, but there wasn't time to think anything further about poetry.

'No, Dad, don't go!' I cried.

As he left us, he looked back at me and said quickly, 'I'm going out now, and I may be gone for some time.' He dashed out of the crowd, through the congregation of cringing Bullyacrists, and he ran towards the machine gun.

I'd have liked to have had Sergeant Wylie there at that moment to see what Dad was doing. Even if I die now, I thought, everyone in the town knows what my dad's made of. I just hoped that enough of us would survive to tell the story.

'So much for Dad being the town drunk now,' I told Bill and Jake triumphantly, but through chattering teeth. I held Emma tight against me and she clutched hard at the writhing shopping trolley.

Dad's original army training showed. He knew how to use that machine gun, and he used it well, swinging the machine from side to side as he mowed down the panthers. My heart beat wildly when one huge beast leapt high and sprang straight at him, but either he shot it, or the soldiers, their courage restored when they saw that they once again had leadership, dispatched the animal. I couldn't say what happened next, because my memory is blurred now, probably by the shock of it all, but I know I was proud of my dad then, and I still am.

When it was over, there were seven panthers dead on the field. Bullyacrists, seven, I thought; panthers, two. Although the two dead people weren't Bullyacrists, strictly speaking, they were members of the unfortunate military. Another reason for Jake and Bill not to join the services.

The people of Bullyacre walked amongst the carnage just as I had read that the people used to walk mediaeval battlefields to inspect the dead, just as Edith Swanneck, Harold's queen, had walked the field after the Battle of Hastings and discovered her husband's body, identifying him by certain marks known only to her.

That's how I recognised the mother cat, by the wounds I'd inflicted on her. She looked smaller dead than she had when I first encountered her. But she was still a very large animal. Two half-grown kittens lay beside her.

The Bullyacrists kicked at the panther's bodies, opened dead mouths to exclaim at the teeth, and surreptitiously plucked hairs from the dead tails for souvenirs of the day. Photographs were taken, and someone used their mobile phone to email one to the newspaper, which is why all the journalists arrived as quickly as they did. If anyone on the planet didn't know where Bullyacre was before this, they would know now.

Just as well the ailing Sergeant Wylie wasn't here today, I thought.

I wondered what the new policeman, Sergeant Fitzgerald, would think when he found out about the incident at the Lions' Park. He hadn't come to the picnic today, pleading that back at the police station he had a load of paperwork from previous incidents to get through. I'd heard him complain to Dad that Bulllyacre had more incidents per head of population than any town he had ever worked in.

'It's all due to that climate change,' I heard Fred Mudge tell Pat Vincent as he poked at the nearest carcass. 'The original genetic structure of the basic animal structure is altering because of those holes in the ozone layer that are letting more sunlight come through to release carbon gas, and that causes something called El Niño which makes the water heat up around the equator.'

'Yair, I heard them ecologist blokes saying something like that,' Pat replied.

'All the water flows down to the South Pole and sets off atomic molecules and radon gas in the form of radiation, the krill population multiplies, which means there's too many whales swimming in the sea, then you get stuff like this happening.'

Pat nodded in agreement, which encouraged Fred to continue his spiel. 'Mutation, it's called. I read it in the newspaper last week. It's all the Americans' fault because they chew too much chewing gum and eat hamburgers and fart. They give off noxious gases, hamburger farts do.'

'That's why we get droughts and flooding rain in Australia,' agreed Pat.

'No, that's been happening for yonks,' said Fred. 'There's a poem about that. I learned it at school. Written by Dorothea McKellar, that one was.'

I hoped he wouldn't recite it, but he did. I walked away to join my family.

'They look just like Cuddles,' wept Emma, clinging to Dad with one hand but still clutching her convulsing shopping trolley with the other as she gazed at the dead kittens lying beside the mother. 'Just a bit bigger. It isn't their fault that they were born to be three-headed panthers. Can we go home now? I feel really sick, Lizzie. This has been a horrible picnic.'

There was a mewling from the shopping trolley which told me that the kitten agreed.

<h1 style="text-align:center">17</h1>

Dad and I sat in the kitchen with our cups of tea on the table in front of us. Bill and Emma and even the kitten were exhausted, mentally and physically, and I'd chased them into the shower (not the kitten, though, because it wouldn't have taken kindly to such treatment) and then sent them all off to bed. Dad and I were tired too, but Dad said he had something important to discuss with me.

'After what you did today, Dad, I'll discuss anything you want,' I said.

My head was still reeling from the sight of Dad taking command of the army platoon, manning the machine gun, mowing down our feline attackers and saving almost the entire population of Bullyacre from a horrible fate. Apart from Sergeant Wylie, who was still recuperating in hospital, and Ms Wylie, who had mysteriously disappeared. It was rumoured in the town that instead of sitting beside her husband's sick bed, she was away cavorting with her ecologist.

Watching people slapping Dad on the back and standing in line to shake his hand was pretty good, though. That's not something I could have predicted would happen, just a few weeks ago.

'The point is, Lizzie, there were only two juvenile cats with the mother,' said Dad. 'And yet we know there were three kittens back in the cave when we first saw her.'

'When *you* first saw her, Dad. The kids and I saw her the night before that. And there were four kittens in the cave, because we've got Cuddles.'

'I stand corrected, Lizzie. But you do agree that we watched the mother carry three kittens away at the time? And there were two half-grown cats with her today. So where is the third kitten?'

'Maybe it didn't survive infancy. There has to be a mortality rate for three-headed panther kittens in the wild. There might be some flaw in their basic genetic make-up. Like tortoiseshell male kittens always dying before they're born so it looks as if all tortoiseshell kittens are female.'

'That's a point, Lizzie. How did you know that?'

'We did genetics last term, and I really enjoyed it. Not all animals survive their infancy, Dad. You know that. We even lose a few lambs occasionally. Sometimes from foxes or other predators, but sometimes just from built-in weakness.'

'I'll agree with that, Lizzie. That third kitten might not have been a strong baby, although, as even Emma said on the day, a mother will always favour the strongest of her litter, and it was Cuddles that she left behind. And as we noticed, Cuddles is much smaller than the juveniles the mother had with her.'

I wondered if that was why Dad always favoured Emma over me and Bill, but I didn't say it. Perhaps humans were different from the rest of the animal world and they favoured the weakest of the family.

'Whatever,' I said. 'Can I go to bed now, Dad? I'm bushed.'

'This is important, Lizzie. The point is, if there is another half-grown panther out there for whatever reason, Bullyacre is still at risk.'

'Why don't we wake Bill up and ask him how many kittens he saw when he was in the helicopter?'

'Good idea, Lizzie.'

We went into Bill's room and shook him until he woke up. I noticed he hadn't turned the light off, and I resolved to say something about that to him. Electricity costs money.

'How many kittens did you see with the mother when you were in that helicopter, Bill?' I asked.

'Three,' he answered sleepily. 'I know there were three. They were all running beside the mother, and they really did look a lot like Emma's kitten.'

'We all saw her taking three kittens away from the cave, but there were only two bodies. Are you sure there were three with her when she was coming down to the Lions' Park?' Dad asked.

'Three,' Bill insisted. 'Lizzie, you said I needed some sleep and now you're waking me up to ask stupid questions. Leave me alone. I just got off to sleep a minute ago.'

'William, this is extremely important. Are you certain that you saw three kittens, or could it be that you *thought* you saw three because you expected three but actually you saw two?'

'I saw three kittens when I was in the helicopter, Dad. I had a good view from up there. I know I saw three kittens.'

'The point I'm trying to make,' Dad said, 'is that maybe one of the kittens died when the mother took them away that day when we went after her in the gully. That's what I am hoping happened, Bill, because otherwise the third kitten escaped from the Lions' Park and it's still out there wandering around in the bush. And those were fair-sized kittens, quite capable of being very dangerous. We can't afford to have another one still alive out there. So try to remember exactly what you saw.'

'When I was in the helicopter and I saw the panthers coming towards the park, I saw three kittens with the mother, Dad.'

My brother's voice shook. Bill was cracking under the interrogation and I actually felt quite sorry for him.

'Lizzie,' he pleaded, 'I know what I saw. And this is the last time I'm going to talk about it. I feel sick just thinking about it, and I've already had one nightmare since I came to bed. It was horrible. There was a panther eating me starting from the feet up. But I'm not changing my story to suit anyone. That's what I saw, and if you want to go and get the Bible from Jake's, Dad, I'll swear on it if that's what you want. So don't talk to me about it any more. I want to go to sleep.'

'All right, Bill,' I said. 'Try and get back to sleep.'

Dad patted him on the shoulder. 'Sorry, mate. We just had to clear it up.'

'I'm scared too, Dad. I'd already worked that one out. I reckon there's more cats out there, too. That's why I've got my cricket bat in bed with me, in case one comes through my window. But I can hardly keep my eyes open just now.' Bill shut his eyes and turned his head towards the wall.

We tiptoed out and I turned the light off.

'No!' yelled Bill. 'Leave that light on. If I'm going to be attacked while I'm asleep, I want the light on so I can see the Beast coming.'

I shrugged and left the light on. Bill probably had a point, although it was a bit muddled.

'Should we ring the police station and let Sergeant Fitzgerald or the army know that we think there's probably at least one more panther out there, Dad?' I asked.

'I'll do it, Lizzie. You get to bed. You look absolutely worn out.'

<h1 style="text-align:center">18</h1>

'It's in the paper. They've got the result of the DNA testing on the panthers.'

'So are they marsupial panthers, Dad?'

'No, Ms Wylie and her friends are going to be very disappointed. It's been proven that it was the DNA for a mammalian panther not a marsupial one. On the other hand, the DNA doesn't quite match the normal DNA for panthers, so it's definitely a new original species, and there are all sorts of discussions and problems caused, because we've effectively wiped it out.'

'So were we supposed to let it wipe us out?'

Dad turned the page of *The Advertiser*. From what I could see, looking over his shoulder, there seemed to be something on every page about the Incident at the Lions' Park.

'The United Nations has appointed a committee of inquiry into the protection of endangered species. We've committed a crime, Lizzie. Australia's in big trouble with the entire international community because we killed those panthers. I might get called up to the International Court of Criminal Justice about it because I was the main assassin.'

'But it was self-defence. What did they expect us to do, Dad?'

'I might have a word with Mr Ryan the lawyer about it. He'll know what to do.'

'Dad, the panthers were threatening human life, for goodness sake. Bullyacre was endangered too. You're a hero. You saved a lot of people from being eaten. You can't get into trouble for that.'

'Look at the newspaper. Greenpeace is furious with us. Ms Wylie and her ecologist friends have started a Protect the Three-Headed Mammalian Panther of Bullyacre Association, and they're going to set up a tent city in Canberra and have demonstrations,' Dad said, shaking his head. 'They've left it a bit late, haven't they? As far as they know, there's nothing left to protect.'

'Well, they're wrong there, aren't they? Did you tell Sergeant Fitzgerald about the missing kitten?'

'Yes, I did, but I don't think he believed me. He says he's got enough to worry about now he has to file reports about the Lions' Park Incident. Apparently paperwork takes precedence.'

'We could tell him about Cuddles, Dad.'

'It's a good thing he doesn't don't know about Cuddles or he'd be filing reports about that, too. And he might tell Ms Wylie's lot and they'd probably want to clone her the way the woolly mammoth is being cloned, so they'd have something to actually protect.'

'But all the panthers are dead, Dad, apart from Cuddles. Unless there really is another kitten out there, as Bill swears there is. And Cuddles is still here. We've got her under control.'

We watched the kitten stalking Toby across the room. The kitten pounced on Toby and the Tabby head bit his ear. The Spotty head grabbed the other ear, and Cuddles, after the briefest of hesitation, reached out and nipped his tail. Toby yelped in pain. I ran over and hit the kitten with Dad's newspaper which I had hastily rolled up into a weapon. Toby crept back and hid under my chair. He lay there, whimpering and whining. I grabbed the kitten by the scruff of one its necks, hoping that it was Cuddles's neck because that was the safest, opened the back door and pushed the animal outside. The Tabby head snapped at my arm but missed. I slammed the door quickly. I handed the newspaper back to Dad.

'Yes,' he said, 'Cuddles is still with us but I'm not sure about how much control we've got over her.' He shook the cat hairs off of the paper, opened it up and continued reading it. 'The Japanese have accused us of crimes against the planet because of killing the cats but, in the reporter's opinion, that might be because they want to take people's attention away from whaling. Some other journalists are saying that wiping out the panther may be a worse crime than the destruction of the Amazon rainforest. The name Bullyacre has been blacklisted worldwide. There's going to be an international boycott of Bullyacre's products.'

'What products? Wheat and wool? And steak from Mr Mudge's beef cattle? How will anyone know if stuff comes from Bullyacre or instead of from somewhere else in Australia?'

'I don't know, Lizzie,' said Dad, shaking his head. 'In this article, the European Union says they'll slap a ban on all Australian produce. And the Americans are accusing us of doing genetic modification on the panthers to give them three heads, and they think our wool might be genetically engineered and therefore not up to their health and safety standards.'

'It reminds me of that row over mulesing the sheep a while back. No one likes doing mulesing, but of course people in the city don't understand that if you don't do it, the sheep get blowfly strike.' I said.

Dad nodded. 'I often wish we'd never laid eyes on those cats,' he said.

'The Curse of Bullyacre,' I agreed. 'Or the Curse of Magnetic Hill. Maybe that's what I should have named the panther. A bit like that plant, Patterson's Curse – *Pantheris cursii bullyacrii* or something like that. I wish I'd paid more attention when we did that semester of Latin.'

'Are you really going to insist that the species be called Cuddles, Lizzie?'

'Yes, I will. I'm going to do it just to spite Ms Wylie and her ecologist friends. And to spite Mr Furphy too. Actually, I think it'll be *Pantheris tricephalus cuddlii* or something along those lines. That nice man at the university said he'll work out the correct way to write it. He said I could even make it *Pantheris cuddliensis epsomii* if I want. Or *Pantheris australistricephalus cuddlii.* That means panther from Australia with three heads called Cuddles. He says it would be pushing the envelope a bit, but he thinks he can fix something along those lines for me.'

'You're a stubborn girl, Lizzie,' said Dad.

'I'm a chip off the old block,' I said. 'You weren't prepared to give in, back at the Lions' Park.'

'Well, the army training usually holds firm. Did you make that cup of tea?'

'In a moment, Dad. Speaking of the army, are the soldiers going to hang around for a bit longer? Did you tell them that we think there could be another cat still out in the paddocks?'

'I did, but unless we can prove it's actually out there, they're going back tomorrow. They've got manoeuvres near Darwin that they have to go to. We'll need the shearers' quarters for the shearers in a month or two, anyway.'

'If we've got enough sheep left to justify holding a shearing this year,' I said.

'There's still a few sheep out there, Lizzie,' Dad said.

As we sipped our tea, I glanced out of the window. I saw that the kitten was sitting at the edge of garden, not far from the spot where the film crew's van had stood on the night of the Siege of Epsom Downs. The Cuddles head had bent down to lick the back of the Tabby head, which turned and stretched luxuriously. Loud purring came from the kitten's belly. Then the Spotty head reached down to lick their communal under-carriage.

Suddenly, as the Cuddles head abandoned grooming Tabby's head and swivelled itself round to help Spotty groom their shared nether regions, the entire animal overbalanced and fell in a writhing mass. There were yowls and growls and screeches as the three heads disputed who had done what to whom and why. The kitten rolled about on the cement path scratching and biting itself in all directions. Fur began to fly and I saw blood on Tabby's ear.

'Would it be such a terrible thing if this species went extinct?' I asked. 'But it probably won't, because if there is another cat out there, the species wouldn't really be extinct, would it, Dad? It'd just be on the endangered list. Because, of course, we've got Cuddles. If there is another kitten, and if it's a male, it could be bred if the world really wants more of them. And if it's a female, perhaps it and Cuddles could be cloned so they could have babies.'

The screeching rose to a crescendo and I struggled to make my voice heard over the din. 'Although I can't help but think perhaps this is one species the world could do without.'

'The whole scenario is still a lot like the original thylacine story, though, isn't it, Lizzie? The Tasmanian farmers felt justified wiping the tigers out because of stock losses. Although I've heard it was feral dogs, not the thylacines, that were killing the Tassie sheep. The Tasmanian tigers just copped all the blame.'

We watched the kitten tear at itself for a bit longer. Things looked to be getting out of hand as the three heads grew angrier. Tabby is quite an evil little thing, I thought. And Cuddles, although she could be sweet at times, was quite a fighter when she was aroused.

'Are you going to do anything about this battle, Dad?' I asked. 'Should I fetch the hose and squirt it?'

'No way,' said Dad. 'It'll just attack us. I've been in enough wars lately. I'm not breaking up a domestic that thing is engaged in. Not unless I've got a machine gun in my hands, anyway. Where's Emma? She'll have to sort it out. She's the only one who can control that kitten.'

'She's playing with her Nintendo. I bought it with the money I got from the interview with Mr Furphy.'

'But you always said you hated those electronic game machine things. You said that you'd read an article saying that kids' brains get cooked from them and that letting kids use them is a cop out by people who use electronic games as babysitters.'

'I know, Dad, but she just went on and on how all her friends have got them and she said she was underprivileged and having a deprived childhood. She insisted that she was suffering enormous stress. I got worried she might report us to the school authorities. So when Mr Furphy's cheque arrived, I decided to buy the toy for her. I'm rationing her use of it, though. No more than an hour a day. She has to do her homework before she's allowed to touch it and if she throws tantrums I confiscate it. I've threatened to toss it down the long-drop loo outside if she doesn't behave herself.'

'Good idea, that, Lizzie.'

'Yes, I told her it'd get caught on those stalactites of shit in the dunny and she'd never get it back, or if she did fish it out it would never work again. I mean it too.'

'And she knows you mean it. So where's Bill?'

'Looking over her shoulder while she plays with the Nintendo, I think.'

The phone rang. I went inside, answered it and brought it back to Dad.

'It's Miss Cobbledick wanting to speak to our local hero. She's got some sort of problem. She won't tell me what it is. She wants you. Have you noticed how, ever since you saved the town, everyone phones you when anything goes wrong? Jake says his dad heard that the people want you to stand for mayor at the next election. Everyone wants to know your opinion about the fireworks on New Year's Eve. Would you abolish them, Dad?'

'I think Bullyacre's had enough fireworks to last it a lifetime,' Dad said, taking the phone from me. 'Yes, Miss Cobbledick. Three chooks yesterday and two today? Do you think it's foxes? It looked more like a big feral cat? How well did you see it, Miss Cobbledick? Yes, I know you're ninety-eight and your eyes aren't all that good in the dark. Oh, sorry, ninety-two. No, I certainly didn't mean to be rude, Miss Cobbledick. I wouldn't dream of insulting you. Yes, I'll come right over.'

'Why you, Dad? What's wrong with the new police sergeant?'

'Sergeant Fitzpatrick is very nice and very well meaning, but the older people in the town just haven't learned to trust him yet, Lizzie. I'll go over and see what's happening. Old Miss Cobbledick says her chooks are going missing, but I expect she's got a hole in her coop. Or maybe there are foxes in the town. I won't be gone all that long. And you don't have to worry that I'll call into the pub. I'm over that now.'

'Do you want me to come with you? Bill can babysit Emma for an hour or so.'

'No, Lizzie. Didn't you tell me you had to complete that science assignment? Something about the Hubble telescope?'

'I handed it in two days ago. I got my marks back last night. Another high distinction. If you've got time, I'll show it to you now, Dad.'

'OK,' said Dad, sounding a bit weary. 'Tell you what, you can come along with me for moral support. I'm not all that keen on facing Miss Cobbledick on my own. Panthers are one thing, old ladies are another. You can show your project to me when we get back from sorting out Miss Cobbledick, Lizzie.'

'No one sorts out Miss Cobbledick, Dad. You know that. It's Miss Cobbledick who sorts everyone else out. By the way, did you know that because of the Hubble telescope, astronomers can confidently say that the rate of star formation reached its peak about five billion years after the Big Bang, and that the rate of formation has been declining ever since?'

'Fred Mudge would say that's due to global warming because a butterfly is flapping its wings in the Amazon jungle and no one's listening. Let's go and see what's wrong with Miss Cobbledick's chooks before Fred hears about it and blames their disappearance on global warming too.'

'Fred Mudge is probably pinching the poultry to make up for losing his prize bull. He'll say he needs them so his wife can make chicken soup to help him over his depression. And he'll claim compo from the government if one of the hens pecks him while he's wringing their necks.'

'Don't be sarcastic about our neighbours, Lizzie. Miss Cobbledick has the monopoly of sarcasm in this town, and she manages to savage not only the entire township of Bullyacre but most of the surrounding farms with her opinions. We'd better get over there before it gets any darker. I'm still a bit nervous about going out at night after recent events, especially if there's one of Cuddles's siblings still on the loose.'

'Miss Cobbledick wasn't happy when you refused to set a rabbit trap for the fox or whatever was taking her chooks, was she? She said she'd seen something nasty in her woodshed.'

'She needs new glasses but she's too stingy to buy them. And I don't care if she doesn't want to vote for me as mayor, either. I didn't ask to be elected and I'm not interested in the position. Mayor Murphy can keep the job. If Miss Cobbledick's vote depends on my torturing dumb beasts, she can keep it. I don't believe in traps that hold an animal's legs with metal teeth so they suffer agonising pain until someone comes and put them out their misery.'

'Miss Cobbledick said all the ladies of the auxiliary want you to stand to be mayor, though. And even Pat Vincent and Mike Young are lobbying for you. I saw a poster on the wall of the police station saying you ought to be elected. Sergeant Fitzgerald's not as fussy about posters as Sergeant Wylie was.'

'Well, they can all go jump in the lake. I don't want the job.'

'But it 'd be great being the mayor's daughter, Dad. Just think of the fame and the glory.'

'I think you've had enough of that already, Lizzie. I did promise that I'd keep coming back to check on Miss Cobbledick's hens every night for the next couple of weeks. And now we've fixed that hole in the wire the chickens'll probably be all right. I wondered if the birds just walked out and couldn't find their way back. There weren't any feathers blowing about, so it makes me wonder whether they were really killed at all. Miss Cobbledick's getting a bit dippy in her declining years. She shouldn't be living on her own, but she refuses to move into the retirement home.'

'Everyone's told her she shouldn't be living out there in that old mansion, but she won't listen. Don't worry about things you can't change, Dad,' I said. 'Anyway, the retirement home people would be devastated if she did move in there. They'd be as miserable as you look right now.' I pulled my school books out of my bag and waved one of them at him. 'This'll cheer you up. You remember I wanted to show you that assignment, the one on the Hubble telescope. Here it is. I told you I got a high distinction. Zoe only got a C and she's furious. She says Mr Gonski doesn't like her and he's marking her down.'

'Well done, Lizzie,' said Dad. 'What's your next assignment?'

'We're back on geology again, and I have to write an essay on the Adelaide geosyncline,' I said. 'Do you know anything about that?'

'Not a thing, Lizzie,' Dad said. 'I didn't even know there was an Adelaide geosyncline. Is it related to Magnetic Hill? Maybe you could contact those geologists, the ones you saved on the hill, ask them about it.'

'Dad, Dad, look out the window!' I pulled him over to the window. 'Look outside, quick!'

'It's just Cuddles rolling about on the cement,' said Dad. 'She's making some funny noises, though. That's strange. Look how Spotty and Tabby are rubbing their heads on the ground, although Cuddles is looking up into the big gum tree. She's probably seen a bird up there and she's trying to persuade the other two to join her in chasing it. I've got to admit I wouldn't like to be a bird in our backyard.'

'We hardly ever get birds in our backyard any more. I reckon Cuddles is acting like a female cat in heat, Dad. You know how they carry on. And that's not a bird in the gum tree.' I squinted so I could see a bit better. 'I can see a tawny body with spots up there on that big branch just above the wood heap. Oh gosh, I think that's the missing kitten, Dad.'

Dad and I both peered through the glass and up the tree. Neither of us wanted to go outside to get a better view.

'Miss Cobbledick must have been right. Something nasty has been taking her chooks. If that cat's a male, it's probably come over here in search of a mate. Probably Cuddles has been sending off pheromones or whatever it's called when the male smells the female from afar,' I said.

'They'd be a bit young for that sort of thing, Lizzie. They'd be about the teenage stage if they were people.' He stopped and looked at me with a worried look on his face. 'They'd be about your stage in life, Lizzie. And Jake's.'

'Don't look at me like that, Dad. I know I'm a teenager, but give me credit for having a bit more sense than a three-headed cat. And Jake's not silly either. He wants to be an accountant. I don't think accountants know about sex. What are we going to do about Cuddles and this cat, though? We know that Cuddles is a female, although there's definitely no pouch on her tummy. If this stranger kitten is a male, we might end up with lots more of the panthers. And the entire problem will start up again. Of course, they're probably brother and sister, though.'

'Cats don't care about that sort of thing,' said Dad. 'They're not worried about close relationships when it comes to mating.'

'Neither did the Egyptian pharaohs,' I said. It suddenly occurred to me that if we Epsoms were Egyptian pharaohs, I'd have to marry Bill. 'It's a rotten idea, though.'

'Well,' said Dad slowly, 'we could neuter the pair of them, although it's probably a bit too late and I don't think the vet would agree to it. It's not a job I'd want to tackle. But if they were desexed, that would definitely mean the species would go extinct and your friend at the university wouldn't like that. Or Ms Wylie's mob. We could contact the army or the police, but they'd want to exterminate them.'

'That's what we probably should do, Dad. For the good of the community.'

Dad held his hand up to silence me. 'We could even get hold of Ms Wylie and her ecologists and offer both the kittens to them, although I don't know where they'd put them. That might prevent a lot of nasty political carryings-on.'

'I'm not donating Cuddles and her boyfriend to Ms Wylie,' I said. 'That would be a fate worse than death for both cats. And what would Emma say?'

Dad shook his head, and I knew he was thinking of the tantrum that Emma would throw if we gave Cuddles away to anyone.

'It's not an easy decision,' he said. He had to raise his voice a bit because Cuddles was making the sort of noises that you'd imagine Cleopatra would have made when she was calling Mark Antony to her side. Only less melodic.

'Do you realise, Dad, we've got the fate of an entire species in our hands? And probably the future of Australia's balance of trade, of our country's economic future, of our nation's standing in the eyes of the entire world? Have you heard that saying, "All power corrupts, but absolute power corrupts absolutely"?'

Dad nodded. 'We could hold the country to ransom, ask for anything we wanted. But we won't do that, Lizzie, will we?'

The stranger kitten leapt out of the gum tree and landed beside Cuddles and her sisters. It turned its backside towards us, and it was obvious that he was a young male. A young male in his prime and full of pheromones.

One of his heads rubbed against Cuddles's head, and then his and Cuddles's necks twisted and entwined. The other four heads were inspecting and discovering each other, and high-decibel purring came through window as Dad and I watched the courtship begin.

'Get the camera, Lizzie,' said Dad. 'This ought to be recorded. Keep Emma and Bill away, though. Where are they?'

'They're both immersed in the Nintendo,' I said. 'I think I'll phone that nice man at the university down in Adelaide. He was telling me he knows some animal behaviourists who are really interested in the life cycle of the panther. I'll see if he wants to send someone up here. He'll know what to do.'

I reached for the phone and dialled the number. It was a good thing that Mr Peterson had given me his private number as well as his office one.

'Mr Peterson, Lizzie Epsom speaking. Lizzie from Bullyacre. I spoke to you about working out a name for the three-headed panther and you said you'd help me work out the correct Latin. Hold on a bit.' I took the phone away from my ear for a moment. 'Dad, shut that window.'

'No, Mr Peterson, I'm not ringing about the name for the panther. We have an awful problem up here in Bullyacre.' The noise outside was reaching a crescendo. I didn't want to look out of the window, but Dad was engrossed in whatever was going on out there.

'I'm sorry, Mr Peterson, it's hard to hear what you're saying because there's a lot of noise this end,' I shouted. 'We've shut the window now.

Yes, I know it's a bit weird. We've been keeping one of the panthers as a pet. Yes, I know I should have mentioned that before.'

Mr Peterson was hard to understand because he was running all his words together in excitement, but I thought I heard him observe that this could mean a unique opportunity to observe *Pantheris austriphcephalus in vivo*. He said a lot more too, but I remembered this was a long-distance call and expensive, so I cut him short.

'Yes, I agree. Only now the kitten's getting difficult to control because it's quite big, and there's another complication because another one's turned up. I think they're mating in our back garden, making awful noises. Can you hear them?' I directed the phone towards the window, held it there for a bit, and then I listened to Mr Peterson's excited voice.

I put the phone down and turned to Dad, who was still watching the cats cavorting on our patio. 'Mr Peterson's absolutely over the moon,' I said. 'He says we're witnessing the beginning of a new era of scientific discovery. He says he'll be on his way to Bullyacre first thing in the morning. He says not to breathe a word of it to anyone until he gets here.'

'That's a bit risky, Lizzie. I still think we ought to alert the community to the danger.'

'He promised he'd bring a team to trap the panthers and take them to Monarto Zoo or somewhere to keep them safe and then we can work out what's going to happen after that.'

'Emma will be furious. She'll be harder to control than the kitten when she finds out.'

'The situation's out of our hands, Dad,' I said. 'We'll just have to play it by ear.'

20

It was fairly quiet until after the food was eaten, but soon afterwards the uproar in the hall became almost worse than when the news of the Beast of Magnetic Hill first burst upon Bullyacre. It was probably even noisier than the tantrum that Emma had thrown when Mr Peterson and his people had arrived and flung nets over the two adolescent cats, which, exhausted after their nocturnal honeymoon, had lain basking in the sun on our patio until their rude awakening and abduction.

The reason the citizens of Bullyacre were gathered in the hall was Miss Cobbledick's wake. She had died suddenly and apparently peacefully while mowing the front lawn on her property a couple of days ago. It was lucky that Jake's dad, the vicar, had happened to call in for his weekly pastoral care visit to see how she was going, or her body might not have been found for a couple of days. The mower had kept going until it hit a frangipani bush, where it had got stuck and ran out of petrol.

Dr Jones said Miss Cobbledick's death was due to natural causes, which was fair enough for a lady of ninety-two. At the funeral, everyone remarked that she'd died doing what she enjoyed most, but some of the community felt a bit guilty for not insisting that she let them mow her lawn. People who had done the job for her, though, remembered that she was never happy with the way they'd done it. She always said she was the only one who could do the job properly.

Miss Cobbledick's wake had to be held in the hall, because it's only venue in the town big enough to hold the number of mourners who'd turned up. Miss Cobbledick, despite her sometimes difficult personality, was well respected in the community and admired for her tenacity, her courage and of course her longevity.

Another reason why there were so many people there was that the local lawyer, Mr Ryan, had announced that, in accordance with the deceased's desire, the reading of Miss Cobbledick's last will and testament would take place at the wake. Miss Cobbledick had never married and, as far as anyone knew, there was no surviving family, so speculation about the disposal of her estate was running rampant in the town.

The ladies of the auxiliary had done Miss Cobbledick proud. In addition to the usual scones with jam and cream, they'd cooked up her favourite dish, sausage rolls. They'd borrowed the pie-warming machine from the golf club to heat them up, and the fragrant smell of fat-laden pastry filled the hall.

'I don't know how Miss Cobbledick managed to survive until ninety-two,' Dr Jones observed, as he bit into one of the delicacies. 'These things are laden with cholesterol. I'm sure the shortening in the pastry isn't polyunsaturated, either. It tastes like butter to me.'

'It's Miss Cobbledick's own recipe,' one of the ladies told him. 'We wouldn't have dared use anything else.'

Mayor Murphy climbed up onto the stage, lifted the microphone, and banged his gavel on the podium to silence us. There was a collective groan from many of the Bullyacrists, who felt that after Miss Cobbledick's prolonged funeral ceremonies and interminable eulogies, they ought to be allowed to mingle and eat in peace.

'Fair go, Mayor,' yelled Fred Mudge. 'We've come for the refreshments and to have a bit of a chin wag about Miss C. And to hear her will read, of course. We don't need any more speechifying.'

The mayor scowled. He obviously didn't want to upset the populace, not with the mayoral elections so close. But, being the fellow he was, he couldn't let the opportunity to speak pass him by. 'Ladies and gentlemen, boys and girls of Bullyacre,' he said.

The microphone whistled a bit and he banged it on the podium to try to fix the problem. It kept whistling until Pat Vincent fixed it. The audience groaned as the mayor lifted the microphone again and looked around the hall.

'We are gathered here today to farewell a prominent member of our community, Miss Muriel Cobbledick. Muriel was well known to each and every one of the people of Bullyacre.'

'Yair, we all know that,' said Fred. 'None of us need reminding about that. She was a bonzer lady, Miss Cobbledick. Nasty temper, though.'

'I would like to take the opportunity while we are all gathered together under the one roof, like the family that we Bullyacrists are, to announce that our esteemed police officer for many years, Sergeant Jack Wylie, has, in part due to the devoted care given him by his beloved wife, Ms Wylie, made a full recovery from the sad affliction he recently suffered – an affliction, I might add, which was undoubtedly induced by the stress imposed upon him by certain junior members of our community.' The mayor paused and glared at me and at Jake.

I nudged Jake and whispered, 'What a load of crap. What about the business of Ian Perkins being killed because he had to go out and put stickers on cars? What about Wylie's devoted wife having an affair with an ecologist?'

Jake put his finger on his lips and murmured, 'Don't say anything, Lizzie. Remember this is Miss Cobbledick's farewell supper. Have another sausage roll before the doctor scoffs the lot.'

We grabbed a couple of sausage rolls from the tray on the trestle table.

'Would you two please sit down and be quiet!' roared the Mayor. 'Mr Ryan, our well respected lawyer, is about to read Miss Cobbledick's last will and testament. It was her wish that it be read out while you were all in the town hall because apparently it has got something in it that concerns us all. So let us have a bit of respect and a bit of silence, if you please.'

Mr Ryan sat at the small table which had been set up for him and opened a large manila envelope. He took out a sheet of paper and examined it carefully.

'He must know what's in it, because he would've drawn it up,' said Bill. 'So why doesn't he just get on with reading it?'

'Shut up, Bill,' said Dad.

'I, Miss Muriel Edith Cobbledick, being of sound mind,' read the lawyer solemnly.

'Well, that's debatable,' said Fred Mudge. 'She told me I was a lying, conniving creep just because I claimed compo for my dead bull.'

'She was right,' said Pat Vincent. 'The whole town knows that.

That bull wasn't worth the air it breathed. It never managed to get my cows pregnant when I borrowed it. I reckon that bull was gay.'

'Silence!' roared the mayor.

'I leave the whole of my estate and property including the contents of my house and all monies held in my several bank accounts as well as any stocks and shares in my possession to the community of Bullyacre to be used for a project or projects to benefit the entire community,' Mr Ryan read. He carefully laid the document down on the table and smiled at us over the top of his glasses. He took his glasses off, polished them with his hanky and laid the spectacles on top of the paper. 'It is, of course, up to the community of Bullyacre to decide just what that project or projects will be,' he said.

'That house of hers was pretty big,' said Fred Mudge, speculating on how much money would be available from its sale. I could almost see dollar signs in his eyes. 'A bloody great mansion. Too big for one old maid to live in. And there's a lot of land around it, too. There's a tennis court, and a swimming pool.'

'Her family had gardeners and housemaids and everything. Of course, she let it all go to rack and ruin. She didn't maintain anything. Except that front lawn. She was always mowing it. She said it was all the exercise she got,' said Pat.

'I would have thought she'd have got enough exercise going up and down those stairs,' said Mrs Latimer.

'She didn't use the upstairs. Just lived in one or two rooms at the back of the house. I've been there a couple of times to see if she was all right. She never let me see more than the kitchen, though,' said Mrs Mudge. 'And that was full of cockroaches and spider webs.'

'We'll sell the whole lot and use the money to improve the golf course,' said the mayor, a huge smile on his face. 'And the club house as well. And anything that's left over can go towards the New Year fireworks display.'

'You've got enough money from those parking tickets to do both those things already,' yelled an angry voice from the back of the hall.

'The local hospital could use some new equipment,' said Dr Jones. 'X-ray machines, more beds, better air conditioning, perhaps a new morgue. None of us is getting any younger.'

'The Lions' Park needs a complete overhaul,' shouted Tom Evans, the municipal gardener. 'It has to be completely re-landscaped after that Incident of yours. There's tank tracks and helicopter damage to the lawns and the rhododendrons, and the rose arbour got trampled by them panthers. Then there's all that blood to clear away. The brass band knocked some of the wrought iron off the rotunda with their instruments when they were running away when that machine gun started up, and there's bullets leaking lead everywhere. Lead's not good for garden plants.'

'Who cares about a garden?' said Fred Mudge. 'We only use it once a year for the family picnic, anyway.'

'Lots of people use the park every Sunday. The kiddies like to feed the ducks in the lake, although most the ducks flew away when they saw the panthers coming and they haven't come back so I'll need new ones, and even the goldfish in the pond look pretty crook. They're swimming around in circles and they're off their feed,' Tom wailed. 'Fixing that park is going to cost money. Big money.'

'Yair, we all need that Lions' Park. My daughter's getting married next April and we want to hold the wedding there,' said Mrs Flynn, 'in the rose arbour, so you'll have to get that sorted out, Tom, quick smart.'

'And my daughter's getting married there in November. So it had better get fixed up very soon for everyone's sake,' said Mrs Boswell, a savage look on her face. 'I vote that Miss Cobbledick's money gets spent restoring the Lions' Park.'

Lots of the townsfolk murmured their agreement to this proposal. But not everyone.

'The school needs money more than anything else in this town,' Mr Gonski insisted. 'Education is our future. We must look after the children's needs before anything else is even given consideration.'

Suddenly everyone was shouting at the top of their voices. They all had their own agenda and their own ideas about how Miss Cobbledick's legacy should be spent for the benefit of Bullyacre, and no one was going to allow anyone else's ideas to stand in their way.

Back in the police station, Sergeant Fitzgerald must have heard the din. I was sitting near the door, which was open a little to let some air in, and I watched as he stalked across the road to the hall and flung the door wide angrily.

'What's going on now?' he demanded. 'Just how much am I supposed to put up with from this town? You're all a pack of loonies. If you're not having some sort of incident, you're having a riot. No wonder Sergeant Wylie cracked under the strain.'

'They won't listen to reason,' yelled the mayor. 'We've been left an endowment to benefit the town, and these idiots want to fritter it away on rubbish. As mayor, I won't stand for it.'

'How much longer are you supposed to be the mayor, mate?' asked the sergeant wearily.

'The elections are next week,' Mrs Flynn told the officer. 'And none of us want him to be mayor any longer. We want Frank Epsom to be mayor.'

'I don't want to be mayor,' Dad protested.

'If you get voted in, you'll have to be mayor, Dad,' I whispered. 'It's for the good of the community.'

'Right,' said the sergeant. 'Someone get a wad of paper, give everyone a piece of it and a pencil and the election can be held right now. Pass me a couple of hats and we'll put the votes in it, and Mr Ryan can count them up. That paper on the desk will do. I'll rip it up into bits and hand it out.'

Mr Ryan clutched the will and held it to his chest. 'You won't rip this paper up, Sergeant. This is the very document that caused the dispute.' He got to his feet and waved the will in the air. 'What everyone doesn't seem to understand is that Miss Cobbledick was an extremely wealthy woman, and there should be enough money to finance most if not all of the projects that have been proposed. Except the fireworks, which I consider frivolous and unnecessary for the common good.'

'I agree with that, Mr Ryan,' said the police officer. 'Those New Year's Eve fireworks should have been abolished years ago. To let off incendiary devices in the middle of the bushfire season is sheer insanity As long as I'm copper here, there won't be any fireworks on New Year's Eve.'

There was a collective groan from the citizens. Although everyone joked about the fireworks, everyone enjoyed them and no one wanted to see them stopped.

'There's never been any problem with the fireworks,' said Mayor

Murphy. 'We conduct them in a very responsible manner and I always have the fire brigade on duty. You can't abolish our New Year fireworks. It's a very important event for Bullyacre.'

The ladies of the auxiliary agreed. 'That's our biggest fund-raising event,' said Mrs Jennings. 'We sell supper that night and that's how we keep our group running. That, and the occasional jumble sale and lamington drive. The auxiliary would collapse without that funding.'

'Speaking of money, I still think it's hard to believe Miss Cobbledick had any,' said Pat Vincent.

'Miss C didn't look like she had two pennies to rub together,' agreed Fred Mudge. 'She used to mow her own lawns, make her own jam, and she sewed her own clothes.'

'She was an old miser, Fred,' said Tom Evans. 'I reckon she still had the first dollar she ever earned. I reckon she had it framed and hung it on her wall. She never even had a crust to spare for the ducks on the lake in the park.'

'She was an only child and the only niece to seven aunts and seven uncles who all died childless. She was an heiress many times over. It was against her principles and her philosophy to spend money so she invested it. And she invested it wisely, too,' said Mr Ryan. 'I suggest we hold the mayoral election as suggested by the good sergeant, and then the new mayor can hold a secret ballot to see how people want the money spent.'

'The way I see it,' said the sergeant, 'there's only two candidates for the office. One is this bloke Murphy over there, and the other one is Frank Epsom, the fellow who almost single-handedly saved the lot of you from being chewed up by wild animals.' The policeman shook Dad's hand effusively. 'This chap, I would like to add, is also the man who set up a branch of Alcoholics Anonymous in Bullyacre, which is about the most community-minded thing that anyone has ever done in this town.'

'Frank Epsom worked single-handed to get rid of Flaherty's illegal still. Flaherty's homemade hooch is the reason why half the town's population has got liver disease,' said Dr Jones. 'Frank has eliminated new cases of cirrhosis in Bullyacre. We owe him our thanks for that. He's an admirable citizen and should be our mayor.'

The sergeant nodded his agreement with the doctor. 'Frank Epsom's a decent bloke who deserves recognition for saving all your miserable lives and you ought to be grateful that you've got him and elect him as mayor. You can see I'm trying to be impartial, of course.'

'You've got to be mayor, Dad,' said Emma. 'No one in my class has got a dad who's a mayor. Please, Dad, say you'll be mayor.'

Paper and pencils were located and distributed. Dad was elected in a landslide victory. There were only two votes for ex-Mayor Murphy. One was in the mayor's own handwriting, and the other was in Dad's.

21

'It's incredible,' said Dad. 'Miss Cobbledick was a fabulously rich woman. I've held the ballot to decide what to do with the money, and I think most people are going to be happy.'

'Well, that's a miracle,' I said. 'I've heard you can please some of the people some of the time, but you can't please all of the people all of the time.'

Dad ignored my statement. 'Mr Ryan suggests we set up a Miss Muriel Cobbledick Foundation to administer the monies. That way it will all be transparent and above board and no one can say we're misappropriating the cash. He says there's enough money to fix up the Lions' Park, re-equip the hospital and the school, re-turf the median strip on the main road, and even give some to the golf club to make ex-Mayor Murphy happy. And there'll still lots be left over.'

'Why are you worried about making Murphy happy, Dad?'

'Well, it won't do any harm. He's still a councillor for his area. I'm drawing the line at contributing to the fireworks show, although I won't entirely abolish it. Sergeant Fitzgerald won't be staying here much longer if Wylie's coming back, so I reckon we can still hold the event. There's enough money in general revenue to pay for that, especially with what Wylie and Murphy pinched from the community with those parking tickets. It won't be as big as Murphy planned, but I don't care.'

'It looks as if power has gone to your head, Dad,' I said. 'All power corrupts, but absolute power corrupts absolutely. I still can't remember who said that.'

'I was thinking, Lizzie,' said Dad. 'The money that's left over from the other projects could be used for something that'd put Bullyacre on the map. It wouldn't do Bullyacre any harm to have a tourist attraction that's unique in South Australia, would it? Especially if that tourist attraction earned money for the town which could go back into the foundation for future use.'

'What sort of tourist attraction?' I asked a little warily. Dad had changed since he'd become mayor. He was more assertive. In fact, he was getting a bit pushy. I was sure he had the best interests of Bullyacre at heart, but I wasn't confident that he could be trusted to make the right decisions all the time. It's a good thing he had me there to be the power behind the throne.

'Emma's unhappy about Cuddles and the other panther being down there at Monarto Zoo,' said Dad. 'And there's been a litter of kittens and the zoo's worried about space. They were talking about swapping the spare kittens for some other animal from another zoo. A flamingo or two if they can get them past the quarantine people, I think.'

'I like flamingos,' I said. 'There are South American ones and African ones, too. They're different varieties, of course. The genetics of flamingos is quite interesting.'

'I'm sure it is, Lizzie,' said Dad, a bit impatiently. 'I had this idea that we could say we should have first claim on them, and we could build a panther enclosure on Miss Cobbledick's old land, and use her house as the keeper's accommodation and gift shop. Maybe even a café that would employ some of the local kids.'

'It's not a bad idea,' I conceded. 'After all, Bullyacre is the original home of *Pantheris austricephalus cuddlii*, so we should have some of them here. And it would certainly bring people in. We couldn't let them out their vehicles, of course. In fact, it might be a good idea if we had a minibus to take them round in. Can we afford that?'

'That and more,' said Dad. 'Much more, in fact. I'll call an emergency session of the town council tomorrow night and put the proposition to them.'

'They'll agree, Dad,' I said. 'They've never knocked back any of your ideas yet, have they?'

'And it'll make Emma happy, too,' said Dad.

'Of course, we always have to keep Emma happy,' I said just a little sarcastically.

'Later on, Emma might be able to get a job looking after the kittens,' Dad mused. 'She's had more experience raising *Pantheris* whatever kittens that anyone else in the country. It could be a good career path for her.'

'And no one would accuse you of nepotism if she ended up running the place, would they, Dad?' I asked, even more sarcastically.

'Probably not,' Dad said. 'They wouldn't dare. Bill's going to have to take over the farm when I'm past doing the hard work, because you said you're going off to university to become a geneticist.'

'Bill's already doing most of the work anyway,' I said, 'because you're always busy being mayor. It's not doing his school work much good.'

'Bill's not the academic type,' Dad said.

'Mr Gonski was complaining about that the other day,' I said.

'I don't know how Murphy managed to spend all that time on the golf course,' Dad said ruefully. 'If I'd only known how much work is involved in being mayor I would never have agreed to the job.'

'It's only more work because you work harder at it. That's why you're a better mayor than he was,' I told him. 'How many kittens did Cuddles have, anyway?'

'Four,' said Dad.

'And have they all got three heads?' I asked.

'Yes, and Cuddles is pregnant again,' Dad said. 'Those things breed like rabbits. So the sooner we get that enclosure built, the better.'

'Ring the zoo first and make sure they'll agree to your idea, Dad,'

'I'll do that right away,' said Dad, reaching for the phone. The phone in the mayoral office was a lot more reliable than the one back at the homestead, and he got through straight away. The voice at the other end of the phone was loud and excited.

'Did you say that the new kittens have got six toes on each foot?' Dad said. He sounded incredulous. 'And you want to isolate them from the rest of the *Pantheris* population because you don't want the new mutation interbreeding in case things get worse? Yes, we'd be happy to take them off your hands. We're working on the enclosure as we speak. Yes, it'll be ready in no time at all. Probably in a couple of weeks.'

'Didn't you take an oath to tell the truth when you were elected mayor, Dad?' I asked. 'Are they complaining that the kittens have six toes?'

'Yes, they're really worried about it.'

'It's not an uncommon variation,' I said. 'The zoo ought to know that. There are people and cats with six toes. Usually the people have the extra digit removed because they don't want to look different. There's a rumour that Anne Boleyn had six fingers and that's why Henry VIII managed to have her convicted as a witch. Well, one of the reasons, anyway.'

'That's fascinating, Lizzie,' said Dad. I felt he was giving me the brush off. 'Haven't you got an assignment on something or other to complete? Excuse me, I've got to make some phone calls and organise that emergency meeting for tonight. We'll start work on the electric fences around Miss Cobbledick's old property tomorrow.'

<h1 style="text-align:center">22</h1>

Ahead of us, just before the sign that read 'Bullyacre, Population 703' near the entrance to the town, we saw a huge bull being attacked by two enormous three-headed panthers. One panther was perched on the bull's back. Two of its heads were engaged in dragging the animal's neck back to allow the third head to sink its fangs in the bull's jugular vein. Another three-headed panther was crouched beneath the bull tearing at the bovine belly with all three sets of jaws.

'Shit,' yelled Jake as he slammed the brakes on the car. 'What the bloody hell is that thing?'

'You're going to have to watch your language now we're back home, Jake,' I said. 'Your father won't approve of that at all. And I don't want your parents blaming me for your swearing.'

'You said nothing ever happened in Bullyacre,' said Amanda. 'You said the place would be exactly the same as it was when you left a year ago.'

We got out of the car and examined the statue at close range. The work was quite well done, as corrugated-iron statues go. Not exactly lifelike, more of a stylised idea, but you could see what it was meant to be. Amanda took photos. Jake found a little plaque on the base of the monument that read '*Sacrifice* by Fred Mudge Artistic Blacksmith. Studio 17 Main Street Bullyacre'.

'It looks almost like Mithras,' Amanda said. 'You know, the Roman soldiers' god who was popular just before Emperor Constantine made Christianity the official religion of the Romans. All that's missing is the human figure wearing a Phrygian cap sitting on top of the bull and the dog running beside him. Of course, there was only one panther on those statues, and it didn't have three heads, either.'

I raised my eyebrows. Jake shook his head. We were used to Amanda finding similarities in present-day life to the classics she was studying, so neither Jake nor I said anything. Amanda kept muttering under her breath. She can be quite boring when she gets stuck on a subject. Jake says I'm exactly the same, and that's why Amanda and I are such good friends, but I can't see it. Amanda was bemused by the statue, but Jake and I recognised it as a monument to the gory death of Fred Mudge's prize bull. I decided Fred must think the event was worth commemorating because of the huge compensation money he had got out of the government for the bull's loss.

'I didn't expect anything this big,' I said. 'Dad did say that Fred Mudge had asked for a grant from the Cobbledick Foundation to set up a blacksmith studio, and he said Fred has got work on display in the town, but I didn't expect his stuff would be on this scale. It must be about three times bigger than the actual bull and the panthers were. What do you think, Jake?'

Jake was shaking his head in disbelief. 'I wasn't there that night. I was stuck in the hall entertaining the kids with my piano accordion. I didn't see the bull die.'

'I'd forgotten that,' I said. 'It was pretty horrible, but the scale of this thing is exaggerated.'

'I can't believe that your dad and the town council agreed to let Fred Mudge put a monstrosity like this at the entrance to the town.'

'Dad always tries to keep everyone happy if he can. Apparently the tourists like it. Didn't your parents tell you anything about this, Jake?'

'No, when Mum phones all she ever does is ask when I'm coming home, and all Dad does is give me advice on how to live my life. No chewing gum, no alcohol, no fast women. That sort of thing. You know what Dad's like.'

'Well, he ought to know that I wouldn't let you get away with any of that,' I said. 'I hate chewing gum, too. My dad's always going on about the farm, the zoo and his plans for the town,' I said. 'You have to admit that Fred's done a good job of it, if you like that sort of thing. His welding is almost as good as mine is. Those joins are really well done. I suppose we'll see more of this sort of stuff all over the place.'

'Your dad must be a busy man,' said Amanda, still photo-graphing as fast as she could. 'Running the farm and the town. Could you two stand together in front of the bull? I'm going to put this on Facebook.'

'Your dad manages to keep in contact with you, even though he's busy,' said Jake, a little ruefully.

I knew that his parents only phoned once a week, and suspected it was because of the cost of the long-distance calls. It's not cheap to ring from Bullyacre to Adelaide. Dad, I suspected, used the mayoral phone line which was his one perk of office.

'He phones you every couple of days, doesn't he?'

'I think he still misses me a lot,' I said. 'Bill and Emma are still a bit young to have a decent conversation with, so Dad phones me. It's different for your parents, they've got each other.'

'Bill's eighteen now, Lizzie. Didn't you say he's left school and he's working full-time on the farm with your dad? And Emma's fifteen. That's the same age as you were when the incidents of Bullyacre took place. Those kids ought be mature enough to talk to.'

'Sometimes I wonder if they'll ever really grow up. Maybe I was old for my age,' I said. 'Or maybe Dad and I had some sort of special relationship.'

'Your little sister's working at the Panther Park part-time now, isn't she?' Amanda asked.

'Yes, and there's a book written about her by Ms Wylie. Dad sent me a copy of it. *The Cat Girl of Bullyacre*. Remember that? I showed it to you both. It's all about Emma and how she's taming the kittens that are born in the *Pantheris austricephalus cuddlii* sanctuary.'

'Yes, I do remember,' said Amanda. 'I remember you throwing the book across the room. I didn't know you had a nasty temper like that.'

'You were furious because Emma signed your copy "From your famous little sister". I reckon you were cross because you're hardly mentioned in the book,' said Jake. 'I thought it was sour grapes, actually. You weren't happy to be overlooked, so you said the book was crap.'

'Well, I still think my achievements ought to be mentioned in a book. That book left a lot of important stuff out. Maybe I'll write my own version of the Incidents of Bullyacre one day.'

'You haven't got time to write books. You've got enough to do with your uni genetics studies, Lizzie.'

'So have you, Jake, with your economics. I'm getting high distinctions, what about you?'

'Do stop squabbling, you two. For two people who are practically engaged to be married, you've got an awful relationship,' said Amanda. 'The way you're going, you'll be divorced before the wedding.'

'It's amazing how Miss Cobbledick's money has stretched to do so much around this town,' said Jake.

I knew he was trying to change the subject. That's a ploy he often uses when our discussions get heated. I decided to go along with it. 'Yes, even though the panther sanctuary did cost quite a bit. But Dad says it's paying its way now. Heaps of tourists come to see it.'

'When can we go to see that panther place?' asked Amanda. 'We've only got a week over Christmas and the New Year to see everything in the area. And both your parents'll want you to spend time with them, too. I'm looking forward to your New Year's Eve fireworks display too. It's all very exciting. It's almost worth not spending Christmas with my parents to be here. Apparently it's snowing in Hobart at the moment. Dad says it's climate change.'

'We should manage to get everything done. But Jake has to help his parents put up the nativity crèche in the church tomorrow. They asked Emma last year and it was a disaster.'

'Yes,' said Jake in disgust. 'She dropped the baby Jesus and broke his arm. They tried to glue it back on, but it didn't work, so they had to send down to Adelaide to get a new one urgently. Mum said the baby's bigger than Mary and Joseph and it's not quite the right colour. But Dad said Jesus would have looked a bit different because of his divinity. Mum just said they'll have to make do with it until they can get a grant from the foundation for a new one. So this year I'm stuck putting up the crèche.'

'Jake, me and Amanda will take a walk down Main Street so I can show her around a bit, so you could go and see your parents now. If Dad's not in the mayor's office, I'll phone him to come and get us.'

'You're trying to avoid my mum, aren't you, Lizzie?'

'It's just that she keeps asking me when we're getting married, and neither of us is ready for that yet. We're both only twenty, for goodness sake.'

'But we've been together a long time, Lizzie,'

'I want to get my degree first.'

'And then you want to do your Masters and probably your PhD,' said Jake wearily. 'We'll be too old to have kids by the time we get hitched.'

Our disagreement was interrupted by a loud American voice. We hadn't heard the car arrive and park beside ours. We hadn't seen the large man and even larger woman climb out of it and waddle over to Fred Mudge's artistic creation.

'Waall, waall, Gene, will you just look at that? I don't think we've got anything like that at home, not even in Texas.'

'No, honey, I don't reckon we have got one of them. Not even in Disneyland.'

'Quick, Gene, get some snaps of it. It's real big, isn't it? And very lifelike. Do you suppose their bulls get eaten by big cats here in Australia on a regular basis?'

'Couldn't tell you, honey. Why don't you ask those kids over there?'

'Hi, kids. Are you from around here?' the strange lady demanded.

'Sort of,' I said warily. 'Some of us are.'

Jake nudged me. 'Don't be rude, Lizzie. These are probably some of those tourists the town wants to attract.' He extended his hand and it was enveloped in the American's huge one.

'I'm Jake Jeffries,' said Jake. 'This is Amanda Todd, who comes from Tasmania, and this is Lizzie Epsom. Lizzie and I come from Bullyacre.'

'Tasmania?' asked the man. 'You mean there really is a country called Tasmania? I thought that was a name Walt Disney made up for his cartoon character.'

I shook my head in disbelief, partially at the bloke's crass remark, and partially because I was looking at the identical Akubras and the fact that they were both wearing outsize moleskin trousers and blue denim shirts. They had obviously decided to dress for the outback.

'Lizzie Epsom?' asked the woman. 'Are you related to that gorgeous young Emma Epsom, the one in the book? Here, I've got it here. I was hoping to run into that little girl and have her sign the book for me.'

She produced a copy of *The Cat Girl of Bullyacre* from her voluminous handbag and waved it at me. The cover showed Emma's face surrounded by a wreath of cat necks and heads.

'Don't do it, Lizzie,' warned Amanda. 'Control yourself.'

'Lizzie is Emma's big sister,' said Jake, a grin spreading all over his face. 'I'm sure she'd be happy to introduce you to Emma.'

'Oh, I'm just so glad we came,' said the woman. 'You know this book is a best-seller back in the States, don't you? And everyone says that this little girl is the next best thing to that Crocodile Dundee fellow you used to have around. The one with the shrimp on the barbie. Do you have barbecues in Bullyacre, sorny?'

'All the time,' said Jake happily. 'The mayor will probably host one next Wednesday. Lizzie is his daughter, so she can put in a good word for you. If you need somewhere to stay in Bullyacre, just drive down Main Street and you'll find the Bullyacre Arms Hotel on the left-hand side of the road, just past the statue of the man with the bullocks.'

'You've got more statues in this town, then? Gene, get that camera ready.'

They drove off in a cloud of dust, and we were left standing.

'How are the mighty fallen,' said Jake, quoting the Bible. 'Your main claim to fame is being Emma's sister, now, Lizzie. Ms Wylie must be making some nice royalties from *The Cat Girl of Bullyacre*. I wonder if she's still living here.'

'Let's go and see,' I said, getting back into the car.

Jake dropped us in front of Dad's office, and I checked that the Americans' car wasn't parked there. It was further down by the hotel, and the man was hauling some enormous suitcases out of the boot, while his wife stood on the veranda, looking about with apparent delight. Bullyacre was living up to her expectations.

'Lizzie Epsom!' said Sergeant Wylie's voice. 'What are you doing back here? I thought the town was free of you now that you've gone off to university. Doing genetics, aren't you? I always did think you cooked up those cats somehow.'

I shuddered. Dad had said Sergeant Wylie was back and that he hadn't been changed much by what had been termed post-traumatic stress disorder.

I forced myself to smile. 'Hello, Sarge,' I said. 'Jake and I've come back for Christmas. This is my friend, Amanda. She's at uni with us. Only of course, we're doing different courses. Amanda's doing classics, ancient Greek and Latin, that sort of thing.'

'Not a relation, is she? She's too pretty to be related to you, Lizzie Epsom. Although that little sister of yours isn't a bad-looking kid. My wife, Ms Wylie, is quite fond of young Emma. She wrote a book about her, you know. Look, there's copies of it in that shop window.' He indicated the window nearest us, which was piled high with copies of *The Cat Girl of Bullyacre*.

'That used to be the coffee shop,' I said, just a little annoyed. Jake and I used to spend a lot of time there.

'Still is,' said the sergeant. 'Only now they've branched out. They sell my wife's book and little replicas of Fred Mudge's sculptures. Only they're made in China, of course. But Fred did the designing of them. The tourists buy them as fast as Fred imports them. The books are the biggest seller, though. The coffee shop's out the back, and Ms Wylie does readings from the book there every Friday afternoon.'

'Please excuse us, Sergeant Wylie,' I said, shuddering. 'My father, the mayor, is expecting us in his office.'

'You won't find him there, Lizzie. He's out at the panther park. There's been another litter of kittens, and he said he has to check whether they've got six toes or not. Tell you what, because you're Frank's daughter and Emma's sister, I'll forget what you did to me in the past, and I'll drive you out there in the squad car.'

I couldn't think of an excuse, so Amanda and I climbed in. I thought it was a bit unnecessary that Wylie put the siren on, but I suspect it was in revenge for old scores. We streaked down Main Street, past the Americans who were still there, taking photos of Hugh Foulkes's bullock team. They took a photo of the police car as it whizzed past them, and I hoped that our faces wouldn't show up and that the Americans wouldn't put them on Facebook or something. Amanda's parents wouldn't be pleased if they saw that their daughter was being conveyed about South Australia at high speed by the constabulary.

'Thanks, Sarge,' I said as I got out of the car.

The panther park was built on Miss Cobbledick's old property. Her lawn had become a car park, and it was full of cars, most of them with New South Wales or Victorian number plates. There was one of Fred's sculptures in the centre of the car park. I went over and had a good look. It depicted Miss Cobbledick and her lawn mower. The plaque read, 'Miss Muriel Cobbledick, Benefactor of Bullyacre'. Amanda took a photo of the statue.

There was a sign over the entrance of Miss Cobbledick's house: 'Tearooms and Souvenirs'. Through the windows I could see people sitting at little tables having Devonshire teas. It looked as if the ladies of auxiliary were running the place, although some of my old schoolmates were working as waiters and waitresses.

I saw Dad coming out of the gate of the panther park with Emma beside him. I rushed over and gave him a hug. 'Hi, Dad. This is my friend Amanda. Jake's gone to see his parents. I'm so glad to be home again Dad!'

'Lizzie, it's great to see you!' Dad said, hugging me tight. 'I've really missed you. Glad to finally meet you, Amanda. Lizzie's always talking about you. And Jake, of course.'

'Hello, Emma,' I said. 'How are the moggies?'

Emma gave me a perfunctory kiss. 'They're not moggies, Lizzie. This is a serious enterprise we're running here,' she said. 'Cuddles junior has just given birth to four more babies. We have ensured the future of the species.'

My sister wore a serious expression and an outfit that resembled the Americans' clothing in its rustic theme. Emma looked more elegant, though, as though she was prepared for TV cameras to roll at any moment. I suddenly realised that the tourists had modelled their dress on Emma's. This was the sort of gear she was wearing in the photos in the book. My little sister had become a trendsetter. Sergeant Wylie and the Americans were right: she had grown into a beautiful girl. I wasn't going to say that, though.

'You've been spending too much time around Ms Wylie, Emma,' I said.

'Have they all got three heads? And have they got five toes or six toes?' asked Amanda.

'Actually,' said Emma, smiling and looking a bit more like the kid she used to be, 'they've got seven toes on each foot. They are so cute, Lizzie, I just want to pick them up and play with them. Only this Cuddles isn't nearly as sweet as the first Cuddles was and she won't let me get really close to them for long.'

'Seven toes on each foot?' I asked, incredulous. 'The rate of mutation is speeding up. Dad, I think I really will do my PhD on the panthers. Can you afford to keep me at uni that long?'

'I'm sure the foundation can afford to keep you there as long as you want to be there, Lizzie. There's been a lot written about the panthers, but the more prestigious academic papers that are produced, the better. And you are a local girl, so it would be very well received. We might have two celebrities in the family then.'

How could it be that even Dad had forgotten the events of the past?

'When can I have a tour of the panther park, Mr Epsom?' Amanda asked.

'Tomorrow might be better. We've just had interviews with about four television stations and a couple of them are still driving around the place. I don't think Emma or I could stand any more TV exposure. Your Mr Furphy was here earlier, Lizzie. You've just missed him.'

'Thank God for that,' I said. 'You know what, Dad, I think I'd rather Emma was the famous person in this family. When I remember what it was like being a celebrity, I think I'd rather settle for the academic life.'

'*Sic transit gloria mundi*, Lizzie,' said Amanda.

'I know that, Amanda,' I said icily.

'What does that mean? Is that Latin?' demanded Emma.

'Look it up on Google,' I snapped.

'Your famous days aren't entirely over, Lizzie. We'll drop in and see Fred Mudge's studio on the way home and you can see what he's working on right now. He wants to unveil it at the New Year fireworks, but I can't see why you shouldn't have a private viewing before that.'

We drove back into town, and as we passed the hall I saw a corrugated-iron statue of Ian Perkins, hand on his pistol, standing in front of the door of the town hall.

Fred was hard at work when we arrived at his studio. There were blinding flashes of light and the sound of hammering coming from within.

'Fred, can you stop for a few minutes, please?' called Dad. 'It's Frank Epsom and some people who'd like to have a look at your art work.'

The light flashes and the hammering stopped immediately.

'Come in, Mr Mayor,' said Fred. 'Always glad to be of service. Lizzie, it's young Lizzie! Welcome back to Bullyacre, love. I told your dad he had to get you to come back this year. I wanted this to be a surprise, but you might as well see it now.'

Fred had constructed a corrugated-iron ute. In the cabin sat a figure which was a reasonably good depiction of Bill at the age of thirteen. And on the tray stood two figures, myself holding a rifle and looking determined and my sister Emma clinging to my legs with a terrified expression on her face.

'How do you do that?' I asked. 'I mean that's corrugated iron you're working with. I can't believe you manage to make it look so lifelike. You're a genius, Mr Mudge.'

Amanda was photographing as fast as she could. Her camera flashes were almost as rapid as Fred Mudge's arc-welding had been.

'It beats raising cattle,' said Mr Mudge. 'I've found my true vocation in life. I'm a happy man.'

'It's huge,' I said, walking around the thing in order to admire it from all angles. 'Where's it going to go?'

'We thought in the Main Street,' said Dad. 'On the other end of the median strip, just along from Hugh Foulkes and the bullocks. It'll make a nice centrepiece. Tomorrow I'll take you out to the Lions' Park and you can see the statue out there, too.'

'Yair, this one's pretty impressive, but you just wait until you see the one of Mayor Epsom gunning down the panthers with the machine gun. I call that one *Salvation*.'

Dad smiled. 'Fred gives all his art works different names. Young Perkins's statue is called *Courage*.

'What do you call this one, Mr Mudge?' I asked.

'I'm thinking of calling it *On the Edge*,' he said. 'I reckon you were on the edge of growing up, Lizzie, which you've done pretty well, now I think about it, and of course it all happened on the edge of Magnetic Hill, didn't it?'

'And you said nothing ever changed in Bullyacre,' said Amanda, taking a photo of me standing next to the ute. 'This is definitely going on Facebook. You're going to be famous again, Lizzie.

Acknowledgements

Thanks as always to my husband Frank, who endured long hours alone while I was off tramping the fictional hills of Bullyacre with Lizzie Epsom in search of panthers. My apologies for the late meals and the phone calls and door bells I didn't hear.

Thank you, Stephen and Brenda Matthews of Ginninderra Press, for accepting my wild story of three-headed panthers and finding it believable.

My thanks for the use of the name Bullyacre to Margaret Travers, whose ancestral home that property was until the 1950s, and many, many thanks to Colin and Ros Bowman, the present owners of the place, who were not perturbed when I told them I had built a town on Bullyacre. Their B&B is called Blue Gum House and I cannot commend it highly enough. Thank you, Colin, for showing us around your land in your ute, and in particular for letting me see the Valley of the Panthers. If I had known how beautiful the Bullyacre countryside is, I might have written a much longer novel. Thanks to John Manion of Orroroo, who told us about the B&B, and to also to Joe and Lynn Grida of the Astronomical Society, who organised an unexpected weekend at Blue Gum House. I am still amazed that we ended up there for a weekend of dark skies and good company.

My IT person, Alexander Worrall, emailed the electronic copy to Ginninderra Press because he knows that his granny is incapable of that sort of thing. Thanks again, Alex.

Thank you also to my grandson Liam, who asked me to write a story his mum would let him read, because she said that *The Blue Roses of Orroroo* is, at present, age-inappropriate for him. I hope *On the Edge* meets Denise's approval.

Lastly, I must point out that *On the Edge* is a work of fiction – in Shakespeare's words, 'Proceeding from th' overheated brain'; that the town of Bullyacre is a mythical place which has no resemblance at all to any town in the mid-north of South Australia or anywhere else; that all the persons and geological clubs mentioned in the book have no resemblance to any persons or clubs living or dead, and that no three-headed panthers, members of the constabulary or of the army were harmed in the making of this book. The only person who was once real (apart from Pythagoras and other historical personages) is my ancestor Hugh Foulkes, to whom I have dedicated a bronze statue in the main street of Bullyacre. Hugh was Captain Charles Sturt's bullock driver. Captain Sturt has a bronze statue in Victoria Square. I have always wanted to give Hugh a statue too, so I did.

Margaret Visciglio 2013